ARBITRAGE

COLETTE KEBELL

SKITTISH
ENDEAVOURS ™

PROLOGUE

Albert Romanov stayed in his office later than usual. No more monthly reports to the Board of Directors. Definitely not that night. Waiting for all the employees to leave the building, including his secretary, he kept looking at the clock and at the attendance register on his own computer, until he was finally sure he was the only person left inside the building.

He again read the Mortcombe dossier, consisting of various folders opened onto the modern burl wood desk, as he couldn't grasp how things had gone from bad to worse. It had started as a game several years before. Requests to open offshore bank accounts, then the money transfer to Luxembourg, which commenced initially as a subterfuge to avoid taxes, as Mortcombe would have said, and then, later, a much larger operation of money laundering.

He hadn't suddenly become a moralist, but if everything had a price in this world, the bill he had found himself liable for was far too hefty. There was no point in delaying further. For the past weeks, he kept accumulating substantial amounts of money in various offshore accounts.

During the years, he had taken bribes, received undeserved bonuses, and even made illegal transfers on one of his bank accounts. The same Mortcombe, the owner of the private bank, had no doubt subtracted his share too. Romanov got carried away by the events, year after year, continuing to play the game because he didn't know what else to do. Stopping and thinking about his own life would only further highlight the oppressive void he had created around him. Not that things were better for those who had decided not to play the game. People suddenly disappeared, others had been found days later drowned in the English Channel, a few kilometres outside Brighton.

Whatever decision he took, it inevitably led to an error.

But when the accident happened to William Digby, Head of Investments, if it was an accident, everything changed. Now Romanov was no longer willing to continue. What could barely appear acceptable if done with an old friend, became immediately horrid and unbearable if handled in isolation. *Jesus Christ, a bad investment could have happened to anyone,* but with the Russian mob, there were no margins for discussion. Old Digby lay in the morgue; they found him hanged at his home by the sea. The investigators had closed the case quickly, suicide, but Romanov knew that things were different. They had planned to rent a boat on that same day, and in Romanov's mind, nothing in Digby's behaviour was suggesting suicide. Indeed, Digby was meditating revenge. They had accumulated several enemies over the years.

Laundering money for the Russian mafia, drugs, arms trafficking; Romanov found himself being a senior executive in an organised crime bank and the sudden loneliness had made him collapse. He had sought refuge confiding with an old friend and mentor some time before, but what his friend had to say about Mortcombe had intimidated him further. Then Digby's death.

He was living a solitary life, his best friend had passed away, and his only interest in life had been his work, apart from getting his hands on as much money as possible. Romanov had given up living years before, saying too many times *Just one more year and I shall quit*, deferring dreams of a boat in the Caribbean, a villa on an isolated place, and why the hell not, some female company. It didn't matter if he had to pay for it.

He had had a long talk with Mortcombe's son-in-law a few days before, and despite the latter's attempts at persuasion, eventually, Romanov was back to square one with his doubts. He stalled. *I have to ponder*, he had repeated over and over to himself, but the decision had already been taken.

He put together the dossier, ready to be shipped to Scotland Yard, and to two or three newspapers, just to be on the safe side, then he would disappear to Switzerland. Maybe to South America at a later stage. With money to spend, a hiding place was easy to find.

He put four copies of the dossier in different envelopes, and he was ready to leave the office, but before that, he had one last thing to do. He opened his bag and took out the USB drive given to him by the hacker. That program could make him disappear forever from the bank logs, or at the very least, obliterate all traces that could lead to his secret accounts. He inserted it into the laptop, plugged into the bank's network, and pressed *enter* on the program. The hacker would do the rest.

Romanov had also organised an 'insurance policy' in case he came to be in danger, another idea in collaboration with the hacker. The slush funds he had just stolen would remain suspended in an inaccessible limbo unless he logged onto a website every twenty-four hours.

This measure seemed excessive to Romanov, but overall it was part of 'the package' paid to the hacker, and so he obliged. He could always disable that function at a later stage.

Vengeance. That was the only word that continued to haunt him in those days. Romanov knew he was guilty, but he had been dragged into that mess a long time ago. It was time to rebel.

He ensured the program was running, left the computer turned on, and walked out of the office. He took the secondary exit at the back of the bank, towards the parking lot.

He had just reached his car when a voice called him, 'Albert Romanov?'

He turned and saw an individual coming out of a black limousine. He couldn't see his face; the light of a torch was dazzling him. The man pointed what, to Romanov, appeared to be a nine-millimetre Beretta and fired repeatedly. Shot in the chest and the face, Romanov slumped to the ground, and the last image he saw was of the assailant collecting his briefcase before leaving the scene at high speed. A downpour ensued; the wet face of Romanov remained motionless while his blood was mixing with the rain.

The limousine headed towards London Road. 'Are you sure he's dead?' asked Bruno Mortcombe.

'Dead as Charon. These are the documents he had with him,' he said opening the briefcase he had just taken from the victim and passed a folder to Mortcombe.

'The little bastard Romanov was going to the police; then planned on screwing me, after all I've done for him. Luckily, Robert warned us in advance. I didn't think he'd have the guts to do it.'

'May I ask a question, Mr Mortcombe?' asked the head of security without looking in the rear-view mirror.

'Fire away, Matt.'

'How come you are dealing with these matters directly and don't leave them to Mr Price?'

Bruno Mortcombe thought about the question for a minute, pondering an answer. 'Robert Price is too ambitious for his own good, and too eager to prove himself. He acts on instinct and doesn't think about the consequences of his actions. I've seen him doing it before. You don't climb the ladder by just marrying the boss's daughter. He will get there eventually, but not before I've kicked the bucket. Let's just make sure it doesn't happen anytime soon and he doesn't facilitate it. Keep an eye on him, will you?'

'I will, Mr Mortcombe.'

They remained silent until they reached the A23. The inside of the car was suddenly illuminated by a bright light. The crash with the 18-wheeler instantly killed the assassin. The impact threw Mortcombe, who was not wearing a seat belt, out of the windscreen. The driver was less fortunate, burnt alive and trapped in the fire that had followed.

****

Mortcombe woke up in a hospital room. From what he could glimpse from beneath the bandages, he shared the room with four other unfortunates; the last bed was vacant. The artificial light was soft, and it took him a long time before he could identify the window, from which he could barely see other buildings outside and the night.

Mortcombe wasn't sure how he had ended up in that place, his mind was still too fuzzy, and every movement caused him excruciating pain in both the head and chest, despite the heavy dose of sedatives and some other drug that was sliding through his veins through a tube connected to the back of his hand. He couldn't see it, but he felt it, a small faint voice hidden by the screaming pain from the rest of his body.

A woman was arguing and shouting with another person in the corridor, behind the closed door, although the content of that animosity was not understandable in the mists where Mortcombe was.

He tried to turn around without success, oppressed by the pain that kept him pinned to the bed. A new stabbing sensation, this time to the abdomen, made him almost lose consciousness for a second time.

After a few minutes, he tried again to look around, without success.

What had happened? he wondered sighing in the semi-darkness of the room. Before he could answer, a man and a woman in doctor's coats entered the room; the man shut the door behind him. He ensured that the remaining occupants of the room were asleep and, as a precaution, he closed the curtains, which served to separate the people and provide additional privacy. He came closer and checked the medical records at the foot of the bed. He seemed to read for an eternity. Mortcombe failed to utter anything due to his injuries. The man examined his eyes, he then turned to the woman and, without caring whether he was heard by the patient, said, 'He is a mess, I don't think he will make it through the night. Give me a dose of Diprivan.'

'Do we know who he is?' asked the woman.

'Yes, the police have already informed the family. They traced his name from the car's registration plate.' Then, directed to the patient, 'Mr Mortcombe, if you can hear me, we need to put you in an induced coma.'

Mortcombe wanted to answer, or at least nod, but failed. He hadn't a God to pray to, and he spent his final moments thinking about Romanov's death, about the fact that he did not deserve to be in the hospital, and about his two daughters. One of which he hadn't spoken to for years. He watched the man preparing the syringe.

The injection lasted a second, the fluid injected in the same pipe connected to the back of his hand, and then there was nothing.

****

The phone rang six times in an office in *Quai Charles de Gaulle* in Lyon before a burly man ran to answer it.

'For Christ's sake!' he swore while the hot coffee which fell on the desk was absorbed by many documents, carefully stacked one on top of the other. It was the private line. 'Hello?'

'I received the documentation. Are you sure that's everything?' asked a baritone voice on the other end of the phone.

'That is the latest information I managed to get. In these matters, there is always room for doubt,' said the burly man, stretching to take a package of paper towels, trying to limit the damage on his desk.

'You assured me they were professionals,' continued the second man.

'Of course, of course. The best around, no doubt about it. Romanov's death is complicating things to a new level though.'

'It was unexpected, that's for sure. So we had to change our plans. Without Romanov, we have to start again from scratch. Almost.'

'How do you think they found out about him?' asked Jordan.

'He blabbed to the wrong person if you ask me. He was extremely worried recently. I'm sorry, I should have foreseen that.'

'Those con artists you suggested, are they still in London?'

'Yeah, the capital is where they operate most of the time. You found the address in the documents I sent you?' said Jordan. 'How do you plan to contact them?'

'I have a half-baked idea in my head, although in the dossier you sent me, I didn't find much that could help me. This Marcus Splinter, for example, he looks like a pensioner.'

'Those are ghosts, my friend, it's not easy to put salt on their tails. They appear when you least expect them, and in no time they have vanished into thin air. Don't misjudge them. Splinter is their boss, and he could fool anybody with that upper crust look he has. If they catch me passing this information on the outside, I'm in trouble.'

The man on the other end of the phone paused. 'There is nothing at the moment that could lead back to you, Jordan, we talked about this. And you'll be rewarded for your services.'

'Of course, if we don't get caught red-handed. I really don't want to spend the rest of my life in jail, even though it would have some advantages.'

'Which are?'

'Visits to the jail once a month, I would get rid of my ex-wife once and for all. Sorry, dear, but I can no longer pay you alimony, force majeure,' said Jordan.

The two laughed loudly. 'Is your ex still after you?'

'Don't tell me. That damn lawyer did not completely close matters, and now, after ten years, she wants more. This time she is in pursuit of my pension, or at least half of it. I either pay, and when I retire, I live in misery, or I run away somewhere abroad. I knew she was a bitch, everyone told me so.'

'I told you myself. There is always a price to pay for our mistakes, that's why I try not to make any. Not lately, I mean.'

'May I know how do you intend to proceed? It's not that you've given me a lot to work with. And in such a short time…' Jordan stood, a dozen coffee-soaked paper towels in his hands which he threw in the bin next to the desk. Some documents had absorbed the drink and now showed a beige halo on the edges. He opened a couple of drawers, but he couldn't find any other handkerchiefs or tissues for that matter. He decided to sacrifice his notepad; he tore away a few pages and laid them where he could still see drops of coffee.

'Better not at this point. Plausible deniability, the less you are involved, the better things are,' said the man on the other side of the phone.

Jordan sighed, unable to even grasp how he had allowed himself to be persuaded so quickly, but it was a matter of money. Money that he desperately needed.

'I'm already involved. It is a complex plan, if you ask me, lots of things can go wrong.'

'I realise that, but I see no other options. When was the last time you felt that kind of adrenaline flowing through your body?'

'Far too long ago. I heard about the accident Mortcombe had…'

'A problem, no doubt,' said the man on the other end of the phone, 'but also an opportunity, that's why I called you. We need to act quickly.'

'I don't like it, there are too many variables and unknowns.'

'Plans never survive the first encounter with the enemy. Relax, we're going to be okay.'

Jordan hung up the phone and walked towards the window, from where he could see the *Tête d'Or* park. He had been lucky in getting this job in Lyon, though the pay was far from being decent and he could barely see the pond from his office. The park was his favourite place and at noon, instead of going to the cafeteria like everyone else, every rainless day Jordan went to the park. Over the years he had acquired a taste for French cuisine, although a little too rich for his cholesterol, and spending a half an hour walking in nature was what he really needed. The trees around the pond were coloured yellow, ochre, and reds in the fall. Or, perhaps he had already grown old inside and was training for when, in retirement, he would go to the park to feed the pigeons, he thought. No, he wasn't finished yet. If what his interlocutor was promising was right, there would be a change in his life. A radical one. Some waves needed to be ridden, despite the risks. If not now, when?

PART 1

CHAPTER 1

1989

Ryan Logan was heading toward London in his new black Jaguar XJS. He had never been a petrol head unlike most of his colleagues, but nonetheless, that car made him feel like he had achieved something in life. Logan briefly stroked his hand across the leather passenger seat and breathed a sigh of relief. Years earlier, while still a penniless student, he had been in love with a London girl, as beautiful as the sun and with two breathtaking long legs. They often spoke about cars, one of the girl's dreams – *What was her name? Monika!* – was to own a black Jaguar.

In Logan's mind, owning that very car had become a point of arrival, he could finally say, 'Look at me, I made it.' Not that Monika could see it at that moment in time, the two had split up several years before, but nevertheless, that dream had been handed down to him. Too many things had changed since then. The law degree and a second in economics taken almost in parallel, a job in one of the most prestigious London law firms that had led him to be the youngest partner, a mansion in the Surrey stockbroker belt.

What hadn't changed was working hard to get results. First at school, with nights spent on books, and then in the office. Ryan never stopped for a moment to reflect on life. That would have put more fear into him than death itself; since he had been a student, he had done everything in his power to avoid that question. After a day of studying came the revelry and drunkenness at night with other students, the parties … However, he always managed to not get into trouble. Not with the police, at least. With the bottle, it was quite another matter. Once he started working for Saunders, Whitehall & Passmore things hadn't changed much. He lived to excess, a candle burning too fast under the night breeze, and often he found himself sleeping in the office, after a night of partying, alcohol, and strippers.

Logan had a reserved parking space, right under the building of Saunders, Whitehall & Passmore, abbreviated as Sandie, a privilege that no one else could boast at the age of thirty-four. The fact was that Logan was damn good at his job. A genius, according to colleagues, even those who didn't like him much.

'Good morning, Mr Logan,' said the security guard as soon as he saw him entering the building. 'Today you are earlier than usual.'

'I came across very little traffic; maybe because of the fog. How are Mike and Simon?'

'Fine, thank you. Simon starts school today; luckily, I am doing the night shift, my wife phoned me and said that the little one raised hell. He just didn't want to go to school. Must have got that from his father.'

'Ah, yes, school, time passes quickly,' said Logan, 'nothing to worry about, they will love every minute of it.' Logan had an innate ability to remember insignificant details, like the names of the security guard's sons. He could never know when an aspect could come in handy in his trade, so he tended to remember everything. He didn't really care about all those details, but he knew they were the key to opening doors that otherwise would remain inexorably closed.

'Do you have kids of your own?' asked the man.

'Who, me? No, I don't have time, but I was a kid once. I speak from personal experience,' Logan said.

'Today's newspapers are by the lift,' said the security officer. He knew the rules, chatting was allowed, but on this occasion, he had stepped too far. Never ask for personal details, especially of one of the partners. He could have lost his job for doing so.

Logan took a copy of the *Financial Times* and glanced at the headlines waiting for the elevator to reach the floor, ignoring that invasion of privacy.

****

'Good morning, slaves,' Logan said to a group of

employees who had spent the night at the office. They were all recent graduates looking for success otherwise, they wouldn't voluntarily submit themselves to the torture of that job. Some would have thrown in the towel, many would remain employed with no real career perspective, others would seek work elsewhere after a few years of hard work under their belt. That was the price to pay, working a hundred hours a week, bill as many hours as they could, and then go somewhere else, and the company knew that. In fact, they had a high turnover, but newcomers looking for their dream job would replace them, in due time. The most tenacious would remain and, after their fair share of backstabbing, lying, elbowing, they would become partners, the same as Logan.

'Good morning, Mr Logan,' they replied in chorus.

'Today's mail, Mr Logan,' said the secretary, a brunette in her thirties, trotting behind him trying to keep pace.

Logan gave a look at the letters and threw them in a rubbish bin.

'Mr Saunders asked if you could join him as soon as possible in his office, and you have a nine-thirty meeting with the Globalstar Financial executives.' The secretary went on regurgitating appointments and deadlines without Logan paying any attention. He was sitting at his desk, back to the enormous glass window from where he could see the skyline of the City, and he opened the *Financial*

Times. Logan preferred to take the day as it came, one appointment after the other, without having to prepare. His memory was photographic and he didn't need much preparation before a business meeting. A quick glance at the files would trigger a flood of information in his brain.

The Moleskine notebook, which he kept in his bag, contained a sentence or an evocative image for each customer, which would unleash a stream of uninterrupted memories, in case any of the partners asked about a particular customer.

He would not move from his desk before having his second morning coffee, which, according to tradition, would arrive there within three minutes.

The phone rang. 'Where the fuck are you, Ryan?' thundered the gruff voice of Newsham Saunders.

'At my desk and I still haven't finished my coffee. What's going on?'

'Get off your ass and come to my office, we need to talk!' And then Newsham broke off communication.

A wasted coffee. Upon leaving the office, Ryan shouted, 'Slaves! I need a two hundred and fifty-page report on the taxation ambiguity in Panama. For this afternoon.' An unnecessary task that had already been completed a year earlier, but by different slaves. Some pressure would keep the newbies guessing.

He entered Saunders' office without knocking. Whenever he entered, a tightness gripped him; the thick mouse grey carpets, three centimetres thick almost resembled a rug, the aluminium windows and the white panels of the ceiling were in stark contrast with the furniture. An antique desk in cherry wood with green skin insert, a Victorian relic for sure. On the walls, there were a mixture of abstract paintings and an ancient eighteenth-century portrait of a nobleman with a sword, definitely not connected to the occupier; a Japanese cabinet with flamingos in relief; a library with a collection of legal books, probably never read, next to a collection of cricket bats. Every time Logan put a foot in that place, he had the feeling of entering a pirate's quarterdeck. A mountain of valuables, which didn't have any relationship to one another because they were the result of raids; nor had anything to do with the current owner, for that matter. They didn't say anything about the owner except cry out bad taste and a lack of style. Logan sat on a black leather chair right in front of the desk.

'So, what's the rush?' asked Logan.

Saunders was head bowed on the desk, trying to separate a little pile of cocaine into several strips with a razor blade. Then he pulled a gold tube from his breast pocket and inhaled the contents through his nose; he looked toward the ceiling and the white panels and then sighed.

'Oh, Ryan, we are expanding,' said Saunders.

'Sure, the awakening of the Kundalini. You know that to refine the cocaine they use kerosene? Tell it to your pituitary gland and to the third eye chakra that it's all an illusion unleashed by the chemistry of the Colombian jungle.'

'Ah, ah, Ryan, you're funny. No, we are not expanding the consciences today, or at the very least, it's not the primary goal. We expand us, a merger.'

Logan held back a couple of comments about his partner burning out his brain, but he merely complied without saying a word. He wouldn't have fallen for the old trick of throwing a bomb of information and then wait in silence for a reaction. Saunders was the first to speak.

'We are in an era of changes,' the partner said, after having suitably rubbed his nose on the sleeve of his tailored jacket. 'Either we evolve, or we die, we have to be laser-focused on success, we expect paradigm shifts …'

'Without forgetting the innovative disintermediation of the markets and transforming the collaborative niches,' said Logan knowing full well that Saunders was hopeless in the field of irony.

'There, you see that you follow me? Well done, Ryan, I knew that we were right to give you the partnership. In October there will be the Big Bang of the stock market, with deregulation promised by Thatcher. I've spoken to the other two senior partners, and we want a piece of the pie.'

'We are lawyers, Newsham, not bankers. We bill hours, we find financial loopholes, we take a percentage, and everyone is happy. No risk involved,' said Logan.

'I know, but this opportunity is too tempting. We are talking here about millions of pounds in commissions, we just need a partner who already works in the field, we will merge, and we are ready to make the big leap. Think about it, if we get in business with a bank or a brokerage firm, we could share large clients, expand even in the legal sector …'

'Create synergies,' Logan completed the partner's sentence. 'We already have good clients, and we're squeezing them like lemons.'

'Ryan, this is a unique opportunity.'

'No this is a colossal fiasco in the making. You made me a partner because I understand finance better than all of you put together. I don't like this idea, and I will oppose it with all my will. My department is the one who brings in the real money in this firm, the one that makes you rich, the one that makes the difference between buying a forty-five-foot sailboat and a hundred and thirty-one. You should remember that.'

Saunders wasn't frightened by Logan's harsh words, and instead, he continued, 'Let's do it this way, prepare me a report on Mortcombe Bank. Dig, make one of your spells, discover, investigate, go and talk to Mortcombe himself. We did some early private negotiations, and everything we found looks promising, but we must not forget due diligence,' said Saunders and then pushed himself headlong into the cocaine.

As soon as Logan exited the office, Passmore, the second senior partner entered the room.

'I told you Logan would pose a problem.'

'I'm not worried about Logan. If the merger goes ahead his department won't be as important anymore, we could even do without him.'

Passmore nodded. It wasn't one of his battles, not anymore. At that point, he was only counting the days separating him from his deserved retirement. Let Saunders deal with it. His only objective was to keep his bottom glued to his chair until the merger was done and dusted, get his rich bonus and a golden handshake. He would retire happy.

The Mortcombe Bank. Who in hell had ever heard of it before? thought Logan.

<u>CHAPTER 2</u>

1989

The Mortcombe Bank building was located in the centre of Brighton, not far from Regency Square. A nontraditional choice for a banking institution, far from any financial route in the rest of England. What was the headquarters of a bank doing right on the seafront in a tourist town? Of course, that area had become fashionable, prices were skyrocketing, and bars and restaurants grew like mushrooms after rain. An ideal place for retirees and young people in search of freedom and a joint to smoke, but a bank?

Logan parked his car in front of the building and lit a cigarette. The architect had been busy, on that there was no doubt, the construction was made of glass and steel and reflected the morning sun on that spring day. The walls were curved, and Logan speculated that the building could look like a four-leaf clover if viewed from above. An anonymous bank, with funds to throw away and based in an inappropriate location. Not to mention the eyesore that that structure represented, surrounded by Victorian houses. He reserved his judgment for after he had been able to analyse the financial aspects. The numbers never lied.

Logan threw the half-smoked cigarette on the pavement and put it out with the point of his shoe. He entered the modern building, noting the wooden floors, and that the plants that adorned the entrance were cleverly arranged. Two receptionists waited at the front counter, both brunettes, with hair tied in ponytails. They didn't seem to have much to do. They were attractive. Logan's footsteps echoed in the half-empty lobby while heading towards the two women. He said his name and signed a register. They asked him to wait, and he sat on one of the grey cloth couches to the side of the reception area. The sofas were elegant but hard as marble. At least they weren't cold. A couple of newspapers lay on a glass table in front of the couch. No brochures on what the bank did. No mortgages or bank account leaflets. Nothing. Every bank had them, happy faces of well-dressed young women who could now afford a mortgage. Men portrayed while discussing a loan with a friendly and smiling employee. Retirees glad to have put their entire savings in a safe place, while staring off into the horizon, dreaming of holidays in exotic countries after a life spent saving. None of this. Zero brochure.

Another secretary came out from one of the elevators behind the front desk shortly afterwards. Logan had had time to look around, noticing that there was no sign of bank cashiers or any other typical components of a bank.

'Mr Logan, Mr Mortcombe is waiting for you.'

Logan got up and followed the woman up to an office on the second floor; everything in the building made him think about an abundance of money; the modern paintings on the walls, even in the hallways, some sculptures positioned to attract attention. It looked more like walking into a Tate Museum corridor, rather than being in a bank. Mortcombe occupied a corner office overlooking the waterfront. It was a very formal office, with modern furniture and defined and square lines. That ample space could have been considered minimalist, almost empty, except for a desk, positioned at least twenty feet from the entrance. A couple of sculptures, a single painting on the wall that Logan identified as a Kandinsky. Maybe authentic. Maybe a copy. But judging by the lustre of that place, possibly genuine. A stack of dossiers was resting on the floor next to the desk. Maybe it was also a modern sculpture, Logan couldn't decide.

Mortcombe was a man of about thirty-five, not particularly tall; he was wearing a blue pinstriped tailored suit and a crimson tie; short, well-groomed hair and a pair of metallic glasses. He moved quickly and precisely, as one who was accustomed to playing sports. As soon as he entered, Logan saw his interlocutor get up and head towards him; a *good sign*, he thought, *at least he's not one of those assholes who pretend to be busy.*

They shook hands and Mortcombe went straight to the point. 'Saunders must have informed you about the merger.'

'Indeed he has. I know enough to find it's a terrible idea,' said Logan and without asking permission, he lit a cigarette.

'There will be benefits for all of us, especially for you.'

'Ah, exactly as I thought,' said Logan, 'you are a benefactor. I understand Saunders' motivations; he is an ambitious and greedy bastard. The more he gains, the more cocaine he manages to squeeze into his nostrils. Your motivations are a little more obscure, though. Where did the money come from? I didn't see half a customer during the ten minutes I waited in reception.'

'Ah, but our customers are special,' said Mortcombe with a fake smile on his face, 'they are received in private offices, they certainly don't go over the counter. And then they leave us to make decisions on how to invest.'

Logan's concerns grew even more significant, if nothing else, however, he had been able to observe his questioner closely. He looked around searching for an ashtray and, not finding one, he put out the cigarette inside a Chinese jar in front of him, probably Ming dynasty. It looked authentic. Mortcombe did not blink.

'Do you have the financial documents I requested? I would like to take them back to the office today.'

'Of course, I gave the order to take them down to the front desk. Someone will help you to load the documents into your car. Ryan … may I speak frankly?' asked Mortcombe. Then, without waiting for an answer from Logan, he continued, 'this merger will go ahead, with or without you. I remind you that you were made partner only recently and your words don't mean shit. I'm not here to discuss strategies with you nor am I interested in your opinion. You wanted the financial statements? You can find them at reception, as far as I'm concerned you can read them or make paper aeroplanes with them, nothing will change.'

The switch in Mortcombe's behaviour was sudden. They had come to that. Saunders & Associates knew that Logan would have objected to the merger and instead of spending hours discussing the pros and cons, causing bad blood among them, threatening to say things that gentlemen shouldn't voice, they had left the task to Mortcombe. A stranger.

It was evident to Logan that Mortcombe was not interested in hearing his reasons and this triggered alarm bells in his mind. Not that he was worried about his role in the new company, he had a list of wealthy clients, and if things were turned for the worse, he would leave taking them with him. The inability to hear was a bad sign in business; vision and determination were necessary, for sure, Logan himself had never pulled back when he faced risks, but this was anything but. The reasons for the merger couldn't be only economic in nature and jump to footer the due diligence activities were not a smart move. He would have done it for a client but not for the company he was working for.

'I understand, I guess this meeting is over,' Logan said finally. It wouldn't make much sense, at that point, starting a battle between alpha males. He knew when it was time to remove the noise.

'You bet your ass it is!'

Logan got up and left the room without saying goodbye. He knew only too well he was being ambushed, strained by Saunders without his knowledge. *That prick*, Ryan thought. Saunders had no financial experience, he had been a criminal lawyer, but his strength lay in political and economic connections. Finding clients, convincing them, make them fork out vast amounts of money, but a merger like this? It was not up his street. It didn't make any sense.

Once he loaded the bundle of documents into the car, Logan departed in a hurry, leaving behind the gleaming building of Mortcombe Bank, and only then he realised what was wrong. The bank wouldn't have needed to do a merger, thought Logan giving one last look at the building from the rear-view mirror; with that kind of money, they could have bought a Saunders, Whitehall & Passmore unflinchingly. If they could throw a hundred million for their headquarters, they could waste fifty odd million to buy themselves a law firm, although perhaps not as renowned as Sandie.

Why? He wondered. Why, why, why?

He was sure he would find the answer in the documentation from the bank and if that weren't enough, he would trawl through every single file in Sandie's archives.

He didn't lack determination.

CHAPTER 3

1989

'Good morning, slaves,' said Logan on entering the office.

The young associates, working heads down for who knows how long, despite it being early in the morning, replied as a chorus, 'Good morning, Mr Logan.'

It was an open office, no cubicles, but only desks placed in different rows; the only separation was a blue panel in the middle with a glass window. Sitting at one of those desks reminded Logan of the visiting room of a prison. Since those promising young rarely had a right to privacy, the comparison suited them perfectly. The buzz was constant, people talking on the phone, employees discussing cases not yet resolved among themselves. The second image that occurred to Logan was that of a farming factory, chickens in a battery would lay their daily egg and, if successful, would survive another day.

'Slaves! You have received the documentation, today we are working on the Mortcombe Bank, it is a priority. If you find something wrong, anything at all, do not wait to do your usual end-of-day report! You come to me directly, and you tell me what you have found, are we clear?'

A chorus of, 'Yes, Mr Logan,' followed.

'Tim, Albert, for the two of you I have a special assignment; come to my office. No need to thank me for the honour.'

Tim Whitley and Albert Romanov turned toward each other with a puzzled look on their faces but stood up from their desks and followed their leader. The secretary was already rushing to prepare fresh coffee.

Logan settled himself on the leather chair behind his desk and turned on the computer, more out of habit than real need, and then rotated towards the two. 'Come on, sit down, you don't have to stand to attention.'

The two appeared fearful.

'This afternoon you shall go searching through all the cases handled by Saunders in the last ten years and find a link with Bruno Mortcombe. If he defended him because he got a parking ticket, I want to know. If he defended a cousin of his for cattle rustling, I want to know. And not a word to your colleagues or others in this company, are we clear?'

'We were finishing the tax avoidance job for Mrs Johnston, the actress. We already have the properties owned by a shell company in Jersey, then we need to divert the compensation and review the contracts with the Studio,' said Romanov. That was one of the main activities done by the working group led by Ryan Logan, it didn't matter if they were a corporation or wealthy individuals, he would do what was necessary to hide the funds from Her Majesty's Revenue and Customs' sight, in a legal way, of course. Not that the HMRC's employees were particularly thorough. They were known to settle incredibly low fines for those who had committed fraud. In fact, they put more effort into making sure that everybody paid rather than check corporates disbursed the fair amount. They were great paper pushers and often accepted gifts in return for favourable treatment. But Logan had never had to resort to this expedient. Why use corruption when a fair amount of grey matter juice would have had the same effect, with the advantage of not seeing their clients exposed on the front page of the British newspapers? That was the real benefit of its working group: elude taxes, not evade it, and get away with it. His group was what brought money into the company, other departments, compared to them, generated handouts.

'Well, my dear little slaves, are you familiar with the *Feynman path integral*, Nobel Prize in Physics in 1965, also known as *the multiple histories*?'

The two young lawyers looked at each other, perplexed, and then shook their heads.

'Ah, today's slaves are no longer what they used to,' said Logan with evident disappointment, 'the ancient Romans used Greek slaves to educate their children, and now the situation is completely reversed, but let's not digress. Feynman's theory, to make a long story short, indicates that at each moment the world separates into two parallel universes and, an instant later, each of the two universes parts also, creating four, then sixteen universes, and so on. In fact, there are infinite parallel universes. In another universe there might be a Martha and James in this office, in your place; or perhaps in another parallel universe it could be you, Tim, sitting behind this desk barking orders, although this would be a highly unlikely universe. Here, ask for help from your duplicates in some parallel universe and finish the fucking job tonight. Do we understand each other?'

'Absolutely yes, Mr Logan,' replied the two in unison. The secretary entered the office at that moment, and the two young lawyers stood up, knowing that their time was running out.

CHAPTER 4

1989

'What have you got for me? Come on slaves, give me good news.'

Tim Whitley and Albert Romanov, standing in front of Logan's desk, hesitated for a second. Bringing bad news to the boss wasn't always a pleasant task. Not that they knew if what they had discovered was of no use. Logan was inscrutable. Sometimes colleagues who thought they had done an excellent job were rebuked with bad words from his office. Other times, their irascible boss lauded jobs that Whitley or Romanov considered mediocre. But one thing they had learned from their dealings with him: the art of listening. Even during the most furious scold by Logan, he spent time explaining the details of how they could have done better. He cited articles and subparagraphs by memory, sentences unknown to most, cases that were long forgotten by everybody, but they were part of the jurisprudence. Many hung on just waiting for the storm to pass, but not Whitley and Romanov. They knew they could learn more in that half hour of abuse than during a whole working week.

Whitley spoke first.

'We searched in every kind of document, and although there is nothing blatantly illegal in

Mortcombe's operations, some things don't add up. For example, Mortcombe is from a wealthy family, but not enough to justify his current good fortune.'

Logan beckoned to continue. Whitley cleared his voice. 'He comes from a noble family but certainly not rich. Mortcombe had studied in Stamford, most likely because they couldn't afford Eton and then went to the Britannia Royal Naval College at Dartmouth. A short career in the Navy and then suddenly he has a brilliant start in the construction sector. He established Jenkins Ltd. which has built a housing estate on the outskirts of Sutton.'

'That eyesore is his?' asked Logan. 'I drive past it every day to come to the office, and I always wondered who had the unfortunate idea to build it. Hundreds of homes around a hillock at stratospheric prices. It seems made with Lego bricks, all the same, and rose like mushrooms after a rainy night. I thought it was an arable area.'

'The fact is that he wasn't rich enough to afford the land purchase in the first place. Although he could have partially funded the construction by selling the houses before they were built, that area is just not economical. Other constructors buy a plot, build, sell, and then buy another plot, simply put they are self-financing themselves. Mortcombe has made a leap that others in the same line of business couldn't afford.'

'Interesting,' said Logan. 'Any idea how the funds miraculously appeared?'

'Total darkness. But since Mortcombe did not inherit a fortune from his parents, old aunties, or forgotten American uncles, we checked, we hypothesise that the funds came from someone else.'

Logan lit a cigarette and exhaled the breath away from the two; they were doing a good job. 'We know how these things happen. You find a figurehead with a shred of aristocracy, and nobody asks questions. No evidence?'

'Nothing,' said Romanov, 'only suspects. I called a friend of a friend who works as an internal lawyer for Jenkins, but they all have their lips sewn tightly shut.'

'OK, then what?' asked Logan.

'From then onwards, he forged a phenomenal career. He moved into the financial sector working for Troy Global Securities and then became CEO of a Swiss Bank, Ranfald & Co, which he led to bankruptcy a few years later.'

'I remember it. It was during the financial crisis. That Swiss bank lost panties and shirt by lending to a bank in Ohio, which failed too.'

'Exactly. Mortcombe packed up, and a few months later, he founded the Mortcombe Bank. With whose money remains a mystery, because there is no record in the documents they provided. They are doing a lot of business with the Russians in New Odessa, disreputable types.'

'We are in the wrong profession,' said Logan. 'All right. Is that everything?'

Whitley looked sideways at Romanov, doubting whether to speak up further or not. Which did not go unnoticed under the watchful eyes of Logan. 'Come on, spit it out.'

'We found no traces of any trial run by Saunders that can bring us back to Mortcombe or its affiliates.'

'But that's not all ...' Logan completed the sentence.

'Last week instead of coming to the office I went to the archives. Don't worry, I worked on my case overnight. There was one detail that haunted me from Mortcombe's CV, and I wanted to check it out.'

Logan beckoned to continue.

'When he was in the Navy, he served on a ship in Malta, and the Captain was Saunders. I mean the old boy, Saunders' father.'

'The Commodore?'

'The one and the same, although at that time he was still a Captain. See, according to my reconstruction, the two served on the same ship for a couple of years. I don't know if it's important.'

Logan thought it over for a moment and then dismissed them. 'Great job, guys, you deserve an award. Take your girlfriends to dinner in a good restaurant and put everything on expenses. The firm will foot the bill.'

The two thanked him and departed in a hurry.

Saunders' father thought Logan. The old boy sometimes showed up in the office and often used to show up during the Christmas party. He was an affable fellow although he often dwelled a little too often on telling stories about his past in the Navy, especially after a few glasses of wine. Probably because he didn't have much else to discuss. Logan made a mental note to have a chat with him at the first opportunity.

CHAPTER 5

1989

The firm had arranged a gala to celebrate the merger between the two companies. *They aren't losing any time,* thought Logan. The event had been at Brentwood Park in Horsham, a XIX century manor recently converted into a hotel. Horsham was supposed to represent a middle ground between London and Brighton, in the minds of the organisers. Logan had no trouble whatsoever finding the hotel. He was a native of Sussex and had driven those streets for centuries, unlike some of his fellow Londoners who screwed up their noses about whatever was outside of the M25. For some, breaching the motorway surrounding London was almost a sacrilege, equivalent to entering a jungle populated by barbarians.

Dinner was a mortal bore, after each course, someone climbed on stage and bored the audience with a slide show. There was the moment of Passmore, one of the senior partners. Phrases like 'cultivate partnerships without friction' followed the 'competitive advantage' and 're-energise hybrid cultures.' Most of the attendants were busy guzzling champagne by the bottle as if there were no tomorrow, except to rest their glass when it was time for the ritual applause at the end of the presentation.

Saunders gambolled around from his table to the stage encouraging those present to ask questions. No one thought for a second about volunteering, so a frustrated Saunders changed his strategy, by interrogating the audience on random topics discussed in the presentation. Most had studied the lesson and were not taken by surprise.

Logan fought to sit near Commodore Saunders. The old man had an age beyond description. He could've been seventy years old as well as eighty. Or maybe less. Snow-white hair and a weather-beaten face chiselled by a lifetime at sea made him look like a piece of old parchment. Saunders Junior was forty-eight. Assuming thirty years before he had a baby, the former Commodore would be almost eighty. Maybe he had been busy as a youngster and had just passed seventy. Difficult to judge. He wore his uniform despite being released from service decades earlier. The medals on display. At that age, there were not many opportunities to show them, and maybe only a few would be able to recognise them.

'You should be proud of your son,' said Logan.

'Ah, yes, yes. If my son had chosen a military career, who knows where he would be by now,' said a tipsy Commodore Saunders. Logan filled the old man's glass for the umpteenth time.

'Charisma and leadership skills can be applied everywhere, even to the legal sector, don't you think?'

'Of course. My son broke a tradition that had lasted for generations, and God knows how much we need good officers, but now they are cutting military budgets everywhere. It is no longer the great Navy we once we were proud of.'

'With the Falklands, we did a good job, I suppose,' said Logan to keep the conversation going. The Commodore was groggy, and between one sentence and the next, he bent his head, like those plastic dogs that sometimes could be seen on the rear of some cars.

'I tell you, those were different times, albeit just a few years have passed, but I agree with you. Times are changing fast. Do you know that that Mortcombe who was on stage a few minutes ago served on one of my ships? A cowardly, gutless twat.'

'That same Mortcombe? Are you sure of that? It's not a common surname, but he didn't give me the impression of being material for the Royal Navy,' Logan pressed him.

'And he was not! An embarrassment to Her Majesty's military forces, but don't get me started.'

'Of course, would you like some more wine?'

'Why not? Is it French? The French are only good at two things: making wines and losing a war. Do you know the story of that Frenchman who placed a rifle for sale? Never used, dropped only once.'

'I imagine during a retreat,' laughed Logan.

'Certainly, certainly.'

'Do you mind if I come to visit you one of the coming weeks? With these corporate mergers, sometimes we have to put into practice some strategies, and there is nothing better than to consult with someone who knows about these things.'

'Of course, come and see me in my home whenever you want.'

'It is very nice of you, as always, Commodore.'

Mortcombe went up on stage and announced the attraction for the evening. They had invited the Bill Conti Orchestra directly from the United States to entertain the guests. The band played the first few notes of the *Rocky* soundtrack, and everyone cheered warmly. Why they were clapping was a mystery that Logan had not yet solved. After all, it was a movie about a boxer who doesn't win and two semi-morons who get together. Parallels on that merger were ironically apparent only to him.

Logan suppressed the urge to shout 'Adrian' out loud, and instead, he concentrated on the dessert they had just served.

It was when he entered the bar, after dinner and the endless presentations, when he saw her for the first time. The woman was wearing an elegant black dress and a necklace of black pearls. Her thick red hair fell over her shoulders. She was alone, sitting on a stool at the bar while sipping what appeared to be a vodka Martini. It was not known if shaken or just stirred. Logan had never seen her before, most certainly she was part of Mortcombe's team. In the two months that followed the merger, he had understood that the only criterion used to hire female staff in that place was beauty. But this woman was different from the other female employees in the Mortcombe Bank. The woman had class, evident from her poise. Perhaps he had been a bit too hasty in judging the merge.

'Which kind of bourbon do you have?' asked Logan to the bartender.

The young man pointed listlessly toward the shelf behind him and kept drying glasses with a cloth. Then, reading the dissatisfaction in Logan's face, he said, 'And we have a bottle of Pappy Van Winkle's Family Reserve, but we keep that in the cellar.'

'Can I order one?'

'Of course.'

'So, go get it. I'll pay for it.' Not that there would have been a problem to put it on expenses, that evening people were drinking rivers of champagne, and the final bill would be massive. He just didn't feel in the mood to share.

'Something to forget?' asked the woman at his side. Not only did she have fabulous red hair reflecting the surrounding light, but she also two amazing green eyes. Hard not to be hypnotised by that look.

'Yes, this merger. I have never liked banks in general, but this one, in particular, smells fishy. And it's managed by an asshole.' Most people know what his position in regard to the merger was. 'They could have at least set up all this circus in London, I could sneak away.'

The woman laughed showing perfect white teeth, and the bartender returned with a dusty bottle; he uncorked it and poured a glass. Then he placed the bottle on the counter next to Logan.

'Would you like a sip of nectar from Kentucky?'

'Willingly. The hotel has a spa, and the garden is not bad at all at this property. Are you staying for the night?' asked the woman.

'Of course. I plan on taking a colossal piss. Why don't you show me these fabulous gardens? There is always the hope they will forget about us and continue with their speeches unaware of our absence.'

'It seems an excellent idea to me. I'm Pamela Mortcombe, by the way, the asshole's wife.'

Logan didn't blink. 'The pleasure is all mine, Ryan Logan.'

The woman took the glass of bourbon and, rising, said, 'Right this way.'

<u>CHAPTER 6</u>

1990

It was a spring Saturday morning in Warlingham, and the dark clouds on the horizon promised rain soon. Logan got out of bed, placed a gentle kiss on the cheek of Pamela Mortcombe, still dormant, and descended the stairs to the kitchen.

He loved the peacefulness of the place, just outside the village and surrounded by trees and the countryside. The only sound he could hear was the wind moving in the trees and the chirping of birds. He prepared a strong coffee for himself and a light tea for Pamela and began to tinker with the bacon and eggs. He had never been a great cook, but he knew the basics; he would not make any mistakes. That rarely happened to him. It had been six months since that first meeting at Brentwood Park Hotel, and since then they had not lost any opportunity to meet. At first furtively, but then, seeing the complete disinterest of Bruno Mortcombe for his wife, more and more frequently. The merger of the two companies had completed months before, and it was actually a real unification. Saunders, Whitehall & Passmore disappeared in the meanders of the Mortcombe Bank. Whitehall had retired from business, Passmore received a golden handshake and moved to Devon. Others, including Logan, had continued working from their offices in London. His department had been halved. Those who remained continued to do the same job, others, including Tim Whitley and Albert Romanov, were routed among the various ranks of the bank.

He turned, hearing footsteps. Pamela joined him in the large kitchen, approached Logan and hugged him. Then they kissed. Logan could no longer think of a life without Pamela. There had been other women in his life, but nothing was comparable to what he was feeling for that beautiful creature who now stood next to him. He sniffed her wondrous red tresses and kissed her again.

'You're missing breakfast in bed,' said Logan.

'How romantic,' answered the woman sitting at the kitchen table. She briefly opened the newspaper from the day before without finding an article of interest while Logan was ready to serve breakfast. He did not move at ease in that large room, often only visited to prepare coffee or grab a beer from the refrigerator. It was a kitchen tastefully decorated by the previous owners, who probably spent every night cooking food. The worktop was in dark marble, the panels of beige lacquered shelves. An Aga was the centrepiece of the kitchen, but Logan had never learned how to turn it on and therefore had installed a gas hob. Not that he used that either, preferring to dine in the pub or in some restaurant in the area. The table where he and Pamela sat was somewhat rustic, vast, and made of oak. No elegance but remarkable features. Ideal for a home with children, that table had definitely resisted weathering from bands of rampaging little whelps and had survived without a scratch.

'Doesn't he care if you're out all night?' That was a topic they had discussed earlier, they both knew it was time for a decision.

'Who, Bruno? He doesn't even notice it. After the birth of Carla, I've become virtually invisible. The important thing is that I attend a few gala dinners and play my part. He has this idea of presenting himself as part of a united family. Do you know he has a lover?'

Logan laid the tea and breakfast in front of Pamela. 'I didn't know.'

'She isn't the first. I was jealous at the beginning, and I even had them followed by a private investigator. But I never confronted him with the evidence. Sometimes he can be ruthless and even if I loved him in the past, it's now all gone. I'm left with doubt about Carla.'

'What doubt?' The two looked each other in the face, no one had yet started breakfast, although Pamela kept sipping tea. The woman put down her cup on the table.

'He has a lot of friends, and I fear that he could get custody of Carla. You don't know what he's capable of.'

'He can't do that. The children remain with their mother, no judge would think otherwise.' He had never dealt with divorces, but the law was quite clear in this respect. Bruno Mortcombe was supposed to prove serious misconduct on Pamela's part to have any chance for custody over their daughter. As far as he knew that option wasn't available to him. Aside from their secret relationship.

Pamela tasted her breakfast; she suddenly stood up and ran to the bathroom. She returned after a few minutes, white in the face.

'I didn't think I was that bad as a cook,' said Logan to relieve tension. 'What is it, it's now one week that you've not been feeling well? Have you been to the doctor?'

'It's not that … Ryan, I'm pregnant.'

Logan stopped in his tracks, unable to utter anything for a few moments. He had no doubt he was the father. Ryan knew the relationship between Pamela and Mortcombe was, in fact, empty. Then he approached her and held her in a big hug.

'Darling … how long have you known?' he asked.

'Only a few days.'

'This is wonderful! We must not waste time and prepare to file for a divorce.'

'As soon as possible, I'm sick of this subterfuge and living this way. Are you sure about Carla?'

'There will be no problems whatsoever,' Logan reassured her. It was time to change his life, he thought. A son, or daughter, would change everything. No more drinking, no more working until late at night for the sole purpose of filling the time. He didn't care anymore about career or living a life of excesses, the only thing he could think of was the idea of raising a family in this very house in Surrey. He didn't care anymore of the daily battles in the office. He knew he would have left after the merger, regardless. Why not now? Cutting the bridges was the most sensible thing to do.

He thought of all those rooms in that house, which seemed to him always empty whenever he returned from work. It wouldn't be anymore.

Logan didn't know how wrong he was.

<u>CHAPTER 7</u>

1990

Newsham Saunders lived in a luxurious apartment at Lowndes Square, Knightsbridge. It was in the heart of wealthy London, and he was indeed proud of where he lived. In some circles, people were judged by their postcode. People let slip during a conversation, *'I live in Knightsbridge'* before even saying their first name. If the other party didn't counter with something more renowned, the hierarchies were established.

That evening Logan was at dinner with the managing partner. No one knew yet of his affair with Pamela, but yes, there would be repercussions after the divorce. He knew he wouldn't stay long in the new company. Contrary to what he had expected, Saunders had assumed an important role, almost higher than Mortcombe. How he had succeeded in that was a mystery.

Logan had arrived early for dinner, and at that moment, he was sipping a gin and tonic in one of the armchairs in the living room. The house had been renovated with taste, undoubtedly the work of some architect, thought Logan, since everything seemed to make sense. The style of the sofa, the paintings on the walls. The place oozed class, and it was ultimately the opposite of Saunders' office. Had he been married, his wife would get credit for such great elegance. Italian marble everywhere, adjustable lights in the ceiling, the Victorian fireplace restored and polished. No, Saunders wouldn't be able to achieve that.

'Good evening, Ryan,' said a voice behind him.

Logan put down his glass on a crystal table in front of him and turned around. 'Good evening, Commodore. Are you keeping me company?'

'Sure, sure, though I should not, considering my age.'

Logan nodded to one of the waitresses and ordered another gin and tonic. It was not the first that evening for the Commodore, nor the second. He was unsteady and visibly excited. He had probably been drinking all afternoon, mixing beers, whiskies, and who knew what else. He was still a sailor, after all. No trace of Saunders at that point, but he had said he would arrive later, so Logan remained in charge of being the caregiver for the Commodore. He had never had the opportunity to visit the old boy and ask about Mortcombe. Maybe this would be the ideal opportunity to do so.

'Nice house, furnished with taste,' said Logan.

'An old girlfriend of Newsham's, an architect,' said the Commodore. As if that could explain everything.

'Newsham should arrive soon,' said Logan, more to fill the silence than anything else.

'We were supposed to meet here this afternoon because of my will, and he obviously forgot.' Then, after a pause, he added, 'I do not like this story, Ryan.'

'What are you talking about, Commodore?'

'About Mortcombe, of course.' The elder, although he was half drunk, tried to keep the tone of a naval officer of Her Majesty. No uniform that evening, only a blue suit and a red tie that had seen better days.

'Not liked by many, but sometimes business is business.'

'Did you know that the man served under me when I was Chief Superintendent? A disgrace to the Navy.' Commodore Saunders began to tell. They were stationed in Malta, and Mortcombe was a young lieutenant on the ship with Saunders.

A malingerer according to the Commodore. One day the local police came out in force to catch a rapist. According to the information supplied by the victim, the offender was a young British male. The poor woman was not only raped but also brutally beaten one evening in one of the side streets of Valletta, not far from the venues and pubs attended by sailors. The description she gave to the investigators was clear and precise. The woman was the daughter of a senior Maltese politician, a girl above suspicion, who was returning home after visiting her grandparents. The local newspapers cried scandal aloud, especially since she later died from the injuries, after weeks spent in a coma due to complications. But she'd been able to provide an adequate description to the authorities.

The police made hell trying to board the two British ships that were in port at the time, diplomatic pressure was applied. At that time, Malta was a strategic port for the Navy of Her Majesty, at the height of the Cold War.

Saunders continued to tell, Logan dangled from the Commodore's lips. After numerous pressures, they ordered all components of the two ships to disembark, officers included, to allow the local authorities to continue their investigation. Unfortunately, the description did not match anyone on board the two boats, which were left to sail away a few days later.

It was only later they understood that a second lieutenant received a bribe from Mortcombe, a hothead but with family money, to hide in a closet in the engine room. No one had paid attention to his absence. To prevent further scandal, the Navy gave a dishonourable discharge to both of them in disgrace but failed to inform Malta about their discovery.

'And how did you come to know about this whole thing?'

That second lieutenant had falsified the attendance log, unbelievable!' added the Commodore, still lost in his thoughts. 'One day during a fire drill, as soon we set sail, they found Mortcombe hidden in that closet. He wasn't supposed to be in that place at that time. The officer involved in the fire drill, at first gave him a reprimand, but the rape story was well present to all of us, and then I was informed. Can you realise? A British naval officer, for God's sake. None of us could believe it. The little bastard spent the rest of the journey in the brig until we returned to Plymouth and then the military police took care of him.'

Logan remained silent. If the old man was telling the truth, and he had no reason to doubt it, that fact complicated things further. Not only was Mortcombe a bastard but he was also capable of violence. He needed to speed things up with Pamela, find a way to keep her safe.

'Have you told anyone else this story?' asked Logan.

'To Newsham, of course, about a year ago. I was reading the *Financial Times* and suddenly, turning pages, what do I find? An article on new banks in England and a picture Mortcombe. Several years have passed but some things you don't forget.'

'They convicted him?'

'Unfortunately, no. The sod got away with a dishonourable discharge. The command decided that it would be better to avoid a scandal. If it was up to me instead ...'

Logan refrained from commenting, but some things were starting to make sense. The sudden decision to merge with the Mortcombe Bank was not a financial move, it was blackmail. The fact that Newsham had acquired a prominent position in the new company and hadn't seemed to stop in his rise. But Logan knew there was always a price to pay. Blackmailers don't ever stop. They get something quickly, and then they want more and keep squeezing. Until something breaks.

Logan changed tack, asking about some nautical club of which the Commodore was part of.

Newsham arrived shortly after, just in time for dinner. The Commodore killed another bottle of Burgundy and when he wasn't able to stay on his feet any longer was taken to his room by one of the waiters. The others were released shortly after, leaving Saunders and Logan alone.

'There are disturbing rumours about you,' said Saunders. They had moved back into the living room, sitting on two cream-coloured sofas opposite each other. Saunders had just lit a cigar and puffed out more smoke than a Cuban bus.

'Of what kind?'

'You're about to go to the competition? I was in touch with Rodderick Finance a few days ago, and they told me you had made veiled allusions to corporate changes. In short, the usual chatter that people make before changing jobs and poach a handful of customers in the process.'

There wasn't much time left. As soon as Pamela made the divorce announcement, Logan would be politely, but firmly, conducted to the door and fired. It didn't upset him in the least, as he had already decided to leave. Ryan had contacted the best customers, and these had given him a nod of assent in the case he decided to open a law firm on his own. But he would have not been alone in this new venture, he would have brought with him a handful of trusted associates.

He had already arranged everything. An office in Chancery Lane, for which he had already paid a deposit, the announcement in two weeks and then the tremendous job of protecting the customers that he stole from Saunders. The partners would go to hell and back trying to recover their clients, they would call them daily, making promises they couldn't keep. They would try to block the funds that Logan held in the company, perhaps they'd take him to court, but those were only tactics that would not have led to anything. Aside from annoying him. No law prohibited changing job and customers were free to choose.

Logan passed a hand through his hair, smoothing them backwards. 'Those of Rodderick are a bunch of morons who couldn't distinguish their own ass from a hole in the ground.' However, if they had spoken to Saunders, it was a problem. Logan would leave irrespective, with or without Rodderick Finance. They were not necessary for his plans.

'Maybe, but the matter got me thinking so I dug a little deeper.' Saunders got up from the couch and walked to a desk near a window. From one of the drawers, he extracted a large manila envelope and retraced his steps. Once he sat down again, he opened it at a glacial pace. They were photographs, of that Logan was sure.

'I had you followed. You know how much those investigative agencies cost? A blunder, they are almost worse than us when it comes to billing a client's work, but in this case, they were efficient. Here, take a look.' And so saying, he laid the pictures on the glass table that stood between the two.

Logan picked one up. There was no need to look at any others. The picture portrayed him in an unambiguous position with Pamela. He was unimpressed, it was not in his nature to lose his temper, but the fact that Saunders knew was an unexpected complication.

Saunders pulled a small container from his pants pocket, disposed a little amount of cocaine in two parallel rows on one of the other pictures, just above the face portraying Logan, and he sniffed.

'So, this is what we are going to do,' continued Saunders, 'when the office re-opens on Monday, the first thing you do is to prepare a nice letter of resignation. Then you bugger off immediately, and if you make a move to take even one of our customers, these pictures end up on Mortcombe's desk. From what we learned, he's quite the vengeful type, and if you care about this woman, well, it's best if you quit silently. What you do after that, is none of my business, open a law firm somewhere in the countryside, take care of buying and selling real estate, draft wills and all the other crap low-life lawyers do nowadays. If I see you in London or if you try to contact one of the other law firms that do business in our industry, I will tell them so many lies on your account they will be horrified at the thought of hiring you. Do we understand each other?'

'Illuminating. So now both of us have a new career in front of us. How is it going your new endeavour as blackmailer?' The disdain was evident in Logan's voice. He deposed the photo on the coffee table; certainly, Saunders had other copies.

'Come on, Ryan, this isn't blackmail. It is simply a business transaction where you got the worst of it.'

'Is this what you told Mortcombe to convince him to merge the two firms?'

For a moment, Saunders hesitated. He opened his mouth to say something but then thought better of it. 'I don't know what you're talking about,' he said in the end.

'Look, your old man does not hold his liquor anymore. He told me about that affair of Mortcombe's in Malta. So, I think this is what we need to do: you take these pictures, and you shove them up your arse. I'm resigning Monday, but if a customer decides to follow me, you're not going to do a damn thing to stop them. And if you don't like it, I can always go to Scotland Yard and give them my side of the story. Mortcombe ends up in a Maltese prison and you in a British one for blackmail. What do you say?'

Saunders put out his cigar and stood up abruptly. Then headed toward the window with slow, measured steps. It was clear he was considering several options in his mind, apparently without coming to a conclusion. It was a few minutes later when he spoke again. He undid his tie and said, 'Bugger off, Ryan. And do it quickly.'

The conversation was over. Logan stood up in turn and walked right out of the apartment. No greetings or pleasantries, it wouldn't have been wise.

When Saunders was alone, he took out his phone and dialled a number he knew by heart.

'Hello?' said the voice on the other end of the phone.

'Mortcombe, this is Newsham. We have a problem.'

****

The Monday morning newspapers reported the news of the gruesome death of Newsham Saunders as a possible burglary in the apartment gone wrong, although investigators did not commit to a clear explanation.

One of the waiters found Saunders on Saturday morning, after dinner with Logan; according to the first reports Saunders was killed with one of the kitchen knives found in the apartment. Signs of a struggle were evident and, according to witnesses, some valuables were taken.

Logan realised something was wrong when he arrived at the office that morning, having spent the weekend in Brighton in an apartment owned by Pamela. They hadn't opened a newspaper or watched television all weekend. They had barely gone out for a walk on the Boardwalk.

The security guard at the entrance of the building had a dark face. When Logan took one of the newspapers, he whispered *condolences* half aloud. Logan took no notice until he was in the elevator and opened the paper. Saunders's face looking at him from the front page, an image that portrayed him in a dark suit and tie and half-smiling. The photo was at odds with the news. He continued to read the article eagerly until he arrived at the floor of his office.

The secretary ran up to him as soon as she saw him. 'Two metropolitan police officers are waiting for you, Mr Logan. I had them sit in your office.'

According to the rules they should have waited in the lobby, thought Logan, but given they were the police and were there due to the death of one of the partners, he decided not to give an earful to his secretary.

'Hello, may I help you?' said Logan upon entering his office and heading toward his desk. The two cops were a woman in her thirties, dark and oily hair held back in a ponytail. The man, of similar age, balding, was dressed in a dark blue suit, surely bought at a discount shop. He wore a pair of turtle shell glasses that he was adjusting on his face every two seconds. It wasn't clear whether this was because they were too big or if it was due to a tic. He looked more like a rugby player than a cop. They showed him two badges. The woman had changed her hair colour from blonde to brunette. The man was unchanged, but with a sad face in the photo. Same glasses. Patricia Willoughby and Jordan Corrigan. He didn't look Irish and had no accents. He was in shape, almost muscular, although from the picture one couldn't have said. The woman was lean and moved jerkily. A nervous type. Logan gave up the badges.

'Can we sit down?' asked the man.

'Yes, of course,' answered Logan, indicating two chairs facing the desk. 'It's because of Saunders, right? I read the news right now in the paper.' The two cops looked at each other's eyes but said nothing.

'Can I get you something?'

'No, thanks,' said the man. He answered for both. No doubt he was the one with greater seniority.

'We learned that on Friday evening you went to dinner at Saunders' apartment in Knightsbridge.' It wasn't a question.

The woman had taken a notebook and a pen from the inside of her jacket and prepared to take notes.

'Yes, of course.'

'Can you tell us about the events? What did you talk about?'

Logan gave a general description of the evening, excluding the attempt of blackmail by Saunders and his threats against Mortcombe. The two nodded and the woman kept taking notes.

'At what time did you leave the apartment?'

'About eleven o'clock. To reach my home in Surrey, it takes about an hour and a half, if there isn't too much traffic.'

'And when you left the apartment, Saunders was alive?'

The question caught him by surprise. 'Of course,' he said, but something didn't add up. If Saunders had been the victim of a robbery gone wrong, why all those questions?

'And you didn't return to Saunders' home later?' continued Corrigan in a monotone voice.

'No, I spent the weekend in Brighton.'

'Can anyone testify you were in Brighton?' asked the woman. She had a shrill voice and a northern accent. Probably Liverpool.

'I shall have to think about it. But what matters where I've been during the weekend? I left at eleven, so the burglary must have happened after that time.'

The woman re-read out loud her notes and then asked, 'Do you confirm what you have declared to us?'

'Yes.'

At that point, the man pulled out from a leather bag a manila envelope, the same one Logan had seen in the hands of Saunders the Friday evening before. He felt the blood stopping for a moment in his veins.

'Who is this woman?'

Logan's face darkened. 'If you want me to answer any more questions, we'll do it in the presence of a lawyer.'

The two looked at each other again. 'As you wish,' said Corrigan. 'You are under arrest on suspicion of murder. You do not have to say anything, but it may harm your defence if you do not mention when questioned, something which you later rely on in court. Anything you do say may be given in evidence.'

With that said, the two agents stood up, and the man pulled out a pair of handcuffs from his back pocket. Logan said nothing but stood up in turn. He knew that before an arrest he couldn't do more than satisfy the agents but meanwhile, mentally, he began to think about who could help him in his defence.

They escorted him out of the building amid the dismay of the other employees.

CHAPTER 8

1990

Gregg Potter disliked prisons, let alone Wandsworth. An abomination built in the mid-nineteenth century and modernised badly. From the outside, it looked almost like a castle, with those two towers of brownstone alongside the main door and the two others at the corners. Behind them, there were other more modern buildings where the prisoners were housed.

He never violated the law, and the mere thought of ending up in that jail gave him the creeps. He did not know Ryan Logan, but due to the insistence of an old friend from university, he had decided to accept the case. It rarely happened that he would take lost causes, but this would bring him minimum visibility and it was a favour for someone he owed a lot to. From the files and the evidence collected up to that point the court wouldn't take long to convict the accused.

He was escorted through corridors painted in cream that could lead someone to think about being in a hospital if it weren't for the iron bars. Everywhere. Cream coloured too. The guard's heavy footsteps resounded in the corridor making it even eerier. One hundred and twenty pounds of muscle, necessary to quell riots, to block violent inmates. Wandsworth gave him the jitters. He handed his bag to another guard and was searched before passing through a metal detector. They left him the case files and a notebook but not the fountain pen. Metal. He received a temporary one made of plastic. Then they accompanied him to a room about four meters square. A laminate table in the middle and two metal chairs fixed to the floor. The walls were cream coloured as well, freshly repainted. As in hospitals.

****

Ryan Logan arrived in the visiting room several minutes later. He wasn't handcuffed, as seen in the American TV series, and he did not even have a uniform. Only a grey T-shirt and gym pants, grey too. In some places, it was better to stay grey, in every sense. Inconspicuous, not to attract the attention of other crooks. Certain colours helped a person to survive in those places. Potter had some documents scattered on the table in front of him.

'What is the situation?' asked Logan.

'Honestly? Simply put, you are stuffed. The police, after having found the corpse, raided Saunders' apartment. They have photos of you with a woman, although they haven't discovered her identity. They've decided not to give the photos to the newspaper for the time being, but they may do in the future. Depends on the situation. They also found one of your cufflinks, with your initials, covered in the victim's blood, under one of the sofas. No fingerprints on the knife but they can be erased. Following the search of your home, they found the second twin cufflink tucked away in a closet. Needless to say, also covered with blood, and half a kilo of cocaine.'

Potter raised his eyes from the papers and looked at his client's face. He looked tired. Motionless. Then he saw the fear in his eyes.

'I've been set up, Potter. I don't own monogrammed cuffs, those are made for hacks who think they are important. As for the cocaine, I don't know what to say. I've never used it, nor have I done any trafficking. I'm earning a mountain of money legally. Saunders made a lot of use of the stuff. If you were to find drugs, his house was the most suitable place. I tell you, I'm being framed.'

Potter scratched an eyebrow. Ninety per cent of his clients said they were innocent. Some were, most not. Yet this Logan seemed to speak the truth. 'The police's main hypothesis is that Saunders was blackmailing you because of the photos. Who is the woman?'

'The wife of Bruno Mortcombe, the banker. We spent the weekend together.'

'Damn! There has been a recent merger between the two companies, right? By the rumours I hear, he is not exactly a commendable fellow. His name turns up from time to time when there has been some crime or other, but nothing that can be proved,' said Potter. 'Maybe we could use her as a witness, but there would be a motive for both of you to kill Saunders. Are there witnesses of your weekend in Brighton? In the documents, there is no mention.'

Logan slumped on the back of the chair and stared at the ceiling for a moment, trying to remember the events. They had brought food from home, and they had cooked together in the apartment. No theatre or cinema, and if anyone had seen them by chance walking on the waterfront, they would have no way to track them. They were two ordinary passers-by to whom nobody paid attention.

'No witnesses.'

'If you plead guilty, maybe we can reduce your sentence,' said Potter.

Logan clenched his fists until they become white. They were at that point. An obvious case to the investigators. Occam's razor would do the rest: why seek a convoluted explanation when all the evidence led straight to him? But pleading guilty was a compromise he couldn't live with. Pamela was pregnant. What Mortcombe would do with her remained to be seen. He would raise the child as his own, or perhaps he would have divorced her, leaving Pamela in the middle of a road. Neither hypothesis was comforting.

Seeing the doubts growing over Logan's eyes, Potter said, 'Look, let me talk to the woman. I can put a private investigator on the case, but it will take time to look for alternative evidence, at least aiming for the legitimate doubt. You are a lawyer, I do not think it necessary for me to explain to you what kind of mess we are in.'

Logan assented. Neither of them had anything more to add.

****

Potter returned several times to Wandsworth. He informed Logan of conversations held with Pamela Mortcombe. After insistence, she revealed that her husband, Bruno Mortcombe, was the mastermind organiser of Saunders' murder. She didn't know the reasons that had impelled him to kill Saunders, but he certainly knew of the relationship between Logan and Pamela. He gave her an ultimatum: continue playing the good wife, showing up at gala parties and in return Logan would serve his prison sentence without accidents. Apparently, Pamela would not testify. From what the private investigator had been able to ascertain through the underground of London, those threats had a foundation and Mortcombe could, in return for payment and the right contacts, do anything he wanted. Kill Logan during a scuffle in prison, Pamela could die in a car accident. Anything.

Logan was sentenced to life in prison. A judgment he wouldn't appeal.

CHAPTER 9

2011

Billy Frazier, known as 'the brick' laid on the bed in his cell at Wandsworth, staring at the ceiling. He wouldn't serve the eight remaining years of his sentence for armed robbery. He wouldn't spend another month in that place, according to the doctor. Pancreatic cancer. Sadly, he'd been neglected by the doctors in Her Majesty's prison service and diagnosed when it was too late. Billy was a chain-smoker and if he had to die of cancer, he at least expected the beast to take it to the lungs. Of lungs, there were two of them, after all. Fifty per cent chance of dying. Of pancreas, instead, there was only one. He didn't even know what the pancreas was for. They explained to him that the pancreas produces hormones and enzymes, but he didn't know what those were. Hormones were the ones which transvestites used to grow breasts, but he couldn't explain how the pancreas would serve a man.

One month to live. Maybe two according to the doctor. But perhaps just one.

He didn't even need to go through chemotherapy as the tumour was too far progressed and that afternoon they'd moved him to the infirmary. They would fill him up with morphine until he was dazed, the only thing left to do was to wait for death to take him away. If it had happened five years ago, he wouldn't have ended up in the hospital. He would have gone to blacks, punched one of them in the face and waited for a sudden knife to the kidneys. In a hallway or in a shower. That would have been a better death. But now, he was sixty years old and had converted to the Catholic religion. Getting killed on purpose was equivalent to committing suicide. He had never been religious, but as the years passed and the fear of dying at any time in that prison, had changed him. He turned slowly to religion, talking to the priest in prison. His cellmate said it was because he was getting old.

'When you get old you become religious,' he said.

In part it was true, he'd committed several crimes, but he wasn't afraid to die. Not anymore.

Eight years in Wandsworth or one month in a bed full of drugs. Maybe two. There was no comparison.

The last time he confessed he had spat it out. All the crimes he had committed, even those he had never been convicted for. He saw terror in the face of the priest, while he recounted. He had no shame for what he'd done, only regret. If only things had gone differently.

In the end, the priest gave him absolution but urged him to speak to the authorities about those crimes. He could take them to the grave with him, he already got the acquittal, but you could never know. Maybe on the other side, they had different rules. Better wipe his conscience clean before it was too late. Who knew where he would be, or in what condition, in a month. Maybe two, but probably one for how it felt that day.

It was at that point that he knocked on the door and called a security guard.

The prison officer winced at his request to speak with the director of the prison, but he finally agreed. He was heard on the same day, just hours before the transfer.

Billy Frazier confessed to having committed five murders, never solved, several more robberies, violent crimes, racketeering.

The director stood at the mention of a name, Newsham Saunders. He remembered that murder and the alleged culprit was in the same prison, although in a wing different from Frazier.

'Tell me about the Saunders murder,' he said.

Billy 'the brick' Frazier didn't know who had ordered the murder, but he was someone who had money to spend and wanted a job well done. The tip and a substantial advance had arrived from a mutual contact, now dead. That night, Frazier entered a flat in Knightsbridge someone had indicated to him. From his previous surveillance, he knew that the owner was alone. Opening the door was easy enough, but when the owner had awakened, Billy had stabbed him in the abdomen. He slumped to the ground. A second stab to the heart had ended his life. It had to look like a burglary and Billy did his best to collect as many valuables as he could. A bonus.

The instructions said to leave a cufflink that had been previously delivered to him, at the scene of the crime. Staining it with the victim's blood was his idea. He had thought of leaving it in sight, but then he had second thoughts, pushing it under one of the sofas. Unless the police hadn't sent a band of incompetents, they'd have found it easily. He wiped his fingerprints from the knife and the doorknob and walked, unseen, to his van, where he deposited the loot. That job had a second part. He travelled to a house in Surrey and planted the twin cufflink and a pound of cocaine. A waste according to him, a few ounces would have sufficed, but those people were no joke. Best to do as ordered.

The director listened, hanging on every word that passed the lips of the villain, noting down every word. Would you make a sworn statement? He asked.

Billy Frazier nodded.

Billy repeated the same story to two apathetic policemen the next day. He signed a declaration, and when asked if he had more evidence, he spoke of the swag. Some objects, two paintings, and a statue were still held at home. No one had ever asked, and he liked those three things, they had class. Something he had never had in his life. He gave a brief description of them, and the two cops eagerly took note. They visited Frazier's apartment that same day for confirmation.

Billy Frazier was transferred to the prison infirmary, and a few days later Ryan Logan was released.

Logan had lost everything apart from his freedom.

He did occasional work to survive, and slowly he put himself back together. Nothing comparable to what he had before prison, but now he had a rented room and some money for a meal. He had read the news about Pamela's suicide years before, maybe he still had a daughter, but he wasn't sure.

The practice to be re-admitted to the legal profession was not complicated. A case of incorrect justice.

There was still the void to fill, but Logan didn't want to think about that. He kept himself busy, the more time he spent working for his clients the less he had to think about the loss he had experienced in his life.

PART 2

CHAPTER 10

Domino Gravis entered the luxury Battersea penthouse, intent on reading a gossip article in the *Sunday Times*; she took off her shoes and headed for the bar. It was late afternoon, and a glass of white wine would help her to finally catch that thought that was slipping into her mind. She chose a chardonnay and headed for the armchair near the large window from which she could see the chimneys of the old power station.

Battersea was renovating. Housing prices in the centre were skyrocketing, and slowly Londoners had moved to the suburbs. The neighbourhood seemed almost a construction site. New palaces stood at every corner, old buildings were torn down to make way for luxury condominiums for those who couldn't afford to make the leap in the most exclusive areas of the capital. The apartment was newly built. There were also plans to convert the old power plant into flats, but until then nothing had yet been decided. She liked her apartment, looking right at the power station and it was like having a three-dimensional Pink Floyd cover available throughout the day.

'Looks like an interesting article,' said Marcus watching her. A ray of sunlight was beating on the woman's hair, making her look almost like an otherworldly creature.

Domino was from Birmingham; she grew up in a tenderloin surrounded by drunks and violence. She left school before age and even if she wanted to work, unemployment was rampant, and at most, she would have found a waitress job in a restaurant. She was attractive and bright, and soon realised at a young age that with a face like hers, people rarely said no. People remained enchanted looking at her, and she understood soon enough that she could ask anything to a man and get it.

In the early years, it was enough for her to borrow a few pounds from the people she met in the pub, while they tried to pick her up. Asking an attractive girl to give the money back? It would never happen. And often the awareness of being scammed by an angelic face passed into the background in front of her beauty. Then came the card games, small scams to raise enough money for the rent. Without realising it, she'd aimed higher and higher, mesmerising jewellers and chief executives of industry. It was a grey winter's day when she met Marcus. She had gone to a fancy restaurant, and a nice gentleman in a pinstripe suit looked just right as her next victim. She would have worked him in about ten minutes. Instead, it was Marcus who made the first move, approaching the girl. He approached Domino in a roundabout way, saying that there were different ways to deal with life. Alone, wasting talent for a few hundred pounds at a time, or with others, where planning and long cons were brought to the extreme, often yielding enormous sums of money.

Domino was not convinced, she worked alone, but she also realised she had limits. That the nice gentleman was dedicated to scams seemed impossible to her. But there was something that drew her into it, not being restricted to the usual deception, seen over and over again a hundred times, the ability to learn new things from experience.

Marcus gave his telephone number to the brunette, who wouldn't have looked out of place as a model at the London Fashion Week, and since then they had always worked together. Ten years had now almost passed.

'There are people in this world who take possession of entire banks,' said Domino without lifting her eyes from the newspaper.

'My dear, nowadays you are either a genius with computers, or you steal money from others, or you make your fortune by inheriting the family fortune. Come to think of it, it has been so for millennia. Apart from computers, of course. I don't want to say that my profits have been obtained illegally, of course, it's a purely academic discourse. Who's the lucky guy?' Marcus would never admit to having done something illegal, despite having been caught red-handed, not even when he was in the company of his associates.

'The lucky gal. A certain Amelia Mortcombe of Brighton,' said Domino showing him the article.

'She is a beautiful woman. And how come you're interested in the social life of Brighton, may I ask?'

'I don't know, in the last few days newspapers do nothing else but talk about her. First an article in the *Daily Mail*, then I find her in other articles in various newspapers online and also today in the *Sunday Times*. She is getting worse than the Kardashians, they don't write of anybody else, apparently.'

'And how much would this fortune amount to?' asked Marcus getting up off the couch. He paced around the room for a few moments and then stopped to carefully admire a painting by Rembrandt. It was apparently a fake, like the Picasso and everything else hanging on the walls. Lenny had made them, who was the forger of the group, among other things. There was no object he couldn't reproduce faithfully. An ancient Roman vase, paintings from the best artists, old bottles of wine. Everything was within his reach, having studied for years with Gavin Neil Tiddington. They were fortunate to have him in the gang.

'It's hard to tell. It is a private bank with accounts for several billion, so I guess it's considerable.'

'Let me read … Oh yes, the father is in a coma, and our young lady is set to take the reins of the family bank. Sounds like an American TV series. Are you getting the Robin Hood syndrome? Stealing from the rich and to give to the poor … meaning us?' laughed Marcus.

'Something like that. We have always operated in London, and there aren't many suckers left.'

'I would disagree on that one. With all the Arabs buying half the town, not to mention the Russians, it seems to me that this is a good country of sheep. London is not over yet, you know? There's always room for another scam.'

'Yes, but we have been looking for the right one for years. The one that will sort us out for the rest of our lives,' said Domino.

Hank, hearing the two talking about of money came up close.

'Lenny, take a look on the internet and browse about this Amelia Mortcombe,' said Hank, 'you never know, we might find something useful.'

The man turned on the laptop in front of him and started typing on the keyboard. A couple of minutes of anxious waiting passed by before he gave an answer. At first sight, she seems to be everywhere. 'Damn it's almost worse than Paris Hilton. Some party, lots of stories on the bank. The father is in a coma in hospital. She is single apparently.'

'What's her occupation?' asked Marcus.

'Hard to say,' continued Lenny, 'maybe she is Beauty without the beast … no, here it is, she is a lawyer. She has a studio in Brighton centre.'

'I wouldn't scruple to scrub a lawyer,' said Hank.

'Considering the one defending you in the last process, it seems to me that the category is long due a lesson,' said Marcus. The man noticed the excitement in the eyes of his cronies, as when blood is thrown overboard in the presence of sharks.

'From what we read, the father is in hospital in a coma. A car accident. The bank is worth billions, and she should take charge of it shortly. In the meantime, she seems to live a worldly life. I'm looking at her on Facebook and LinkedIn; she has a sister who doesn't seem to do anything in life, aside from being committed to going shopping and going from one party to the next. The brother-in-law works at the bank and looks like a big shot, he is in charge of investments. He looks like an asshole.'

'What makes you think that?' asked Marcus. Any information they could find at that point would facilitate the engagement if they wanted to con them.

'Well, he is spitting life, death, and miracles of his work on LinkedIn. It sounds like a lot of big words to explain to the world that he is more important than he actually is. He doesn't have a Facebook profile, but his wife posts enough pictures to get an idea. An expansive house, even for an executive, a sporty BMW, typical of those assholes…'

'Hank has a sporty BMW,' said Domino.

'Exactly!'

'Guys, let's not digress,' said Hank, as if stung. He had always had a passion for fast cars, although often he drove under the speed limit so as not to attract the attention of the police.

'There is nothing, however, leading us to believe that this Amelia is eager for money,' said Marcus. That was a pivotal point to locate a good target.

'What do you think, gentlemen, is it worth sending a couple of our teammates to test the waters?' asked Hank.

'A few days break in the lovely town of Brighton?' said Marcus laughing. 'Can I bring one of the guys with me?'

'Of course,' said Hank, 'we still have a lot of money from the previous scam, this Mortcombe is worth the investment.'

'Before going though, a little lesson on slyness for Chaz,' said Marcus. Chaz was the youngest of the group and often the target of taunts. 'Do you want to bet a beer that I can tie a napkin without letting my hands leave the edges?'

Chaz thought it over. For knotting a towel, he would have to remove a hand. 'OK, I'm in. But if you lose you buy my cinema tickets for a week.'

Marcus placed the napkin on the table and formed it into a triangle. Then folded his arms and using his fingertips grabbed the two extreme sides of the napkin. He straightened his arms, and in doing so, the fabric knotted, leaving the young man in dismay.

'You owe me a beer, boy,' declared Marcus, but it was time to leave the apartment and go to Brighton. They couldn't formulate a precise plan until Marcus gave the OK. Studying the victims on paper was not sufficient, in their craft they had to understand the personality of the victim, what motivated a person. Only an inspection in the field would give those answers.

And all those millions were an incredibly strong incentive.

<u>CHAPTER 11</u>

It was a gloomy day in Brighton, and the drizzle made the outlines of the buildings indistinct. It wasn't the first time they had met at Café U Týna, they had already seen each other on previous days, and a few times they had also exchanged a few quick words about the weather and the hordes of tourists invariably gathered to explore The Lanes. Having lived in Brighton quite some time, Amelia hardly even noticed them while for Anders it was still a novelty. Both were waiting for a gap in the rain, and when Amelia looked around to find a table, Anders did the same, albeit more slowly. 'May I sit down with you?' he asked, after observing other tables and their occupants. The man was standing with his cup in hand, uncertain about the answer he would get.

The woman was very classy, in a grey suit and heels. She had carefully folded her coat and stowed it on the chair beside her. The man, a few years younger, looked like a model. Not only due to his beautiful facial features and physique, but also because of the clothes. He wore a dark suit and a bright shirt that looked like one often seen in fashion magazines.

Amelia still had an hour before her appointment at nine a.m., and she did not want to be alone. Small talk with a stranger, was more appealing than spending a whole hour thinking about what would happen later so she nodded at him to sit.

'Thank you,' he said, his slight accent catching her attention. 'What are you doing in Brighton?'

'I'm a local, lived and worked here all my life and every Saturday morning I try my best to entertain handsome tourists in this café. I can't seem to place your accent, though?'

'That's funny! Well, I'm not really a tourist, let's say I like changing venue and live my life in a less conventional way. And yes, my father is Swedish and my mother English, so with my time spent abroad, I do have a less then easy to identify accent. I'll take you up on the entertainment offer. Tell me something about yourself that I wouldn't guess easily.'

'OK, my father is in a coma at the hospital, and today I have to take charge of a private bank.'

'I'm sorry.' Anders wanted to say something different. He felt the falsehood in its reply, a sorry thrown there, for an unknown woman, about another unidentified individual. He wanted to add something else, but nothing came to mind.

'No reason to be sorry. The old man is a jerk,' said Amelia unperturbed, without showing the slightest glimpse of emotion.

'I meant I'm sorry you own a bank now. Bankers are pricks.' Amelia's laughter came after a brief moment of astonishment, making the heads of some of the other occupants of the café turn. The waiter also threw a furtive glance in their direction, perhaps he was checking if they had finished the coffee yet. Shortly after that, the café would be filled to the brim, and he would want them to either leave or at least to order breakfast. He passed a wet sponge along the marble counter and resumed his chores.

'And you, what are you doing to Brighton, tell me more about your "unconventional" way of living?' Amelia asked in turn, her retort to that first question.

'I'm travelling around Europe, for the time being. I work as a model, catalogues, nudes for some local artists, and I paint too. Maybe you have a job to offer me, in that bank of yours?' Amelia's hand ran down to the bag she had between her legs as if fearing that it could disappear into thin air all of a sudden.

'It's not mine, and I don't think I want it either. I'm expected to sign some paperwork today. Jesus Christ, I don't even know where to begin.' The absurdity of the situation did not escape Amelia, sitting in a café with a stranger talking about her private affairs. *Whatever,* she thought, *rather than make me think about what awaits me.* And the idea of offering him a job? So out of hand, without even knowing what experience he had. Ridiculous. This wasn't what she'd learned at the Imperial College in London, surrounded by books on economics and marketing. But Anders seemed like the only friendly face she'd seen in a while, and that gave her something to think about.

'Maybe there is an opening. Do you have a phone number?' she asked; if she'd thought about it further, she would find a thousand reasons to ignore that meaningless request. Especially with what was happening in her life.

Amelia looked at her watch knowing she was running out of plausible excuses to linger more. She would willingly have drunk a glass of wine; maybe even something stronger. Amelia wondered what they would think at the bank if the new owner arrived a little tipsy. She seriously considered it a second time, she smiled to herself and almost ordered a glass of whisky, when Anders jotted down his number on a paper towel. He pushed it toward Amelia as quickly as you might pass a bribe.

'If there is anything, I'll let you know,' said Amelia and stuck the napkin in the expensive purse she'd bought the day before, just to give herself confidence and to play the part once in the bank.

'You can call me even if you don't have a job for me,' remarked Anders unperturbed. He looked her straight in the eye as if he were trying to extract a secret, making her even more uncomfortable.

'Show me where your bank is,' said Anders, he had no desire to stay there any longer. He had nothing else to do for the rest of the day. 'You don't have to let me in and introduce me to the Board of

Directors,' and then added, as an afterthought, 'if you don't want to.'

'Well … no, I mean, yes … I mean, I'd like it if you could accompany me. It's not very far.' The idea of going to face her destiny suddenly made her less afraid, knowing that maybe she could go with someone, even a stranger. They stood up, and Amelia wobbled for a moment, sudden dizziness caused her to falter and rest her hands on the table, the stress had gripped her for days now, as the night was consistently plagued by insomnia. Anders was next to her in a flash and, supporting her by the arm, he made her sit again. Removing a handful of pounds from his wallet and leaving them on the table without counting them. When Amelia seemed to have recovered, he helped her to get up. There was something in the way Anders spoke that made her feel secure, comfortable. She hardly opened up to strangers, but there was something different about him, that she could not explain. He made her feel at ease and nervous at the same time.

'Come on, you need some fresh air. You are as white as a ghost.'

They sauntered slowly, Anders supporting her, and when they reached the café threshold, he threw one last look at the bartender who was busy washing glasses. He didn't look at them nor saluted.

'I've heard many excuses for not paying for a coffee, but that takes the cake,' said Anders while they walked in the general direction of Kingsway, he had pulled a wool cap out of his pocket, letting go of her arm for a moment.

Amelia laughed to cover up her slight embarrassment. 'I'm inviting you for lunch soon, to reciprocate.'

'Who knows what you're going to invent than to avoid paying, I'm curious.'

They had just reached the waterfront when Amelia checked her wristwatch and said, 'I need to make a phone call. Do you mind waiting a moment?' Anders shrugged and walked away from her a few steps, unsure what to do.

'Ryan,' said Amelia, 'anything new on the Bradley dossier?' Amelia spoke with authority, but often it was just part of the façade she wanted to present to whoever was around.

'No, Amelia. I guess it will take a couple more days. Are you there yet?' asked the interlocutor.

'No, I'm still walking, I will let you know. I'm tense.'

'Don't worry, everything will be fine.'

The two talked for a few more minutes, then Amelia closed communication and put the phone in her purse before reaching Anders.

Ryan Logan would work until late as usual.

'Is everything all right?' asked Anders.

'Yes, it was my colleague Ryan.'

'He's at work early.'

'He doesn't go anywhere else. When I leave the office, he is still intent on working, and the next morning I find him already there. Sometimes I think he sleeps in that study.'

Without a specific reason, Amelia began to tell Anders about Logan. Procrastinating on worrying about the appointment in the bank was perhaps the only loophole that was left to her.

'You know, Ryan is a bit like an uncle to me. For a time he was one of the best-known lawyers in London in the financial sector,' said Amelia.

'How come he is not anymore?' The two had stopped on the Boardwalk near a bench. Amelia thought for a moment if she wanted to sit. It had stopped raining, but the seats were wet. She looked at the horizon in the direction of the French coast, not visible, and continued.

'Ryan has always been self-effacing about what happened during that time. I don't know much else about him. He reappeared a few years back and an old family friend, Albert Romanov, did everything he could to convince me to bring him into my firm. He said, "Just make sure of two things, that he doesn't turn to the bottle, and that he doesn't work more than forty hours per week." The second is a lost cause.'

'Sometimes working helps. You can bury yourself in work and forget other things,' said Anders thoughtfully.

'That's what I also believe. There isn't work enough to justify those hours, but probably it's a habit that's hard to break. I'm not complaining, I give Logan the worst cases, divorces, which I hate, cases from Legal Aid and everything that I don't like in this profession. We live in love and harmony.'

'Shall we continue?' asked Anders. He took her by her arm without waiting for a reply and kept silent up to Regency Square.

'Then you will leave the legal profession to become a bank owner?' asked Anders. He liked that contact against the heavy overcoat, probably cashmere, and walking together. It seemed a gesture of other times walking around like that.

'I don't think so. I'm a lawyer and probably will continue to be that after. And then I hope it's only temporary, while my father is in a coma,' said Amelia and asked, 'What about you? What did you do before going around being a model?'

'You've got to stop repeating my questions and begin to ask your own, brand new ones,' said Anders. The lack of ideas went hand in hand with lack of imagination, and at that moment Amelia was short on both, topped by the weight of the events of that week.

'The bank is right there in that building,' she said to her companion, stopping. The idea of going through the main door and entering was scaring her. If she crossed that threshold and entered, she could no longer go back.

'Are you bringing me in there with you or are you leaving me outside like one of those dogs sometimes seen waiting for their master in the doorway of a supermarket?'

'Well … I don't know … it's a private meeting and then … The way you're dressed …' Amelia was cursing inwardly, she was hardly ever at a loss for words and often had no qualms in telling outright lies. Yet, she was in awe, she had not been able to take the thread of the conversation and keep it in hand. Anders was as good looking as a god and with eyes to get lost in.

'Is that a coffee shop in front of the bank, there on the waterfront?' asked Anders squinting.

'Sort of, it's a brewery. Why?'

'I'm going to stay there for a while; at least I'll get rid of a bit of moisture from my bones.'

Without waiting any longer, Anders dragged her across Regency Square. They arrived in front of the bank and stopped for a moment.

'Well, I'm going in,' said Amelia, reluctant. She couldn't put it off any longer.

'I got an idea,' said Amelia, 'Why don't we have lunch together? Today? I'm not asking to stick around but maybe we can meet here at half past twelve?'

'Are you sure? Will you not be too busy with that bank of yours?'

'I'll make time. What do you think?'

Anders popped a kiss on her cheek and said, 'It's a deal. Let's get in touch later.'

They headed in opposite directions, each one lost in their own thoughts.

<u>CHAPTER 12</u>

Amelia entered the bank as if it already belonged to her, with a decisive step and look of ice. The coat, slightly wet from the rain, released water droplets on the marble entrance, raising the squeal of rubber soles of rare passers-by who roamed that morning. The fear that had gripped her until a few moments before was gone when she walked through the door of the building. She announced herself at the reception and none less than a group of five people, all in grey jackets, white shirts, and red ties, came to welcome her. She recognised one of them as one of the bank's internal lawyers. They had occasionally used her firm in the past, but it happened only rarely.

They sat in the main meeting room where several papers laid on the table, waiting. Some folders were already open, others stacked one above the other. From what the lawyer had explained, Amelia would take the absolute majority of the bank, which although was not listed on the stock exchange, was substantial. At least until her father had returned in full possession of his mental faculties. The other two owners were a Russian oligarch, whose name Amelia heard a few times in the news, a close friend to the Russian president, and an American lobbyist, but also with a name of Russian descent. How they had come to associate themselves with her father remained a mystery, and still, it wasn't necessary for them to be present during that transaction.

They began to review the papers and pretty soon her thoughts went to Anders, sitting in the brewery on the other side of the road, drinking coffee, and watching the faces of passers-by. While other lawyers were continuing to explain procedures, accounts, and balancing, her gaze went for a moment toward the window facing out towards the street. She wouldn't be able to see the brewery from where she sat, but maybe if she raised from her seat for a moment … She asked for a suspension, and while secretaries were unleashed to prepare coffee and pastries, Amelia rose to peek out of the window. Much to her dismay, she found that, although she could see the brewery from where she stood, the two shop windows and the entrance of the room reflected the light of the day, preventing her from seeing inside.

Amelia kept an eye on her watch and when it was almost half past twelve, she called for a break.

'Are you sure, Ms Mortcombe?' asked one of the lawyers. 'If we push through lunch we should be done in an hour or so. There isn't much left to discuss.'

She already hated that bank. A bunch of people following her at every step, people stepping aside in the corridors to let her pass, but most of all she hated that bunch of obsequious lawyers. One of the many reasons why she cherished her independence, working in her own firm with Logan, not having to deal with all that corporate nonsense.

'Yes, we take a break now and continue in an hour's time.' Her tone was categorical. Perhaps more so than she intended to, but she was looking forward to getting out of the building.

'Maybe we could have a quick lunch in our canteen. It will save us time ...'

'No, I'm done here. I'll be back in an hour or so.' Without waiting Amelia picked up her bag and coat and walked out of the meeting room before anyone could say anything further on the matter.

She took a deep breath of fresh air as soon as she was outside and started walking towards the brewery. Anders was walking towards her from the centre town.

They kissed each other on the cheek. 'Do you think they will have food in there?' he asked, pointing towards the brewery.

'Nothing too fancy but I know they do seafood and small plates. Let's give it a go.'

The brewery was modern in style, handwritten on a blackboard behind the bar was listed the house specialities.

They sat at a small table with a view of the sea.

'So, what do you do in your spare time?' asked Anders once the waiter walked away with their orders.

'Let me think. Long walks on the beach, watching the sunset, and candlelight conversations with a glass of wine.' Laughed Amelia. 'But I throw all that away as soon as the winds pick up and I have a chance of doing kitesurfing.'

'You do kitesurfing?'

'Yes, you too?'

'No, but it sounds exciting. I did a bit of sailing and windsurfing though. How long does it take to learn?'

'Not much. For the basics, two or three days training just to avoid ending up in France or on the shipping lane. If you want to jump over the pier, much longer.'

'Jumping the pier? Are you kidding me?' asked Anders.

'No, look …' said Amelia picking up her phone and showing a video on YouTube.

'That's so cool!' Anders watched, amazed at that short clip.

The food arrived and Amelia told a few kitesurfing stories. Anders talked about himself, his youth in Sweden and when he moved to the UK. The time passed quickly, and before she knew it, it was time for Amelia to go back to the bank.

'I'll stay a bit longer,' said Anders. 'Can you recommend where they teach that kitesurfing thing?'

'You are a brave man. There's one by the London Road train station, and another one in

Hove.' Amelia picked up Anders' phone and bookmarked a couple of addresses.

'Maybe if I crack on, I can take you out next weekend?'

'It's a date. Now I really have to go, though. I've got your number.' They both stood up and Amelia gave Anders a kiss on the cheek, a bit too close to his lips. Then she walked out of the brewery without looking back.

A date. She liked the sound of those two little words.

The meeting resumed and continued after lunch, where finally the last thing to do was to sign the papers for her to take possession of the bank. Amelia felt her stomach turn, not knowing what to do. She knew that she couldn't hold the reins directing the bank, continuing into a position her father had begun decades earlier, often at the expense of affection for his wife and two daughters. The only reason she was there was because her father didn't completely trust Robert Price, her brother-in-law, to take the reins of the bank.

Maybe I could sell it off, and eradicate Daddy-dearest, she thought for a moment. This was pure revenge, and even if it wouldn't make any difference to her father while he was in a coma, it would at least give her some relief. On the other hand, she knew that revenge was never pursued to punish an opponent but to make the one who implements it feel better. *No, it would take too much time.*

Amelia knew what she should do; so she gathered the most essential folders in a binder, she asked them to send the remainder to her office and started to leave. A choir of voices of disappointment arose, voices that Amelia heard no more. She phoned Logan to inform him that the documents would reach him that day and maybe they would see each other before closing the office. Without further postponements, she ran out and headed for the brewery on the opposite side of the road.

She looked around quickly, searching Anders out as soon as she reached the entrance, but she couldn't see him. She headed to the bar and ordered a glass of white wine, knowing full well beer wouldn't be enough and peered around again, table to table. He had already gone.

When she arrived at the office a couple of hours later, she'd drunk more than usually acceptable to herself, and she'd even bought a pair of outrageously expensive shoes. Logan was already at work on the documents shipped by the bank, surrounded by boxes and sheets that had now invaded the room. When he saw Amelia in that state, he did not want to hear reasons and called a cab to take her home. Instead, Logan would have a lot to do with all those documents. He prepared fresh coffee and ate leftovers from the day before as the night progressed inexorably.

On the following Monday Amelia woke up early to go to the office and stopped in the same café where she'd met Anders, without finding him. She had thought of calling him or sending a message, but what could she say? She had tried random phrases in her mind, more targeted ones and she'd also given answers to them. Between one case and the next, she'd dialogued with imaginary Anders for at least three hours without having the courage to dial that number. The reality was that for some reason, she now preferred being in Anders' company, even if he was only in her mind, than deal with her day to day life. He brought a spark, a novelty in what was a serene but monotonous life, with no surprises.

There was security in knowing how each day, and the next, would pass: smooth and without a hitch. What would happen, she wondered, and where would she be today if she'd abandoned her studies, thrown caution to the wind like Anders and lived unconventionally, or if she'd taken a boat headed to South America like her grandfather's cousin had done at the beginning of the century?

It was an unusual gesture, sometimes quoted at family dinners which still required her attendance from time to time. Someone said he had made a fortune in exporting meat or perhaps, as someone else said, he had bought half of Buenos Aires speculating on real estates. Amelia awoke from her thoughts, she gave a second look inside the bar just in case she hadn't noticed Anders, paid more than necessary for her coffee and walked out, heading to the office. She thought for a moment if she shouldn't try the brewery, the one near the bank. For some strange reason walking a couple of miles would have been more comfortable than a phone call, but then resigned to doing so. Probably Logan was right when he told her she needed to dare, to take the reins of her life in her own hands, to take risks.

'You only live once,' he said to her, 'you're the sole master of your own destiny.'

Logan was already working, and looking at the documents which were placed on the floor like an abstract painting, he'd spent all weekend on them, she realised. The office always made her relax. It was an old converted apartment with high ceilings. Although the desks were modern, over time she'd acquired some antique furniture, used mostly to host journals and books; she was pleased with the end result, it made the office feeling cosier, less intimidating. Amelia spent more on furniture for the office than for her own house, and sofas and chairs that would be suited for a London apartment were well placed at the entrance and in the waiting room.

'It is amazing,' Logan was kneeling between the hallway and the kitchen, trying to peer into a file.

'What is amazing?'

'These documents, for example, I'm trying to find out who actually owns these accounts in Switzerland,' he said, pointing a finger to a piece of paper right in the middle of the corridor, 'and one of the companies is the Gerald Tore Capital Management. They receive funds from the bank, but I tried to go back to the parent company, and I'm lost, having followed the tracks in Luxembourg, the Cayman Islands, the Isle of Man, Panama, and back. It doesn't seem to have any parent company.' He was fascinated, like a child intent on rebuilding a puzzle, although financial, trying to put together pieces that rarely matched.

'I'm confused, Ryan. What do you mean?' Amelia smiled to herself looking at the partner crawling on the floor.

'I need a couple more days to check, but usually this Chinese box system serves to hide a lot of money with the intent to evade taxes. If not worse.'

'Worse?' asked Amelia, halfway between intrigued and worried.

'Usually it's illicit acquisitions, but they could hide money from the mafia, arms trafficking, drugs. Are you sure you want to know what's really behind it?' he asked inquisitively.

'My father made some bad choices, of this I am aware. I want to know what's behind it before making a decision, we've been through this.'

'There are a lot of documents signed by Albert Romanov.'

'Albert?' Amelia flashed back to the last time she'd met Romanov, right in that office and the lively discussion which had followed. She was sorry, but by then it was too late to apologise. Romanov had been killed, and she couldn't recant. 'All right. You keep digging and let me know.'

Amelia went to her office, but she couldn't concentrate on work. Anders, the bank, the potential trafficking by her father. Everything was happening too fast.

CHAPTER 13

There would be a battle, thought Amelia. It was amazing that she had the power of representation of all that her old man possessed. But there were rules to follow, it was not the case that Amelia could actually close the bank and give all the money to charity. Her sister wouldn't be involved, she was weak and didn't understand anything about finance. A completely different matter was her brother-in-law, Robert Price, who had done everything to try to set foot in the bank. He'd succeeded after the marriage, but not in a prominent position. He managed mostly Russian customers in the private banking sector.

The Russians were coming in droves, and they were buying half of England, building after building. They were no worse than the Arabs, who, in summer, descended upon London in droves with their supercars and blocked Knightsbridge. But they weren't any better.

Robert Price wouldn't accept being left out from the management of the bank and would have certainly tried to persuade her sister Carla to do something. He couldn't do much as, the documents spoke: Amelia would handle the family fortune. She didn't care, and at that moment the only thing she cared about was the truth. There would be time to act later.

Her thoughts went to Anders. Amelia couldn't grasp how she'd reacted to that meeting. Anders was of striking beauty, tall, blond, and with a physique cultivated in the gym, no doubt, but still, there was something else she was intrigued by. Perhaps his determination, acting as if he had all the answers. And the way he looked her in the eye, almost without even blinking, as if searching for a clue to the depths of her soul.

She looked again at the paper towel with a scribbled phone number on. It was strong handwriting. She picked up her phone and dialled the number. One ring, two, and then three. Nobody answered, not even an answering machine to leave a message.

'I believe there is a shortfall of several million, maybe more,' said Logan coming into Amelia's office; he entered without knocking, his eyes still immersed in the documents which he flipped through giving Amelia chance to compose herself and banish the fantasising about Anders, in which she'd been submerged.

'What do you mean, a shortfall of millions?'

'Yes, here, look at these transactions. The bank has made regular transfers to these subsidiaries' accounts, but from this day,' he said, pointing to a date on a report, 'they'd messed up. Enormous sums. The documents from the subsidiaries show other movements to other companies in the group, but at some point, the money disappears into thin air.' He was almost embarrassed about not being able to solve a mystery.

He was a proud man and cared about a job well done. For some reason, not being able to tie up loose ends bothered him, he was utterly absorbed in those papers and now it was a matter of irritation.

'Let me see,' said Amelia, but financial accounting was not her forte, and if her colleague had failed to untangle the knot, she would hardly understand much.

'Damn! It is about ten million!'

'Welcome to creative finance, where the money miraculously disappears and reappears somewhere else,' announced Logan. 'If once Houdini, Penn and Teller, and David Copperfield were the magicians, nowadays the real magic happens in the financial environment.'

'For the time being, continue to investigate, I want to know what shady business my father was involved with. If we cannot understand, we'll ask an auditing firm to intervene; we don't have much time left.'

'I know. Take your brother-in-law out for lunch, give him a shake. If there is something dodgy, he must be in the know.' Logan picked up all the documents and left.

The phone rang at that moment, and a brief look at the display revealed it came from Quentin, her former boyfriend.

'What do you want?' asked Amelia in a peremptory tone, almost bored.

'I wanted to know how you're doing,' said the man on the other end of the phone. Quentin had a deep voice, almost hoarse, which still made her quiver.

'I'm stuck in a job that I don't enjoy and, guess what, I'm overworked. Didn't we decide to take a month off?'

'That has already passed.' There was a pause where Amelia cursed herself for not having marked that date.

Amelia would gladly have spent another month, or maybe even a year without feeling the need to meet him again. She didn't know what she still felt for Quentin and, especially during the past few days when her mind had wandered more in the direction of Anders, rather than her former boyfriend.

'Look, I'm a little busy these days …' she tried to end the conversation.

'We could meet for dinner, maybe this evening? We don't have to talk about anything in particular, just a dinner between two people who've known each other for a long time,' he said. 'I won't eat you.'

Nothing better. Amelia still couldn't grasp how Quentin took it lightly. Was she the only one in the world to have feelings, to suffer and get angry when things weren't going the right way?

'See you at the Gotika, about eight o'clock. Now I have to go, I'm busy.'

'Eight it is then. Kisses.'

She hung up the phone and immediately panicked. The restaurant was near the office, although on the other side of The Lanes, and it was a pub, not too pretentious. Local food, frequented by both tourists and locals, with ample opportunity to complain about the food, the noise or anything that could attract his attention and give her an excuse to leave.

Do I trust him? Because if I don't trust him the very foundations of our relationship falls apart, she said to herself.

She had never got to the bottom of the matter if Quentin had betrayed her or not, but the suspicion burnt within her. She was pretty sure, and perhaps it might have been better to know the full truth. She would be able to start afresh, instead of continually fretting inside. Instead of doubting his every gesture or word. She had thought about leaving him several times after her suspicions, the secret messages he received on his phone and immediately erased. She also caught him getting too close to that blonde chick in the marketing department where he was working, but nothing definitive.

Her mind drifted back to Anders, that short space of time together had made her feel alive. She panicked. On the one hand, there was Quentin who wanted to start over and on the other Anders, who had her mind wondering about the possibility of an unexpected adventure. *If only the bastard would answer the damn phone*, she thought.

You have to dare, said Logan's voice in her head.

She picked up the phone and dialled the number. Again, Anders didn't answer.

She had to face Quentin.

<u>CHAPTER 14</u>

'What do you mean she hasn't signed yet,' asked Price in a peremptory tone. He was on the second floor in the same bank that Amelia was now the principal shareholder in, a spacious office looking right on the Boardwalk.

'She decided not to sign and took the documentation with her, to analyse it without hurry,' said the clerk.

'And why wasn't I told sooner?' pressed Price.

'I don't know, sir, I can check with the legal department? Maybe they didn't think a small delay would be an issue, given it was a Saturday,' said the clerk, who suddenly seemed extremely interested in the tips of his shoes.

'All right, you can go,' said Price. *Clueless people,* he thought as soon as the employee was gone, *they had only one job to do, make her sign those bloody documents;* he would take care of the rest later, but that was a mishap he did not expect. Amelia was supposed to sign and then ignore any matter related to her family as she'd done since she was a teenager. On the contrary, this abrupt change of mind was going to change everything and maintaining control over the bank would be a problem.

Price began pacing around the room. Gaining full control of the bank was necessary to continue to work with the Russian mafia. There were accounts for hundreds of millions, and in addition to those, the mafia's personal accounts. The bank wouldn't stop without a defined owner but moving the slush funds would be riskier. And the clients he operated with did not tolerate delays or errors.

He took an encrypted phone and dialled a number he had memorised years earlier.

'We need to meet,' he said.

'Are there any problems?'

'Some, requiring your skills.'

'How many people?' asked the woman on the other end of the phone.

'Only one. It should look like an accident.'

'They always look like an accident, that's why you pay me a fortune,' said the woman confidently. 'Bring the dossier and half of the payment.'

'All right.'

Money, always money. Everybody asking for damn money. The Russians never had enough, his wife was possibly the worst and every day she found new, creative ways to spend it as if she did it deliberately to anger him. The killers cost a fortune, and a man with a little ambition had to navigate through all those obstacles to achieve some minimal result.

The Russians wouldn't have waited much longer, despite Price's attempts to stall.

****

That evening, Amelia arrived deliberately late to her meeting at the Gotika. Quentin was already seated at a corner table and was savouring a local beer. He stood up when he saw her enter and the waiter accompanied her to the table.

'Amelia, you look wonderful,' he said watching her and dwelling for a moment too long on her breasts, before helping her to sit. That was Quentin; knowing how to be a gentleman and a cheating bastard at the same time.

'Do not exaggerate, this is one of my usual work outfits.' She taunted, shifting her focus onto the inside of the restaurant, which was oddly uncrowded.

'I'm sorry I couldn't attend Romanov's funeral, I know he was a family friend,' said Quentin sensing that Amelia did not wish to speak about herself. Not yet.

And instead Amelia answered simply, 'No big deal.' And then, 'He's underground now.'

'I never had an affair, you know?'

Amelia felt her heart lurch. She was still in love and being in his presence made her wish she could smash a fist into his grinning face. Or make love to him.

God, let's hope he didn't notice, she thought. Quentin could read her like an open book, or at least he was able to do so until a few months before.

'It doesn't matter if you did it or not. It's what I'm convinced of that does matter.'

'What did you do during our break?'

What had she done? She was ready to answer but a waiter came to take their orders. This gave Amelia time to think about it some more. About the previous month and the one before, the fact that in love truth is never essential, but how we perceive things is.

They ordered a seafood appetiser and a main meat course. In that, they had not changed, always choosing the same dishes from the menu, independently. Two people so different, sharing the same tastes.

Quentin poured the wine and, once he reposed the bottle, he grazed Amelia's hand; she did not flinch. They were such large hands, strong-willed, which had caressed her and had been caressed countless times. For only an instant she compared him to Anders, also fairly muscular in body but with a sadness which ran through his eyes. She understood she could remain infatuated by two such different people, although one belonged to the past and to her real life while the other was just a dream, a wish. She wanted to leave with the urge to call Anders, once again, and resisted almost for a whole minute, only to retrace her steps.

'Do you mind if I go outside a moment for a smoke?'

'I thought you'd given up, it's a bad habit,' said Quentin watching her putting her jacket on.

'Only one per day. I usually smoke it when I have to sort things out.'

'I never took you for someone who needs excuses for smoking.'

'I don't need an excuse,' said Amelia crankily, 'I was just informing you.' And having said she walked toward the exit.

The need for a cigarette was real, but the urge to call Anders was even stronger. She lit it in a hurry and tried the number again. As usual, no answer. *Damn it, why do people get a phone if they are never at home,* she thought. *And who nowadays does not have a mobile phone or at least voicemail.*

Angrily, she put the phone in her coat pocket, she cursed silently for not being more insistent and went back to the pub.

They kept talking like two old friends even though they both knew they were lying to each other. When Quentin kissed her, suddenly and by surprise, just outside the restaurant, Amelia let herself go between those strong arms that huddled her close not wanting to let her go.

'Sorry, I'm not going to do this!' she said, wriggling out of his arms and stepping away from him.

'Amelia… I thought…'

'You thought wrong. Sorry but I'm going.' Of one thing Amelia was sure, she didn't want Quentin. There was too much history between them, of the wrong kind.

'May I call you later?'

'No, Quentin. I was wrong in coming here, I just realised that.'

She didn't wait for a reply. She walked away without a backward glance. She only stopped for a second when she reached the seafront to take a deep breath.

Anders, where are you? she thought.

CHAPTER 15

Marcus Splinter was 'the hook'.

He had now reached sixty years of age and had been in jail a few times. On other occasions, he had been very close to it. Marcus was fluent in four languages, and he could have done any job he wanted to choose, but instead, he dedicated himself to scamming people. Educated at Eton and with a degree in literature from the University of Cambridge, he had stopped working after two weeks in his first job. Working in an office didn't suit him and despite always appearing calm and in control, the tales of the unexpected was what made him feel alive. It didn't matter if they were short cons for some quick money or the long haul ones that could provide hundreds of thousands of pounds; given a choice though, he preferred the second. Feeling the adrenaline flowing in his veins and the challenge was what made him move.

Instead of settling for the path decided by his parents, taking responsibilities in the family business and marry a nice girl he preferred a life of poker, frauds, and deceits.

He was sitting in the restaurant of a downtown hotel pretending to read the menu while in fact he was carefully observing Robert Price, a banker in Brighton with access to numerous wealthy clients, sitting at a table next to him. He had discreetly followed Amelia Mortcombe and, thanks to a generous tip, a waiter had secured him a table next to the two.

Price had complained of the impossibility of taking significant decisions without a definite direction, and Amelia had replied she wouldn't make any decision until she'd cleared up all aspects of the bank. When she informed her brother-in-law about the millions of pounds which had disappeared into the ether, the man became pale; he promised to open an internal investigation, but anyone could see that this information had troubled him deeply. The time for pleasantries had long gone, like mist evaporating in the sun. The two were in open conflict. The woman's accent was definitely Oxford, with a slight London inflexion, while Price was definitely American, Texas or probably one of the southern states; the latter spoke with that slow cadence typical of those states.

The watchful eye of Splinter saw Price paying with a credit card, but without being noticed by his partner, not leaving even one pound of a tip. Amelia Mortcombe seemed an incorruptible person, driven by morals rather than by a desire for easy money, according to Splinter. Price was a very different story. He was a greedy man, anyone could see it from a mile away. Which made him an ideal target.

Once Price and Amelia left the restaurant, two gentlemen sitting nearby began to comment.

'Nice guy that.'

'Who, the one that just left?'

'That's right, Price. My wife plays tennis at the same club as his wife. You wouldn't believe the stories she has told me. Greedy, attached to money, like no other. His wife is related to those of the Mortcombe Bank, I believe she's the owner's daughter. That's why she's still able to do what she wants; otherwise, that guy would pass her money using an eyedropper. Such a miserable, stingy sod.' They continued to talk and gossip, without noticing that Marcus Splinter was listening to every word of their conversation.

When the two patrons left the restaurant, Splinter's teammates approached him.

The first was Hank, the brains of the gang who had waited near the bar and the second was Domino, an attractive woman but with an intellect that would be the envy of many.

'Made any progress?' Hank asked sitting at the table.

'Not really,' answered Splinter, 'but from what I could see there are developments.'

'What do you mean?' asked Domino.

The group had laid eyes on Amelia Mortcombe during the previous weeks. A British tabloid had reported the news about the Mortcombe Bank and had done an article on the most beautiful heiress of Brighton.

Intrigued, Marcus had done an internet search and had managed to find a variety of information. The father in a coma, the killing of the second-in-chief to the bank.

'That well-dressed gentleman you ran into is Robert Price, brother-in-law of our beautiful victim and head of the department for private investments. A seriously greedy and unscrupulous guy if you ask me.'

'So, we have a new target?' asked Domino.

'What makes you think he's the right person to con?' asked Hank, who had started reading the menu. He looked around in search of a waiter. The room was modern, and Brighton was slowly moving up the ladder regarding restaurants. A couple of them had already been awarded a Michelin star, and it clearly showed that the town was continually evolving, vibrating with novelty.

'Just a hunch, I'm hardly wrong. I have seen many like Price. From what I heard of their conversation he's not quite the half figure we had thought of. In fact, at the heart of the bank are the private accounts that are under his management. If I have to bet, he's the one running the show. I have to work a bit to get more information, but it will take funds to hook him up. He was on a rampage, although he didn't want to show it, for a shortfall of several million and because Amelia Mortcombe hasn't taken possession of the bank yet.'

'Then we forget about the woman?' asked Domino sipping from the cup of hot tea. Brighton weather was inclement, and although it was sunny, the cold was much more intense than in London. She was not accustomed to it, despite heavy clothing.

'Not yet. Let's see how things evolve.'

'What we have in cash shall be enough?' asked Hank.

'In my opinion, it's going to take at least a million pound. Maybe more,' said Splinter considering some options in his mind.

'If it goes wrong, it's going to leave us with our arses on the ground.'

Hank managed the money to devote to frauds and often was the one who had the last word about a job, even for others who were not present at the meeting.

'If this job goes all right, we can retire once and for all,' mused Marcus aloud. The scams were his life, but somehow, he always failed to get the big one, the one that allowed him to forget about everything and retire in a tropical country drinking Martini by the sea aboard a yacht. Nobody would scam him out of his lifetime of earnings, nor would that happen to his teammates.

'How do we proceed, then?' said Domino.

'Cautiously,' answered Splinter. 'First, I have to hook Price; maybe we can even pull in Amelia Mortcombe, although at this point, I'm not convinced. I heard from some friends that she works with a Ryan Logan, and the guy, besides being one who knows how to spin money, has some skeletons in the closet. If I can't convince him, we can blackmail him.'

'And who is this Logan?'

'He was known in London a while back. He worked in a law firm and apparently doing spells with accounting books. Things at a high level, for big companies who wanted to avoid paying too much tax. He has also spent several years in prison.'

'Blackmailing could be a dangerous game.'

'Are there any circumstances in which blackmailing is a safe option?' said Splinter. 'Can we trust him?' asked Domino.

'No, but we can control him, I wouldn't worry too much,' replied Splinter.

He didn't know how wrong he was.

CHAPTER 16

Amelia awoke at almost ten o'clock. She should already be in the office by that time, but the advantage of having her own law firm gave her the right to take days off whenever she wanted, even though it happened infrequently.

She looked at the time on her phone and noticed a message. The number was unknown to her, and she hurried to open it.

I saw that you called me. Try this number, I'm not often at home. Anders.

Her heart skipped a few beats. First came the excitement and then the anger. If only Anders had answered before. Maybe she wouldn't have wasted time with that loser, Quentin. And then why he hadn't given her his mobile number straight away?

Anders looked younger than her and nothing might have happened between the two, but somehow, she was intrigued by that man. Not that she was old herself, Amelia was just twenty-eight years old, but Anders was indefinable, he looked younger, but thinking about his confidence, the way he spoke, his angle in judging things, he seemed much more mature. She decided to respond. *To hell with Quentin*, she thought, *if these things are not done when we have the chance, when we are old, or worse, dead, we no longer have time.*

She began writing.

When can we see each other?

Even today, I don't have much to do.

Amelia felt remorse at having to miss a whole day's work. With all those papers from the bank, Logan would have progressed a little. She was annoyed to have to leave him alone, but she knew within herself that meeting Anders again was a priority. She'd woke late anyway, better take advantage of the situation.

There's a classical concert, a quartet, playing close to downtown in the afternoon. Would you like to go?

I love classical music.

She opened her purse in search of the leaflets that she'd taken a few days before and wrote the address and time in next message.

She still had a few hours to prepare and decided to take a bath before choosing her outfit. As usual in her life, the problems came all at once. The bank, Quentin, and now Anders. Everything needed to be done in a hurry, decisions, choices on unlikely futures, dreams that collided with reality.

Sometimes she desired dropping everything and running away to some distant country and living a simple life. But those things don't ever happen in real life. If she left for the Caribbean to make a living as a waitress, the problems would doubtless follow her. People imagined that by going somewhere else problems would vanish, but the truth was different: there were mortgages, the issue of having to live on minimum wage. Even if she'd decided to become a little shepherdess on the top of a mountain, there'd be veterinary bills to pay, a building to repair, and walls in need of repainting.

People were always enchanted by the romantic side of things, ignoring the facts. She understood only too well, being a lawyer, the ugliness that people had to deal with daily. No, it would be much better to continue with what she was doing. Better to cry in a luxurious apartment, if you had to than in a cold mountain hut.

She decided for casual attire, jeans, a white blouse, and a light jacket to wear under her coat; the only concession would be her Burberry handbag, which she was rarely separate from.

When she arrived at the rendezvous, Anders was already waiting. He was a sublime beauty. This time he was carrying a shoulder bag, those used for laptops. His dress, though unusual, was of excellent quality.

They sat and watched the day's program in silence. They didn't notice the woman seated two rows further back observing them.

Margot carefully scrutinised the blond guy who had accompanied Amelia, and she didn't like him at all. She had encountered similar people throughout her career; they usually were tough cookies, ex-military; full of resources. Margot didn't let his stylish clothes confuse her, he was anything other than what he appeared to be at first glance. She would have to revise her plans.

<u>CHAPTER 17</u>

'There's been an unforeseen circumstance,' said Margot into the phone.

'Of what kind?' Robert Price was getting impatient. Unscrupulous friends had recommended the woman, and she still hadn't accomplished anything.

'She was accompanied. I don't know who the guy is, but I think he's trouble.'

'What makes you say that?'

'He moves confidently, he looks around to absorb every detail, the way he enters in front of her. I've met a lot of guys like that, after a while they don't even realise how they act as that posture becomes second nature for them. The exact moves of a bodyguard. You didn't mention this when I took the contract.'

Price scratched his beard of two days. As far as he knew, Amelia had left her boyfriend a month before, and he wasn't aware she was seeing someone else. A bodyguard then. Good to know. He had done well following the advice to hire a professional to do this job.

In the past, he had acted on impulse, thinking he could handle a similar situation and had almost ended up in jail. *Shit! Even Mortcombe almost ended up in jail*, he thought. That issue almost ended his career; what saved him was the fact he was married to Mortcombe's daughter. It took years to regain the smallest amount of confidence from the old man. No, this time he would be cautious, he would have someone else handling the dirty work. It was his chance to prove to his father-in-law what he was really worth.

He had found the shortages reported by Amelia and had managed to hide them by playing the three-card game, withdrawing from other private accounts and letting the owners believe that he was investing the money, but they would soon learn the truth.

From an initial investigation, it looked like Bruno Mortcombe was the one who had extracted those millions, but that seemed far-fetched to Price. Mortcombe knew better than he who they were working for. The computer geeks had found a virus, or a Trojan horse as they called it, that was potentially used to steal Mortcombe's log-ins. Everything had yet to be proven.

He either fixed the issue rapidly, or he would have a lot to answer for. And his customers were not people to involve the lawyers. They would extract the truth from him using beating and torture.

Margot's services would cost a fortune, but he realised that in certain matters, he was only an amateur. Better let the professionals do their job.

'How are you going to proceed?' he asked after a long pause.

'I want to see how things develop,' said the woman, 'if that guy is hanging around her, there might be a valid reason. There is definitely something going on here, and if we don't understand what it is, we risk doing more harm than good.'

'I have faith in your skills, do what you think is necessary.' That was the phrase that Price always used when he couldn't take a decision. Leave the initiative to those who knew, or believed to know, more. It was a useful trick in his work, allowing him to take risks and drop the responsibility onto others. This, however, was a different game. In the event of failure, his clients wouldn't accept excuses; he would find himself in trouble up to his neck.

'I'll keep you updated.'

Margot turned off the phone and went back into the room where the concert was about to end. It was a spacious nineteenth-century building off North Street. The interiors were exquisite and, with the oak inlaid floor, they were in an elegant room. Margot wondered what it would have been like living in one of those houses during the previous century. It was not unusual for ancient buildings to be used for concerts and in recent years it had become more popular. Tourists or business people passing through frequented most of them. In the streets, there was always somebody distributing flyers about the concerts. Most were students, including musicians, who earned some pocket money that way.

When Anders and Amelia left, Margot pretended to talk to the man sitting next to her; that gave her the opportunity to watch the couple again. The young man leaned his left hand on her back as he looked around, peering into the faces of the people who had attended the concert. A typical gesture made by bodyguards used to analysing a situation quickly and making decisions. She refrained from locking eyes with him and waited a few moments before she followed them. Better not risk it.

'How's it going with your bank then?' asked Anders as they walked through the narrow streets of The Lanes without a set destination.

'It's not mine yet. You'll have to wait for that job.' Amelia laughed, but without conviction.

'Don't worry, I knew I had little chance of getting one. Hey, I started that kitesurfing course you suggested.'

Amelia stopped walking. 'Really? How is it going?'

'According to the instructor, I'm a natural.' Laughed Anders. 'Give me another couple of days and the right motivation, and I could jump that pier of yours as well.'

'Ha, ha, ha, I'd like to see you trying.'

'Ok, maybe that would be a little premature, but I'm sure I'll be ready for a bit of kitesurfing this weekend, if you're up for it?'

'I wouldn't miss that for the world. Take some cash with you, just in case you haven't learned yet how to go upwind. You know, for the taxi home.'

'Ha! That's funny. Do you want a coffee? We could go to the same café where we met.'

'Why not? But first I should go to the office, to see if everything is in order. It's not far from here.'

They set off down a side street, and Margot decided not to follow them. If her suspicions were founded, the guy would have surely spotted her. She would have to recruit the entire squad for complete surveillance. Alternating people, changing appearances and places, different cars. *Damn, this would cost*, but she saw no alternative. They were still too close to the centre to try something. She could kill them in the street, that was sure, but the orders were to make it look like an accident. With Bruno Mortcombe in a coma and the death of Romanov, killing her in the street would have unleashed a hornet's nest. She decided it was better to wait.

They arrived at the office building and, when Anders suddenly stopped, she said, 'You can come in, it's only a matter of minutes.'

It was an old building, with wide stairs leading to the upper floors. The office was on the second floor which had always attracted Logan's grievances, but she liked it as it was. Remote but not too far from the centre. Professionals mostly occupied the building. A dentist, a general practitioner, and a firm that Amelia had never understood what kind of business they were dealing in.

She opened the door and walked toward her own office.

Logan, hearing noises, came out from behind a corner, said, 'Oh, Amelia, there you are. I have news …' But he stopped, seeing the man behind her. The two briefly glanced at each other and Logan nodded with his head. People who had been in jail always recognised each other, in one way or another. Even those who had been in different prisons. He started to say something, but he was interrupted by Amelia.

'I'm just passing through. So, were you able to make any progress on the bank's matters?'

The embarrassment at being recognised was apparent on Logan's face, who did not wish to discuss the firm's affairs in front of strangers.

He pondered for a moment what to say and then alluded to nothing. 'Well, yes and no, there are still many things to review,' he said changing tone, to equivocate. 'By the way, there's a package for you; I put it on your desk.'

Amelia nodded and headed for her office. She returned with a large brown envelope in her hand. 'I'm taking a few days off, Ryan. You should too, sometimes. It would be a novelty.'

'I'll think about it,' he said not averting his eyes from Anders, as if to measure an opponent before a duel, 'will you be in the office tomorrow?'

'Yes, don't worry, tomorrow's business as usual.'

Logan wanted to say more, but something caused him to hold back. He would have time later, he thought.

'See you tomorrow then,' said Amelia exiting the door, followed by her silent friend. She seemed happy, almost different, but the instinct of the old lawyer wasn't slipping.

Once out of the building they headed towards the main square, not noticing that Margot was following them.

'Look at that gadget of yours,' said Amelia looking at Anders, who was checking emails on the latest generation mobile phone, more to break the silence between them than anything else.

'What can I say, I'm a bit of a geek. Computers, connected watches, tech toys. I don't do cosplays though.'

'Ha ha ha. OK. What other secrets do you have to confess?'

'I like rich heiresses. I don't even look at a woman unless she has at least a bank,' he said earnestly, looking her straight in the eye to elicit a reaction.

'You are in trouble, then. I'm a very mean heiress and I don't own a bank yet.' She knew that the bank, in one way or another, would change her life dramatically and she still couldn't bring herself to allow that to happen, she had far too many demons to contend with where her father was concerned to make this decision lightly.

'I could always make an exception,' he said, and when Amelia stopped trying to find a proper answer, Anders took her in his arms and kissed her. He stood over her by at least three inches, although she wore heels, and she felt enveloped by the warmth of the muscles holding her. Anders was strong, he clutched her, and she wouldn't be able to avoid it even if she wanted to. The kiss lasted forever and when they separated her head started spinning, like when she did too much exercise, or had drunk more than she should.

'I don't live far away,' said Anders.

Amelia looked around as if she were afraid of being spotted in the company of a stranger. As if the few bystanders could read from her face what she was thinking or they knew she'd only met Anders, by accident, a few days before.

'No, we go to my place.'

He took her arm in his, as he had done that first time, and they departed in the direction of The Lanes.

****

Logan, alone in the office, looked at the phone for the umpteenth time and then he dialled a number he had memorised long before. 'I have a doubt, and hopefully you will be able to put me at ease,' he said to the man on the other end of the line.

<u>CHAPTER 18</u>

'We must find a weakness if we want to hustle Robert Price,' said Hank looking out the window of the hotel, not focussing on anything in particular.

'Greed is not enough?' asked Domino.

'No, it's not,' Marcus Splinter said, 'he is rich, he married one of the daughters of the banker, and even if he has put his hands on his wife's wealth, it's certainly not the money that's missing.'

To engage someone in a long con it was necessary to study the habits of the target. Understand what made him act, his innermost passions.

'We could sell them Shergar's descendants, an entire stable of horses. From what I've read, he likes to gamble,' said Domino.

People laughed out loud in the room; the kidnapping of Shergar had made the headlines in Ireland and throughout the world, in the late 1970s. A famous racehorse that had been stolen by individuals armed with guns, the IRA was suspected, and the horse never recovered.

'Hmm … It wouldn't work. Even if we sell him a couple of horses, the most we could reach would be a few million. We need something bigger,' said Splinter. 'Maybe we could revisit the shares con. A new company to be quoted on the stock exchange.'

Hank was undecided. He strolled back and forth in the hotel room as if he were in a cage. 'These are bankers, they'll see right through it, and if we make a mistake, and that might well happen, goodbye investment. And those people are better than us at stealing money. Too risky.'

'I wanted to be the one who invented the LIBOR manipulation. That was a stroke of genius,' laughed Splinter.

'They are ahead of us regarding theft.'

'No, we need something different,' said Lenny standing up from the couch and heading toward the bar. They had rented a suite in the best hotel in Brighton, no expense spared when it came to hooking a victim; appearance was everything in their craft. 'We must focus on the feelings, passions, and dreams of the victim.'

'Maybe he's an art lover. We could sell the first abstract painting by Caravaggio. Or we make him believe that one of us is the only one of Hitler's living relatives who has access to the Nazi gold buried in the vaults of a Swiss bank and waiting to be found. I zizn't mind imitating ze German aczent before.'

The group laughed loudly. Throwing ideas around was not only fun but also a way to invent new scams. In time, they happened to stumble across an idea so absurd that someone, sooner or later, would have taken it as real.

'No, this time we can't leave anything to chance. We need to study the habits and weaknesses of the victim. We don't have much time.'

The group had been working together for ten years. They came from different backgrounds, but each of them had a reason for pushing to be outside of the law. Hank was raised in a Welsh mining village; after seeing his parents consumed by their efforts, his mother as a maid and his father as a miner, he had decided he would never do an ordinary job. He had seen them growing old and bent under the hardships of a life of misery; his father had died when he was young because of an accident at the mine and the company he worked for didn't even bother to send a note of condolence. Hank was tired of reading of all those celebrities in the papers who were acting up for trivial things. Of billionaires who got rich to the detriment of poor people; of those spending millions for yachts and villas that they would use only occasionally. That society gave him the creeps, and somehow, he had always tried to make them pay, those greedy, monster exploiters.

****

Chaz didn't usually intrude in those discussions. Splinter had selected him personally. Others insisted it was a waste of time, he would never learn, but Splinter claimed there was potential in the boy. Apart from working hard and driving the car as if he were a formula one driver.

'Somebody got in touch with Ryan Logan?' asked Hank looking around.

'He should be here any minute,' said Domino. 'Steve went to pick him up, and they should be here by now.'

'Chaz, it's time for a new lesson,' said Marcus. The gang turned their eyes to the newcomer.

'Right now?'

'Of course, any time is a good time to learn. How are your legs? No pains?' asked the elder.

'I played rugby until yesterday, of course, I have no aches or pains,' said Chaz. 'I'm fit as a fiddle.' He was aware he would suffer another trick, but no matter how hard Chaz tried, he had never managed to get the better of Splinter.

'Then you're in good shape. Very good. Shall we bet that I find a way, without tying you or forcing you in any way, to stop you raising your leg? I won't touch you either. If I can't, I'll pay for your dinner for a week. Otherwise, you buy me a beer.'

The boy thought it over for a moment, then said, 'OK, let's see how you do it.'

'Here,' said Splinter asking him to approach the wall. 'Put the left ankle to the jamb. That's right. And now lean against the wall, knee, shoulder, and cheek.' The boy did as ordered, staying with the left side of his body in contact with the wall.

'And now try to lift the right leg.'

Chaz made as much effort as he could, but he soon realised there was no way. In that position all the weight was on his right leg, he couldn't move it despite the efforts. 'I give up!' he said finally.

'A free beer and an old trick taught. Not bad for a two-minute job,' said Splinter.

He just finished the sentence when they heard a knock at the suite door. As a precaution, Hank hid files and paperwork on the table while Domino walked toward the door.

Steve was a six-footer, short brown hair and wore a made to measure suit from a tailor in Bond Street. He kept with him a dark brown leather briefcase and was accompanied by a slightly overweight man, personable, with grey hair and with a pair of black plastic glasses.

Steve introduced Logan and made him sit on the couch.

'Thank you for coming, Mr Logan,' said Splinter in an affable tone, while serving a shot of whisky to the newcomer. 'We have a deal we'd like to discuss with you.'

'I don't drink anymore,' said Logan pushing away the glass in front of him. 'You could make an appointment; I was told it was an emergency, a testament ...' he said looking Steve directly in the eye. It was clear that he had lied to him.

'I'm sorry if we had to resort to a little subterfuge to get your attention,' continued Splinter, 'but actually we are interested in some of the financial skills you have shown in the past.'

It was clear to Logan to what they were referring to. It was about his work at Saunders, Whitehall & Passmore, the financial tricks he had learned over years of practice, the fact he had been in jail. It didn't matter if they had eventually acknowledged his innocence, twenty years of prison over his head were a reality, whoever knew would doubt him.

'I haven't done those things for years, I have a job, and I don't want any trouble,' he said looking around the room as if to seek an ally, which he didn't find.

'We're not asking to make it a regular occurrence. It will be only once. We're interested in your knowledge and old contacts you could possibly restore,' said Splinter, 'obviously you will be rewarded handsomely.'

Logan knew exactly what they wanted, they were interested in his old bag of tricks, from his years in the financial sector.

He listened to what they had to offer.

CHAPTER 19

For a moment after she entered her apartment, Amelia was troubled.

This is stupid, she thought. Anders was as beautiful as a god, but she knew nothing about him really. She'd never done anything like this before.

'Would you like something to drink?' she asked not knowing how to dispel the swirl of conflicting emotions that promised to leave her paralysed in the middle of the room.

'A fruit juice,' said Anders, 'it's not even dinner time.'

'Yes, that's right. A juice.' *Damn,* thought Amelia, *now he'll think I'm an alcoholic.*

She walked to the kitchen and poured the juice into two glasses; for good measure, she added a dash of vodka to her own. And then yet another.

Shit, Amelia, do you really want to take him to bed? Just like that, without thinking about it for a minute? She tried to shake off the sudden fatigue that was gripping her by gulping some more vodka straight from the bottle. It wasn't physical fatigue, but rather mental. Created by years of quarrels with her family, differences of opinions; from a job she loved but that at the same time held her captive. What was the point of making money if she had to live the same life, day after day, unchanged? Divorces, trusts, mortgages, after a few years they all looked the same, as the clients had started to resemble each other, all worried about the same thing, the same miseries and misfortunes. Each day at the office brought Amelia joy and sorrow at the same time. She loved the independence and hated the repetition; her life had reached that kind of bottom. Repeating the same gestures, passing the same paperwork day in and day out. The only distraction, Logan's sense of humour, which made the days less mundane. If it weren't for Logan, she would have lost it a long time ago.

Hell, she said to herself, *you only live once*; and so, with a new determination inside her, she headed toward the living room, where Anders pretended to be interested in certain abstract paintings on the wall next to the balcony.

She handed him the glass and drank hers in one gulp. Her companion raised an eyebrow. Amelia laid the glass on a small table next to her and grabbed Ander's jacket, she pulled him toward her, kissing him hungrily. Neither of them expected this sudden change of events, not yet, but neither showed any sign of second thoughts. Anders lifted her from the ground and embraced her with his powerful arms. They continued to kiss each other all the way up to the bedroom, trying to undress each other without ever losing contact. Once they reached the room, Anders dragged her onto the bed and started to undress her. They were slow gestures, measured, but Amelia wouldn't have any of it. She grabbed him by the neck dragging him towards herself. They rolled on the bed, and the man took the lead once again, this time with increased passion. Kissing her neck, her lips while his hands were seeking a gap between the underwear. Amelia girthed him with her own legs, so as not to give him a chance to escape.

They made love in that darkened room and then again. Amelia had not felt so alive in years, and Anders was about as far from a life in a law firm as she could imagine. She paused to contemplate the muscular body, the tattoos on his arms that narrated a story unknown to her. She admired the contrast of that black on the white skin, a stylised falcon just below the chest muscles, a tiger coming down along his arm as if to bite into the forearm. They made those arms look even stronger. She would have liked to have seen those he had on his back, she'd briefly glimpsed them in the twilight of the room while they made love, but Anders was sleeping. She got up after a while that seemed endless to her and went into the kitchen to make a cup of coffee.

****

'They are still in the apartment,' croaked a voice on the radio.

'Roger.' Margot was thinking about what options she had in front of her. They could force the door, go in and get it over with it once and for all. A robbery gone wrong, the hosts surprised the thieves, and it all ended in tragedy. No, it wouldn't be enough. First Amelia was not alone, and that guy who she'd brought with her to the apartment reeked of trouble from a mile away. There would be a struggle, they would leave traces. 'Are the microphones working?' she asked as if awakened from her thoughts, 'I cannot hear a damn thing.'

'The lovebirds were busy for a while and went at it hard until recently. I guess now they're playing the rest of the warrior,' said another voice that Margot recognised as Kaleb, a former legionnaire who, on this occasion, was stationed on the rooftop opposite the apartment.

'OK, keep your eyes open. No matter what they do. If they say anything, even whispering, if they go to the bathroom, if they put their fingers up their noses, I do want to know.'

'Roger that.'

'Kaleb, have you got a good view of the apartment?' said another voice.

'Good enough. The bedroom has the curtains drawn, I saw only shadows until recently. The rest is illuminated. Wait … The woman just walked into the kitchen. She is opening a cupboard. She takes a cup for coffee. She is naked and has a pair of juicy tits.'

Margot cursed herself for asking to be given every single detail. The voice continued, 'She is preparing an instant coffee. A spoonful of sugar. Are you sure that we need to get rid of her? She is quite pretty, a waste.'

'Kaleb, try to do your job,' said Margot crossly.

'Roger. She is coming back into the living room. I've lost visual. It's up to you, Yuri.'

'They are not talking, all I hear is indistinct rustling.'

'What are we going to do, boss?' said a voice on the radio.

'We wait,' answered Margot.

****

Amelia sat down in the armchair in the bedroom and pulled her legs against her body, keeping the piping hot coffee between both hands. She sipped slowly and she watched Anders' body. There was a time when she'd wanted to get a tattoo. It was during a holiday in Cyprus and some friends, some of them a bit tipsy, had decided to take the plunge. She would have liked a butterfly on her back or somewhere else it wouldn't be easily seen. The guy who ran the store told her to be cautious, against his own interest, *tattoos are for a lifetime, you can't remove them when you're tired of them,* he said. There wasn't much difference with the sorrows of life, thought Amelia at that moment, even those remained indelibly etched in people's memory, maybe even in a more permanent way than tattoos. Pain could change lives, transform them. A tattoo wouldn't be too dissimilar. But when the man made her try the needle, without ink, just to see what she would be subjected to, she changed her mind.

She saw at least five of tattoos on Anders' body, all large ones. Who knew what drove people to go through all that pain?

She took another sip of coffee while checking messages on her mobile phone. She read a couple of texts from Logan and then she cancelled them immediately. She ignored another. She snapped a photo of Anders' sleeping face and then got up, and with light steps,she put on some sportswear. Anders was fast asleep and rather than sitting in the lounge doing nothing, she decided to go for a jog. She had skipped her morning routine for a few days and she missed it. Running was one of her favourite sports since she gave up Judo a couple of yours before. Half an hour to run three miles, she wouldn't try to break her personal record that morning.

The brisk wind enveloped her as soon as she stepped outside, making her shiver for a moment. She ran towards the beach, finding her rhythm.

When she returned home, Anders was preparing breakfast. After a quick shower, she joined him at the kitchen table.

'Do you have a kitesurfing lesson today?'

'The course ends this afternoon, why?'

'Nothing. There's a brisk wind and I might tag along. I guess there will be a few people out there today, and I want to ensure you don't end up in Devon.'

'No chance of that. The boss said I don't need the kid training kit anymore and he's cutting me lose today.'

'So, you are a natural, after all.'

They spent the morning wandering around town and in the afternoon they went to the beach where a few people were already assembling. Amelia exchanged a few words with the kitesurfing instructor, a long-term friend who gave her permission to take Anders for a spin.

'We are heading east,' she said to her companion, who was busy checking their kit was in order. They sailed away few minutes later.

'Just follow me and don't attempt to do anything stupid.'

Amelia loved the feeling of freedom she got every time she was surfing. Riding freely on the waves, being taken away by the wind but at the same time being in control, being able to change direction, steering as she pleased. If she only could steer her life in whatever direction she pleased …

Anders was doing well. He wasn't elegant in his movement but he was effective, and thanks to his muscular build and possibly an innate sense of balance, he was able to stay close to Amelia.

They stopped on the long beach of East Blatchington to catch their breath.

'This is the life!' said Anders, laying down on the pebble beach. A couple of fishermen not too far away looked at them with curiosity.

'Am I not keeping you away from your responsibilities?' asked Amelia.

'What, modelling? No way! I still have a reasonable amount of cash and this is what I do. Work and then enjoy life at my own pace.'

'So, no plans of settling?' asked Amelia cautiously.

Anders talked about his dream of setting up something in the south of France, being somewhere by the beach all day and it one day at a time. Maybe a bistro, maybe renting out jet skis.

'I was aiming for a flock of sheep in the Welsh mountains but I think your dream is far better.' They laughed.

'Here, let's take a selfie.' Amelia took out her phone from a plastic bag and took a snap of herself and Anders. She sent the picture to Logan with the caption 'On holiday! You should try it sometimes, it is FUN!'

'Shall we head back?' asked Amelia half an hour later.

'Let's go.'

They spent the following few days together kitesurfing, sightseeing, getting to know each other, and making love, unaware they were under surveillance.

****

Amelia couldn't sleep. She got out of bed and picked up the envelope that Logan had given her few days earlier.

There was little light to read in the room and turning on the lamp near the armchair could have disturbed Anders. She decided to put a robe on and head for the living room. The couch was a little old, not in line with the modern style of her apartment, but Amelia was reluctant to change it. It was a grey cloth couch, worn in several points on the seat and armrests. She'd bought it years before while still a student and she'd spent days and nights studying on it. The first significant purchase she'd made with her own money from doing odd jobs and she couldn't bear to part with it, but maybe one day she would have it reupholstered.

She opened the envelope and began to read a letter handwritten by Albert Romanov. Romanov was like an uncle to her. As she read, her apprehension grew, grasping the pit of her stomach. She had seen many things as a lawyer, but this was above all the others. Amelia was sipping a now lukewarm coffee and re-read the letter many times and was about to start again when she felt two hands grasp her shoulders. For a moment she felt lost, and she jumped.

'Sorry, did I scare you? What are you reading?' asked Anders from behind her shoulders.

'It's a long story,' said Amelia folding up the letter.

'Well, we've got time.' He walked around the sofa and sat next to her. *Luckily, he is wearing his underpants*, she thought. *I don't have the energy or desire right now to make love again.* She reflected for a moment and then unfolded the letter again. Romanov filled the gap her father had left during the years she'd grown up. She called him "uncle" even though she knew he wasn't her real uncle. He was the person she went to when she needed advice and the one who gave her the chance to be who she was today. During those years, he had become a mentor, a dear friend, and a confident. But also the fatherly presence she had needed.

'It's from an old family friend. He died recently after being shot. And he stole ten million pounds from the bank I'm supposed to take possession of.'

'Damn. What's he doing, giving it back to you?'

'Not quite. Romanov knew that there was bad blood between my father and me, so he is giving me a chance to destroy the damn bank,' said Amelia, thinking again about the contents of the letter.

'You don't look like a happy heiress, right now. What happened between you and your father?'

'We have never gotten along. The only love of his life was money. For which, he ignored family and affections. My sister was perhaps the only one in the family he had truly loved.'

Amelia told of how her father rarely showed up at home, and those rare times, in her memory, he was never in a good mood. Of how her mother had endured one betrayal after another: secretaries, clients, and even prostitutes.

Bruno Mortcombe was a bastard who didn't care about anything or anybody but himself. He was married to an Italian who worked for a local museum and who had become enchanted by his strong jaw, his determination as a businessman, and the sense of risk that oozed from him. She knew she would be marrying a jerk and somehow maybe she'd accepted the challenge, trying to ride the tiger and tame it.

But the years passed, and Bruno Mortcombe rarely bothered the family. Get rich, by any means possible, was his passion. And be a skirt-chaser.

The arrival of Carla had not helped to reinvigorate the shaky marriage, and maybe it had worsened it. Several years later, when Amelia was in her early teens, her parents quarrelled worse than usual, maybe about the umpteenth of her father's escapades; the fight lasted for hours, her mother threatening divorce and her father threatening to take their daughters and throw her out on the street. It was later when everything seemed quieter, and the sisters were in bed when the house resounded with the shot of a pistol. A single shot, loud, almost like one of those of firecrackers that kids threw out on the streets in the days around New Year's Eve. The girls were kept in their room, a maid kept them company until someone was able to reach the nanny by phone. The lights of police cars and an ambulance were clearly visible through the window though to

Amelia, the younger of the two, it quickly became clear that a tragedy had just happened. She just wanted the body covered with a white sheet, that they were loading in the ambulance, to belong to Bruno Mortcombe.

From their room, they could hear the voices of people and policemen who walked around the house. It was only much later that peace returned. But neither of the girls managed to get to sleep, despite the presence of the nanny. The next day other policemen visited her father, and maybe Amelia saw a large envelope changing hands between her father and a police officer. Only later, many years later, she grasped the significance of that gesture.

According to the report, it was a suicide, but Amelia knew that even if that had been the case, it had been her father who pushed her in that direction. Their already fragile relationship with their remaining parent, typical of early adolescence, was hopelessly compromised.

Amelia finished university and was looking for a job when Albert Romanov, an old family friend, proposed to her the deal of the century. To buy the studio where she now worked and keep the existing customers, for a reasonable price. She obtained a loan from a bank, thanks to Romanov. Then he introduced her to Logan, who also began working in the studio. After some time passed trying to keep the business afloat, tightening their belts and not paying themselves a real salary, thanks to Ryan Logan's financial skills, eventually they had made it.

'A nice gesture, Romanov's,' said Anders.

'Interest's at fifteen per cent for that loan, I've just finished paying off debts.'

'Would you have accepted a gift?'

'No, I don't think so.'

'Maybe your father leaving you the bank is a preparatory gesture,' continued Anders.

'I don't think so. My sister is incompetent, and my dad doesn't trust Price. There were no other choices.' Her father was well aware of the hatred that flowed in her veins; he knew she would never want to deal with that bank, with whatever came from her father. Romanov's letter confirmed her feelings. But maybe he also knew that Amelia was basically honest.

'He tricked me, no doubt about it. If I refuse to take control of the bank, I do what he expected of me, if I keep it, I carry on a past I always denied. There is no exit.'

'What does that letter say?'

'Read it.' Amelia handed him the papers that were on the coffee table in front of the couch.

Dear Amelia,

If this missive reaches you, it means I'm dead. It may be that I died under natural circumstances, or of a heart attack. Or perhaps in a car accident. Don't believe it, I have been killed.

I worked for the Mortcombe Bank for a lifetime, and I curse myself for having spent all that time accumulating money for others instead of thinking about my own family, my beloved ones, and especially of my daughter.

As you may have guessed, Mortcombe Bank is not what it seems to be on the surface. They launder money on behalf of the Russian mafia, and so it has been since the beginning. Bruno was an ambitious man who wouldn't have stopped for anything to succeed. Some people are motivated by love and want to get rich, to give hope and a future for their children. Or just because they have enough talent to do it. Bruno was different, he always sought success as an end in itself, for his own pleasure. Nothing in the world could stop him in his quest, he would (and did) falsify papers to succeed, to feel important, to be able to drink from the cup of success one more time.

Sorry if I'm hurting you with my words, your father was a good friend to me for all these years. But I'm at a point in life where what I say is no longer relevant. Now that I am a dead man, I think I can afford to express whatever I feel.

I met Bruno during the merger with Saunders, Whitehall & Passmore and we met again in London several years later when we were looking for our own space in this corrupt and brutal world. Before the Mortcombe Bank, Bruno worked at Ranfald & Co and had already made a name for himself in the financial sector. He was a person with few scruples, even then, and he was considered a shark that wouldn't back out of anything. He took incalculable risks and bet ridiculous amounts of money, other people's money, and for some years he was admired. Young people regarded him with respect, a model to aspire to. Until he made a lousy investment borrowing money from an American bank. What you may not know was that the bank was a cover for a Russian underworld organisation in New York. He made bad investments in another bank of Ohio, who later went bust. They could have killed him for that mistake, but instead, he came out, as always, being the winner.

He managed to find a way to hide funds and earning the esteem of people who rarely have respect for anything or anyone. Needless to say, maybe you've already guessed, that Bruno had managed to do so through illegal practices. The result was to bring back the money lost by the Russian mob and keeping a substantial amount for himself. Thus, the Mortcombe Bank was born.

He needed trustworthy people, with strong ambition and I was one of the first directors to whom Bruno turned to, after the merger. I didn't have many scruples at the time, although I feel ashamed now, and I started working for him. Slowly I learned about racketeering, but I closed one eye. Then both.

The same lust for power which had taken Bruno had also taken possession of me. But over the years I started feeling the weight of what I did, and I changed my mind about what was important in life.

If you are reading this letter, it means that they found me and I'm a dead man. Please apologise to Ryan for what I did. I'm a scumbag and always have been. But they will never find the money I stole. The money is suspended in a sort of financial limbo, and even if they capture me, they will not be able to get the information because even I don't know where the money is. I split the account numbers and passwords into three sections. I attached one part to this letter, the second I sent to my daughter. This information alone is not enough, I paid a hacker to take the third piece of information. This person will receive a letter like this. It will be his decision whether to run the risk of contacting you or ignoring the question. If he chooses to contact you, I promised him an additional million dollars, as compensation. Of the remaining nine, I leave it to you and my daughter to take the decision of how to use it.

I'm sorry to have brought you this news, you probably still remember me as Uncle Albert who came to visit you laden with gifts at Christmas. I'm sorry I've ruined that memory.

If you decide to meet my daughter, tell her she has always been in my heart, though I've never shown it, even though she may not believe a word of what I'm saying.

Uncle Albert.

Landau Bank, Cayman Island – 674566456-34 xxxxxxxxxxxxxxxxxxxxxxxxxxxxxxxx

Messner & Co, Zurich – xxxxxx xxxxx 456123/xxx/

Colman Affiliates, Panama – Chris Xie x xxxxx/xxxxxxxxxx/Mrs. Belkin

36331232/xxxxxxxx xxxxxx XXXXX Financial Holding, –/xxxxxxxxxxxxxx/Mr. Johnston

Anders laid the letter on the table and, for a few minutes, did not know what to say. 'What are you going to do?'

'I don't want a bank that's associated with the Russian mafia, of that I'm sure. What were my father's plans, it doesn't matter at this point.'

'And the ten million?'

That was a more difficult question. She could understand Albert's gesture, she'd thought several times about disappearing, although she couldn't tolerate the challenging position he had put her in; the options she had were dwindling fast.

'Nine. I have to think about it.'

'If it's the mafia's money, they will want it back.'

'It's nobody's money at this point, we don't even have the full information necessary to retrieve the loot.'

'And then,' Anders repeated, 'what are you going to do?'

'I should at least get in touch with Albert's daughter. Let her know how things are. I will decide what to do at that point. You know, I don't even remember her? She was a young, brunette girl who sometimes came to dinner for Christmas when I was growing up, but I don't even remember her name. Her parents sent her to Switzerland to study; my mother always threatened me with the same when I was acting up, to send me to a boarding school in Switzerland … Damn, what was her name …

Dimitra. Being sent to Switzerland was mine and my sister's bogeyman.'

'Do you have an address?' asked Anders.

'No, we have never been close, I barely remember her. Maybe I can do a search, with all these social networks and Google, you can't really hide anymore.'

'Even from the Russian mafia, for that matter.'

That too was a valid point. Not that she knew much about the subject, apart from something she'd read sometimes in books, or seen in Hollywood movies, but disappearing completely, even for individuals with resources, wouldn't be an easy task.

'What do you know about the mafia?'

'Not a damn thing, but if what you say is true, you're in trouble up to your neck.'

Amelia began to feel uncomfortable and stood up for a second cup of coffee. Having all those millions or not wouldn't have made any difference. If anyone knew she had a key to that money, she would be in danger.

****

Margot slipped her phone out from her jacket and dialled a number.

'Robert Price,' said an irritated voice from the other end.

'I've got news.' Margot told him about Romanov's letter, of the suspended accounts, and the ten million. She hadn't gotten her hands on Romanov's letter, but it appeared there were partial instructions to recover lost funds.

'Are you sure Romanov's daughter has the remaining instructions?' asked Price.

'So it seems, although the only certainty would be to read that damn letter. We could kill those two immediately and take that, and then introduce ourselves undercover to Romanov's daughter.'

'It might not work, we don't have all the info,' objected Price, upset by being called while he was having dinner with his family. He had kept this double fronted face for years, kind and thoughtful with his family and cruel and unsympathetic at work. 'Let's avoid any risks; follow them and take action when you have all the information available.'

'Roger that.'

CHAPTER 20

'As I was saying, Mr Logan …'

'You can call me Ryan, let's cut short the formalities.'

'Well,' Splinter continued, 'I won't beat around the bush. We are interested in your ability to make money disappear and have it magically reappear somewhere else, without anyone knowing or have a way of tracing it back. Of course, for a fee.'

'This can be done,' said Logan pensive. They had chosen the easy road, oiling the wheels was always more effective than blackmailing. The fact that these guys weren't greedy made the proposal most interesting.

'And in addition to making them disappear, we'd also like to have a system to make them multiply,' interjected Hank.

'If I knew how to multiply money, I would have my own personal investment fund, and we would speak on a beach in the Caribbean.'

They all laughed except Logan.

'Let me explain. The idea is to set up a system, an investment system which appears to be bulletproof. You don't really have to multiply the money, it just has to look like it, even under an expert's analysis.'

Logan was beginning to understand. 'A scam aimed at a few individuals or at a large number of people? Because there is a world of difference.'

'We'll limit it to one individual,' said Splinter.

'I need something more, who he is, what does he do for a living, how much money are we talking about,' insisted Logan fondling his chin, as he always did when a situation was intriguing him. 'It's not that we can improvise such things.'

'We will let you know the details in due course, but just to give you an order of magnitude, think about tens of millions of dollars, perhaps hundreds.'

'Ha, ha, ha!' Laughed Logan. 'To invest tens of millions you have to have a real organisation behind you. Don't get me wrong, you might be very good at what you do, but here we need people in the trade.'

Hank did not scare from those claims, but Logan continued, 'And then it takes funds just to start. You cannot create money from nothing.'

'Don't worry, we have funds for that.'

'Don't you even consider the insider trading story. That story is as old as Noah, and only the pensioners fall for it.'

They looked at each other. Someone in the gang had actually proposed it, but then the idea had been rejected because having to cheat people who worked in a bank wouldn't have been feasible. In fact, they were almost to despair, they could easily pull off a con from a few million, but that wouldn't have changed anything. What they wanted was the final blow, one that would allow them to retire and make a good life forever. No matter what industry people operate in, the dream of winning the lottery was always the same, equal for everyone.

The fact Logan had agreed to take part and provide his expertise was unexpected luck, maybe the only opportunity to carry on that scam, that last one, the one that would make history.

'According to you, Ryan, how could we defraud a guy like Robert Price?'

At that point there was no need to drag this out too long, thought Splinter. Sooner or later they had to reveal the target's name and equivocating wouldn't be useful to anyone.

'Price or the Mortcombe Bank?' asked Logan, half amused and half dissatisfied.

'Does it make any difference?'

'I might have a conflict of interest; Mortcombe's daughter is my employer and maybe the new owner of the bank.'

Domino interjected, 'Would this conflict be removed, let's say, by a generous compensation or a percentage of the profits?'

'We should think about it. You know that old Mortcombe was in cahoots with the Russian mob, right? You don't mess with those guys.'

That was a piece of information that took the crooks by surprise. They had come to the point of understanding that Robert Price was working with

Russian clients, but that the bank was colluding with the Russian mafia was news, something they had not considered. Domino kept to herself and moved toward the window, thoughtfully. Hank said nothing, but it was evident he was thinking about a possible response, which didn't arrive.

Splinter was the one to save the day at the last minute. 'We are aware of the risks, but there are ways to disappear, or at least to let the cheated think it's not worth chasing us.'

Logan was doubtful, and he made no effort to hide it. It was at that point that Splinter decided to explain the basics for a scam.

The first rule is that you can't cheat an honest man. There are types of people that are best suited for a scam. Greedy people, with a dark soul. The idea is to let the target think he faces a unique opportunity. This must happen by chance, or at least must appear as such. Every move must be assessed as if you played a game of chess, and convincing a target becomes an art. The target must maintain its ability to decide, to accept a risk or to call it out; we have to anticipate every possible move the target might take. When the prey makes a choice, he has to do it with his own head; the main work of the scammer is in helping him make that decision, relying on his weaknesses and his desires.

Splinter showed confidence in front of Logan but had not yet recovered from the news about the Russian mafia. They would have had to revise their plans, make sure they covered every possible detail.

No one wanted to end up in the hands of those types.

'As I said, I have to think it over. Not only for what binds me to Amelia Mortcombe. Finding a way to fool a banker and convince him to invest won't be a cakewalk.'

Logan stood up, to make it clear that that meeting was over, and, after the usual pleasantries, he left.

'It sounds more complicated and riskier than any scam we've done before,' said Domino, 'are we sure we want to continue?'

'Marcus, if we are not careful, we'll end up in a lot of trouble.'

The elder fraudster poured a drop of brandy, and for an interminable period he remained immersed in his own thoughts, rotating the liquor in the glass he held with both hands. Eventually, he spoke, much to the relief of everyone.

'The bigger the risk, the higher the reward, my dear friends. I don't have the strength anymore to continue making hundred thousand pounds scams at the time. This could be an opportunity to end this game and get over with this life.'

Each of them was immersed in their own thoughts about how their life could change. Someone would have loved to go to live on the west coast of the United States, someone else thought about an apartment in Central London and maybe at a villa in the Kent countryside. The dreams were always the same, although people were different;

they all wanted the same things: recognition, stability, and security. The difference was in how much they were willing to risk obtaining those rewards.

They went back to work, the concern clearly visible on their faces.

CHAPTER 21

That Saturday morning, Amelia received another message.

She cursed herself for having forgotten to turn off her mobile phone. They were back in bed, and she was still in Anders' arms. She reached to the bedside table to see who it was. A message from Quentin inviting her for a stroll along the seafront and then to lunch. She glanced at the clock on her phone, it was nearly eleven o'clock in the morning.

Quentin.

She had completely forgotten about him, but he was continuing to pursue her relentlessly and she would have to tell him bluntly where her mind was. Why not do it now? Of course, she couldn't consider Anders a boyfriend, and he might not even want to be that. *What's wrong with dreaming a little and getting carried away by events?* she thought. For an instant she felt alive again, in the middle of an adventure, taking risks while life around was screaming at her not to. *To hell with Quentin,* she thought, *for now, I want to live, and I don't care about the consequences.*

Quentin, stop texting me, I don't want to see you anymore…

How much had it cost her to write that message? Little. She had acted on impulse, but once she pressed the 'send' button, she was sure. Quentin wouldn't be part of her life.

Are you sure?

I am through with you. For good.

She waited for a few minutes for a response that did not come, and so she turned off the phone, resting once again in Anders' arms.

'Good morning,' he said stretching himself in bed.

'Good morning to you. Do you want some breakfast?'

'I'm starving, why don't we go out instead of tinkering with pans and stoves?'

It wasn't a bad idea, and slowly they got up to go to the bathroom for a shower. Anders pulled her to him and kissed Amelia hungrily. They were still half asleep but already willing to make love again. The lukewarm shower jet washed over the two tangled bodies and became hotter and hotter. Anders lifted her up and pushed her against the wall, holding her weight, while Amelia wrapped her legs around his hips. They made love again while the water rushed in their mouths. Amelia was the first to reach orgasm, nailed to the wall by a bundle of muscles that moved her like a twig in the wind. Anders gave her no respite, he kissed her and held her, moving slowly against her body until it was all over. They washed each other, exploring each other, looking into each other's eyes like two old lovers, without actually knowing anything about each other.

****

'Stand by. They're coming out,' said a voice on the microphone. Margot was visibly tired. During surveillance, it was always hard for her to sleep. She had slept at times in her car, reclining the seat slightly, but tensions were running high. Also, it was a difficult task, and despite years of practice she'd never managed to shake off the desire to control every aspect of a mission personally, down to the smallest details. It was a mixture of arrogance and distrust. She was adept at her work, and she often went on a rampage when the rest of the team did not put the same care and passion into a mission. But there was also a sense of insecurity that would force her to keep the situation under control. The fear of delegating and, in doing so, stumbling across an irreparable mistake. And then, the only reasonable option she had was to check everything until she was inevitably worn out, holding the reins until the end.

Margot was ex-military, and she'd served in Iraq with the coalition troops during the second Iraq war, though she still remembered Desert Storm, from when she was a kid. Margot had been with German troops at that time and even if newspapers called it a 'peace operation', Margot had done her part in that battle, killing an unknown number of Iraqis. After the three mandatory deployments, she'd returned for another two years as a mercenary, although they claimed to be an organisation protecting civilians who were rebuilding the country. When Margot returned to her homeland she soon felt the lack of adrenaline. In Iraq she could manage her own life, even to kill when necessary. Margot would never adapt to make a living as a bartender or working in an office. The only skills she'd ever had she acquired during the war. She decided to put them to use, no matter what.

'Kaleb, get off that rooftop and go to the end of the road,' said Margot into the radio. 'Yuri, you and Aleksey are seconds. Ivan and I will continue the stakeout as third. Taras, get to Kaleb's and await instructions.'

'Roger,' came as if a single response to her orders.

'The couple are headed toward the centre.'

When a distant voice, not heard by either, cawed on the radio, 'Two moving subjects. They are not aware. They are heading for the waterfront.'

'How many passers-by?' asked Margot.

'Not many but enough,' replied Kaleb.

'Roger. Keep going in silence. Aleksey, move towards the seafront and wait. Kaleb will leave at that point.' Margot was studying a map of the city trying to anticipate where the two were headed. The worst was The Lanes, they could lose them easily between those streets or be spotted, but if they kept walking, it wouldn't be a problem. They alternated security staff to prevent the same face appearing behind them too frequently.

The couple kept walking, oblivious to the group that was following them. When they reached Marine Parade, Anders and Amelia stopped for a moment to observe Brighton Pier in the distance.

'Don't stop,' said Margot to Aleksey, who had replaced Kaleb. 'Go to the shops and pretend to be a tourist.'

Aleksey was too close to Amelia and Anders to answer and made two clicks with the radio to confirm that he had received the message. The man he was following looked at him intently as he passed them in a hurry; looking at the ground as if minding his own business, but he felt that look continue to follow him. He said nothing for fear of being rebuked by Margot, although he had made no mistake. *Who in hell are these two?* He thought as he walked to a newsagent. He bought one and kept walking on the opposite side of the road to where the two were walking. 'They are heading toward the pier,' he said with a faint voice on the radio.

'Taras, reach the pier and pass wherever you can, stay near them until they reach their destination.'

'Roger.'

'They've stopped. The targets are walking into a café,' said Aleksey.

'Roger. Everyone into position. Taras, stay where you are. Aleksey and Kaleb, stay on the opposite side of the street, we'll take them when they come out.'

'Roger that.'

****

They ordered two cups of coffee, a croissant for Amelia and some sausages for Anders. 'I would like to go to Romanov's daughter. At the very least I should try to find that missing money,' she said aloud, but in fact, she was talking to herself.

'And if she has one piece of the puzzle, what will you do?'

'I don't know yet, but I have already decided that I won't keep the bank,' said Amelia.

'And when did you make that decision?'

'This morning. I don't want anything to do with my father or my family's past. They can all go to hell.'

Anders watched her with admiration, it wasn't an everyday occurrence to find a person willing to give up a fortune. He wondered if, in the same situation, he would have done the same. He failed to come up with an adequate response in his mind.

'I don't see you running away with Romanov's loot.'

They both laughed. The waitress came with their dishes, and for a while, there was silence again. Anders wasted no time in attacking the sausages, worked with knife and fork as if he had not eaten for weeks.

'No, I can't see myself running either. Ten million is nothing nowadays, you're not going to get very far, I would need at least five hundred.'

'And what would you do with all that money?'

'I would buy the biggest shoe store in the world.' They both laughed. 'What would you do with all that money?'

'I've never thought about that, I don't even play the lottery. I'd probably do what I do now, touring the world and meeting people.'

'So you're here visiting?' asked Amelia. Her companion laughed out loud, which caused some diners to turn their attention to them.

'I don't know yet. I think I need the motivation to leave a place. Change is always difficult, depends on what binds us to a place.'

The waitress returned, asking if they wanted something else. Sometimes timing was everything when running a restaurant, interrupting a conversation before someone could ask an embarrassing question or reveal a thought. How many lovers were saved in a bar, we will never know. The two were at their beginning, at the stage where you tried to find out who was standing in front of you, without succeeding. Sometimes an interruption was enough to bring people back to the right pace, to not proceed in a hurry; it's the mirror of our life, the bar, which reminds us that there's always a hitch, an unwanted break in front of us. And a price to pay at the end.

'I have to go to the bathroom,' said Anders getting up and excusing himself from his partner.

'I was thinking of going to the Romanovs' today, would you accompany me?'

'Sure, why not?'

'Can I use your laptop? I think I found her on Facebook and I wrote her a message, and I'd like to see if she's replied. Like an idiot, I left my phone at home.'

'Go ahead, it's in the bag.' Anders jotted his password and login on a napkin, before heading towards the back of the room.

Amelia turned on the computer in front of her. The bag, half-empty and flaccid, was placed by her chair, she avoided looking inside it. She started tinkering with the computer and eventually managed to find what she was looking for. Anders returned after a few minutes.

'Did you manage to find her?'

'Yes, she answered. She lives up north, in Scotland. We used to go on holiday there when I was a kid, and my sister has a home near Aberdeen, although I don't think they've used it for years.'

'When would you like to go?'

'Today, she's given me her address. We can stop in Leeds for the night, we'll find a nice bed and breakfast.'

'I have nothing else on, and this story has begun to intrigue me.'

'Would you like something else to eat?' asked Amelia, who had become nervous and wanted to leave immediately, so she stood up without waiting for an answer making it clear she didn't want to wait. She blushed as soon as she realised her mistake.

'No, I'm fine. Let's go.'

CHAPTER 22

Igor Sokolov came to Brighton that afternoon. In the sphere of Russian mafia, he was as feared as he was detested. Someone had even nicknamed him 'the woodcutter' for his habit of carrying an inlaid sixteenth-century German axe, which he used for some jobs. Those who knew him well, few, knew about the history of that axe, taken by his grandfather as a war trophy from a German army colonel during World War II. Nobody knew who the owner was, but during a battle, Sokolov's grandfather came face to face with a German soldier who had stopped the car near a grove, right before the Russian counter-offensive to liberate Leningrad took a foothold.

The man came out from behind the trees as if he had suddenly materialised, he killed the driver with a knife and began to hit the colonel with his bare hands, leaving him bleeding and unconscious on the side of the road. Searching the unlucky man's luggage, he found the inlaid war axe, probably a family heirloom. Its twin can still be admired in Dresden Museum nowadays. It was with that that Sokolov's grandfather had torn the colonel to pieces.

The axe passed from father to son until Igor, who had chosen it as his privileged tool to kill his enemies and for 'small works of persuasion' as he used to say. The ferocity of Igor Sokolov had no peer, it had been cultivated for years, polished, refined in every detail, first as a special-forces operative and later in the service of the Russian mafia.

Having to face Sokolov was a powerful message for anyone, often equivalent to receiving a business card from death itself.

The car, a Mercedes Maybach, travelled through the downtown streets until it arrived at their destination under a Victorian building in the centre. The driver opened the door, and Sokolov entered the building, heading toward the elevator. The building was facing the sea and had probably cost a small fortune, but with what they paid Robert Price, he could probably afford it. Sokolov was not keen on houses or apartments, and despite the tailored pinstripe suit that made him look like a businessman who had just arrived in town, the woodcutter preferred spending time in the countryside, far from too many memories and the noise of the city. Even when he was in Moscow, he avoided the apartment he had received as a gift from the mafia, preferring hotels or even sleeping on a makeshift bed at a friend's house. He had never been accustomed to luxury, unlike so many with whom he worked.

The doorbell rang and a blonde, an attractive mid-30s woman, came to answer. He introduced himself as a client of the Mortcombe Bank while in the background he could hear the shouting of children busy arguing over a few games. She asked him to wait in the lounge while Price's wife went looking for her husband, holed up in his home office.

The room was furnished with modern, plush designer sofas, contemporary paintings on the walls and a few pieces of art, mostly bronze, scattered around the room. It was not clear if they had taken advantage of a decorator or if it was the work of dear Carla Mortcombe. Sokolov made a mental note to ask at the first opportunity.

Price's expression switched in an instant from surprised to terrified before settling on irritated, as soon as he saw his guest. 'An unexpected visit,' he said coldly, shaking hands with the guest who meanwhile had stood up from the armchair. Sokolov was an imposing man, six feet three and bulging muscles, clearly visible even if he was wearing a suit and tie. A slither of a tattoo raised from the neck, slightly jarring with his clothes.

'We have an important transaction to carry out, and the boss has seen fit to send me here, to avoid hitches or delays that would be ill received.'

'Obviously, obviously … The accounts are all in order,' lied Price.

'We just sold a large quantity of weapons and drugs, and with that money, plus what we have in our accounts, we'd like to invest in an insurance company in Germany. As you say, diversifying investments is always important.'

'Do we have to talk about it right here?' asked Price looking in the direction of the hall, irked by the fact that his wife, unaware of his real business, could reappear at any moment.

'Of course, we do. With old Mortcombe we had an established relationship, which we've been in for years. We just want to make sure that the new management … you know, keep our interests in mind.'

'About that … There could be complications. My sister-in-law has control of the bank, but she has not yet taken over. There may be delays.'

'That's why I'm here, to avoid those and get rid of any mishap,' said the Russian with a phoney smile planted on his face. Price knew the guest's methods; he had witnessed his rampage once before. When he started to get his hands dirty with the sordid affairs of the bank, Sokolov invited him to a demonstration of what would happen to those who betrayed the organisation. The poor guy was lying nude on a table in the back of a butcher shop. Sokolov had started to cut him, piece by piece until he had confessed. This, however, had not given him the right to a quick death. The woodcutter went on for hours hitting him and cutting him with the blade of that sixteenth-century axe. He worked skilfully, causing pain and at the same time avoiding getting the job done too quickly. Price would have vomited his own soul after seeing that havoc, but nobody was allowed to leave the room until the execution was terminated. You could even forget Sokolov's face.

The face was not significant. Nobody would have overlooked the axe.

'You could come to the bank next week, we will release the funds as soon as possible. Sometimes we invest money, it's our task as a bank to make you earn as much as possible.'

Sokolov nodded and stood up, heading for the door without saying a single word. There was no need.

When he left the building, he paused for an instant before getting into the car. A waiter in a nearby café was trying to ward off a stray dog that hadn't bothered anyone, apart from looking at customers consuming drinks and some sandwiches. Instead of leaving, Sokolov entered the bar, bought a ham sandwich and began to feed that ragged dog right in front of the waiter. One look off Sokolov was enough to stop any action by the waiter. When the dog finished eating, he let the waggling tailed creature onto the backseat of the Maybach. That gesture would have not been enough to erase all the atrocities he had committed, not even scratching the mountain of sins he was guilty of; he was aware of that.

The car drove off shortly after, while the darkness fell on Brighton, and the pier lights were lit.

CHAPTER 23

Logan slumped on a chair in his office and sighed. He cleaned the lenses of his glasses using part of his tie as he often did when he had to find a solution to a problem. His gaze went to the ceiling and to a long crack that had been there for a few years. He had to find a solution.

He mentally listed the pros and cons before deciding what to do next. Among the advantages, he definitely put the fact that Bruno Mortcombe was in a coma as a positive. At least he wouldn't create complications. What about Albert Romanov? He had taught him a lot, but after twenty years people changed. Or was it twenty-five? There was still Thatcher, he thought for a moment, but he hadn't made the exact calculation. After Logan came out of jail, Romanov had done everything possible to bring him closer to his daughter Amelia. He had also acted as a filter against Mortcombe. Not that there was a need, Amelia had already broken those bridges on her own, but it was a gesture Logan had appreciated.

The original idea of taking revenge on Mortcombe was Romanov's. They talked about that often, whenever they met in London. For years Logan had meditated revenge, a thousand different ways to kill Mortcombe, but deep down he knew he would never commit murder. He had not changed despite years of detention. Romanov was different, more secretive and warier compared to the young man who had worked for Logan years before. Then came the job offer by Amelia.

Romanov persisted with the idea of cheating Mortcombe and Logan kept going along for fun. Talking about a scam eased the pain and exorcised the desire for revenge. Over time the plan was refined, discussing pros and cons, possible errors that investigators would discover. It was a game. Until they ran out of ideas.

The plan was simple. Utilising a hacker, Romanov would obtain Mortcombe's username and password, then he would transfer some money to some offshore accounts. Logan's task was to make them disappear, moving it through several shell companies. Last, deliver to the authorities evidence of Mortcombe's involvement with the Russian mafia.

What had made Romanov change his mind was a mystery, but when he was killed all sorts of alarm bells rang in Logan's head. Sooner or later someone would have made inquiries, and the friendship between the two was well known. And he had to protect Amelia. The fact that Mortcombe was in hospital bought him some time, but he did not know how long. He was not angry with Romanov who, after all, had tended to Amelia all those years during his time in prison.

His mind returned to the meeting with Marcus and how to defraud a bank.

****

He picked up the phone and called Amelia. 'Hi, Ryan.'

'Hi, just in time. Do you remember those missing millions from the bank?'

'Yes, of course.'

'Well, I found them. There are approximately ten million scattered in various accounts around the world,' said Amelia.

'Where are you now?'

'I'm driving toward Aberdeen to see Albert Romanov's daughter.'

'Look, try to be careful. Romanov was also associated with the Russian mafia, like your father. What his daughter's involvement in Romanov's affairs is all a mystery.'

'Do you think she has any interest in what happened?' The M6, which passed on the right of Birmingham was pretty busy and Amelia decided not to overtake the bus in front of her. Anders, sitting in the passenger seat, slumbered. He looked like a god at rest.

'I don't know. From the documentation I've seen, Dimitra's name doesn't come up, but you never know. The fact that someone killed Romanov keeps me awake at night. It is a lot of money, and

I'm sure several people want to get their hands on it.'

'I still cannot explain how he managed to make it disappear without anyone noticing.'

'Romanov was good, not the best, but he knew what he was doing. It would have taken months for the bank to notice, given the number of transactions he created, but it has left traces. You say that Albert's daughter has got the money?'

'No, Romanov wanted to keep them for himself. But in case of sudden death, if you know what I mean, he sent me a letter with the details on how to retrieve them.' Amelia explained to Logan the contents of the letter, bank accounts and, after some hesitation, even the latest about Anders.

'Proceed with caution.'

'All right,' she said embarrassed. She wouldn't have liked to explain what she was feeling at that moment if it wasn't necessary.

'OK, be careful. Have you been back to the bank?'

'I want to stay as far away as possible from that place. After the trouble which happened to Romanov, who knows what surprises await me in that den of vipers. Send back the documentation. That should please my brother-in-law, he's drooled over that bank for years. But not too quickly.'

Logan thought it over for a few moments. Maybe he ought to give a second look at those documents; he would need all the information possible. In particular about the accounts managed by Robert Price. 'I'll start to work on that by Monday, and I will send them back, don't worry. Let me know how things go with Romanov's daughter.'

'You can count on it. I'll talk to you later.'

After the conversation, Logan returned to his desk between files and containers of documents, the only place where he could really concentrate. It wasn't always so. Formerly a cheerful person, especially during his university years. He had wanted to be a comedian, on more than one occasion, friends encouraged him to go on stage to tell something funny. He knew he had a great sense of humour, but had never thrown himself into the fray, he had never found the courage of really trying. His parents had made sacrifices to allow him to study, and he always understood how much they had done so to give him an opportunity. Giving up everything for a dream? It wasn't like him.

It's funny how life changes you, he thought, I'm not that different from the honest person I was thirty years ago, nor am I different from these hustlers I'm working with now.

He picked the documents once again in search of a stratagem that would do the trick.

He began to leaf through his agenda, and after a few minutes, he stopped on one name in particular. And a phone number. He picked up the phone and dialled it.

'Tim! It's Ryan Logan, how are you?'

'Ryan? Bloody hell, it's been years since we've been in touch, where have you been?' said the voice on the other end of the phone.

'A long story. Look, I could use some advice.'

'I can't believe it. Ryan Logan asking for advice. This is news to me, when we were working for you everyone hung on the words from your lips.'

'I'm serious,' said Logan, trying to mask the embarrassment in his voice.

'OK, shoot. Although I doubt can … do you remember when we did that thing with the Kenden Insurance accounts…'

Logan interrupted him. He was not in the mood to dig up the past, albeit with that phone call he knew he didn't have alternatives. 'I need a way to make money. A lot of it and fast.'

Tim Whitley paused. 'Legally or illegally?'

'It doesn't matter, whatever works.'

'You are cornered, right? Are you planning a supplementary pension?' asked the questioner, laughing.

'Something like that.'

'If you want to make a lot of money, quickly and legally, you have two options: you create your own stock exchange, or you start working in the arbitrage field.'

'I always thought that the story about arbitrages was an urban legend.'

'Not anymore, old boy. Now that's where you make real money. I'm doing that myself, I pocketed my bonuses from Barclays, and now I'm going to the United States. I'm leaving next week. Look, why don't you come to London next week before I leave? I could use some money, and I'll tell you about the new business I'm undertaking. We can help each other.'

'Why not? Shall I find you at this number?'

'Sure, old chap. Jesus Christ, what an honour, working again with the old Logan. Who would have thought?'

The two lingered to talk at length. Whitley had been a shy young man when he started working for Logan. The company where he was working at the time had gotten into trouble due to insider trading and Logan had been called to clean up the mess. Beckett, Wool & Perry was famous at that time for two things. Making a lot of money and not caring about the law. Whitley, in those days was a rookie, and he was pushed a little bit beyond the customary practices of the company. Logan had been called to put it all to rest. They had become friends after that nasty business, and Logan had seen potential in that skinny guy with a nose too long for his face. Logan solved the problem and took Whitley with him to Sandie as a third-year associate; for half the salary, but he had taught him everything he knew. Or almost. Apparently, his old love for finance was not dead in Whitley, and maybe it was time to repay the debt.

When he put down the phone, Logan knew he had a chance.

He poured a glass of cognac, sniffed it for an interminable time, and then emptied it in the sink, opting for Coke. He shouldn't even have a bottle, he hadn't touched alcohol in years, and even if this were a special occasion, he wouldn't slip back into that old habit.

Then he picked up the phone and dialled another number he had learned by heart.

'Hello, Domino. I was looking for Marcus, I might have something that could solve our problems,' said Logan, upon hearing the soothing woman's voice on the other end of the phone.

'Just one second.' There was a pause, and then the stern voice of Splinter came on the phone.

'Did you find anything?'

'I think so, and if things go as expected, maybe it's also legal. I mean, besides conning Price. We should take a trip to London as soon as possible.'

There was a pause on the other end of the phone. 'The whole team?'

'No, just you and me … and maybe Domino.' Logan knew she wouldn't serve much purpose, but Domino was a beautiful woman and to have her around was always lovely. There was some difference in ages between them, which Logan ignored, and waited for the answer.

'I will call you back as soon as we book the trip. How long we will stay in London?'

'One or two days will be enough,' said Logan.

The big con was set in motion.

CHAPTER 24

'Here we are, the house should be the one on the left,' said Amelia pointing towards an isolated building, painted yellow. They entered the driveway leading to the house and stopped in front of the gate. Anders got out of the car to open it and slowly walked towards the house. The gravel made a noise under the car wheels, which occasionally were losing traction. A dog barked in the distance, probably in some nearby home. It was now dusk, and Amelia rang the doorbell. Amelia felt exhausted due to the long drive, despite having spent the previous night in Leeds.

'I'm Amelia Mortcombe,' she said trying to recognise some resemblance of the little girl whom she'd met years earlier. They entered an elegant but not luxurious, house. The furniture in the living room was old fashioned, with a large sofa upholstered with a flower-patterned fabric; it resembled an elderly person's house.

'I remember you, from when we were teenagers,' said Dimitra picking up a picture from a nearby shelf. 'Careless me, haven't introduced myself yet,' she said turning toward Anders and shaking his hand. 'Dimitra Romanov.'

'My pleasure, I'm Anders Nilsson.'

She walked toward the fireplace and weighed a framed picture for a while, before giving it to Amelia. 'Do you remember this one?'

It was a picture that portrayed them as children in a playground that Amelia couldn't recall. She lied, 'Yes, I remember, vaguely.'

'You came because of my dad's letter, right?'

'Yes. As I said, I received one too.'

'Can I see it? It is difficult to comprehend that these were my father's last thoughts before he was killed.'

****

'They are in the house, the living room is at the front of the building,' croaked a voice on the radio.

'Roger.'

'Have you positioned the microphone?' said Margot.

'Wait … Now we should hear something. Kaleb, are you in place?'

'I have a visual of the living room, I'm in a car across the street, about three hundred meters away. I could kill them at any time,' said the North African stroking the rifle on the passenger seat.

'Roger. Stay where you are.'

Margot listened attentively to the conversation that was taking place in the building, using a microphone that had been placed on the outside of a window.

'Karl, Aleksey, Ivan, give me your position.'

'Karl. I'm in the front with Taras, near the main door.'

'Aleksey. I'm covering the back of the building, there is only one door to the garden. I have it in sight.'

'Ivan. I'm near the garage, not far from where they parked.'

'Stand by,' said Kaleb on the microphone, 'the man is nearing the window. I've lost visual on the two women. Wait. I see one of them now, I think they're still in the lounge.'

'Roger, stand by.'

****

Meanwhile, inside the house, Dimitra was carefully reading the letter written by her father to Amelia. She had reciprocated by showing the one she'd received a few days earlier.

'I can't believe it. My father was a criminal. Stealing all those millions when he had enough money to live a good life. I do not understand.' Dimitra handed the two letters to Amelia. She turned them over in her hands for a moment, as if she didn't know what to do with them, before placing them back in her jacket pocket.

'I think it was the mafia's money, Dimitra. If it's any consolation, your father's last gesture was to take it away from that criminal organisation. He was not a saint, but it's something you should take into consideration.'

Anders did not say anything, continuing to walk up and down the room, first near the window, then headed for the living room door, as if he were a caged animal. Amelia followed his movement now and then from the corner of her eye, unable to understand his sudden restlessness.

'It is amazing how all this money,' continued Dimitra, 'ten million dollars, are frozen in these accounts. He also left instructions on how to get them back.'

Her mind began to wander, and although Dimitra had an excellent job in one of the town's spa houses, she couldn't help but, even for one moment, fantasise. Every person in this world has had dreams about an unlikely winning of the lottery, but it was the real possibility of changing one's life that made her tingle. Changing lives. Few people were really able to rationalise that concept.

'It's blood money, Dimitra,' repeated Amelia.

'I know, I know. It's just that for a moment …'

The phrase was left incomplete. Amelia heard a sharp sound of breaking glass and Dimitra fell down to the floor, hit by a gunshot to the forehead. Amelia remained motionless for a moment, incapable of utterance in the face of the death of this woman. She had fallen to the ground, a patch of blood wafted across the Persian carpet and was absorbed by the fabric. She stood looking at her as if in a trance, and unable to move. It was at that point that the lights went off and a voice roused her from that torpor.

'Get down!'

Amelia crouched in front of the sofa. She could see in the dimness the unmoving body of Dimitra and almost smell the metallic stench of the blood that wafted across the floor. A bang on the door made her turn her head towards the hallway. Anders, in the twilight, had struck a belly blow to a man who had just entered the house, leaving him sprawled and gasping on the ground, and was preparing to engage with a second. He grabbed what looked like a submachine gun with both hands and gave a headbutt to the second man, making him stagger. Taken by surprise, the stranger slammed violently against the door jamb and Anders struck him with a knee to the ribs, followed by a second hit. The man fell to the ground. For good measure, he kicked the first intruder in the face. Then shut the door again.

'Come here,' he hissed to Amelia.

When she approached, she saw him put the gun strap across his shoulder and slipping a pistol into his pocket which he had taken from one of the two killers, along with a couple of magazines.

'Is she dead?' he asked turning his gaze in the general direction of Dimitra. Amelia did not reply, still intent on watching the two killers lying on the floor.

'Is she dead?' he repeated.

'Yes, I think so. Anders, she was shot in the head.'

'Stay close to me, there will be others.' He took her hand and walked towards the kitchen. Amelia started to complain, but Anders had laid his forefinger to his lips. There would be time to explain later. In the darkness of the room, he looked briefly out the window. He couldn't identify anything, for good night vision he would have to wait at least another ten minutes; time that they didn't have. Soon, very soon, others would come, probably entering the house from different directions. Time was a luxury they couldn't afford. He again checked the gun and motioned Amelia to stand behind him. He opened the door, and suddenly he shot several rounds toward the most likely place where someone could have been waiting, a bush on the left side at the bottom of the garden, from where they could have a clear view of the kitchen door. A gasp followed shortly. *Good sign* thought Anders. *Hopefully, there aren't any others.*

'We have to run to the bottom of the garden and then climb over the fence. Keep your head down.' Amelia nodded, which Anders did not see, and took her by the hand. They began to run at breakneck speed, and when they reached the fence Anders jumped it with a bound, he then aimed the gun in the direction of the building which they had just left. Amelia was intent on climbing the fence when a figure appeared at the kitchen door. Anders for good measure dropped an entire magazine against the pursuer. Amelia was back at his side. They continued to run through the garden and jumped into another and then another one. Finally, they arrived in a small side street which probably led to garages, but they kept running. They had to put as much distance as possible between them and the trackers. They kept on running, zigzagging between buildings. Anders knew it wasn't so much the distance from pursuers that mattered, but how many corners they could put between them. Changing directions often would have served the purpose. At least for a while. They could hear the dogs barking in the distance and soon after they heard the noise of sirens in the night. It was time to find a means of transport.

****

They arrived near a tree-lined street and saw, not far away, the lights of the city. Anders approached a vehicle parked in a quiet driveway, he looked around for a couple of minutes to make sure nobody was looking and began to pick the car lock. Amelia saw him fumbling with something metallic in his hands that she did not recognise. After that, Anders opened the trunk and began rummaging around until he found a screwdriver. It was an old car, of which she did not recognise the brand in the darkness. Anders motioned her to approach and enter the vehicle.

****

She saw him remove the ignition key cylinder, and then with an abrupt gesture, force the steering wheel, first in one direction and then the other until she felt the steering lock break. Only then did he begin to tinker with the ignition wires.

Once the car was running, they headed toward the centre.

'If I tell you to bend down, do it immediately and without any objections,' said Anders.

'OK. If we were going to steal a car, we could have gotten at least a decent one.'

'Those guys are still out there and as far as we know there may be others. Best to keep a low profile.'

'And who would these others be?'

'I haven't the faintest idea, but if I had to guess, I would say they are hunting for ten million. Romanov was killed for that.'

Something was wrong, she thought. Romanov had been killed before they found out about the ten million shortfall, surely there was another reason for that death. But the attack a few minutes before was definitely a move to recover the money.

'One thing I haven't understood. Even though we have two letters, those are not enough to recover the money. Romanov's letter is clear, there is a hacker somewhere who has the missing piece.'

Anders did not answer and drove towards Inverness. Going directly to the south would put them in danger again, if they headed in another direction, maybe they would cover their tracks. Unless the pursuers had unlimited resources. In that case, it'd be trouble. He returned to thinking about what Amelia said. 'Maybe they don't know that they are missing the third piece in the puzzle.'

'What do you mean?'

'Think about it, we never spoke aloud. We read Dimitra's letter, and she did the same with yours, but not aloud. She mentioned taking possession of the money, but we never mentioned the hacker. If anyone was listening, they could have misunderstood the whole story, thinking we had the entire key to getting to the money.'

'Hear us?' asked Amelia. 'How?'

'Maybe they kept Dimitra under surveillance; it doesn't take much to install a microphone, you leave the house unattended for a moment, and they do the job.'

'You seem knowledgeable about these things.'

'I have read many crime fiction books,' said Anders. Silence fell as they drove towards Inverness. Fatigue was replacing the adrenaline, and Amelia felt she needed to sleep. She leaned her head against the side window, and she fell asleep instantly.

CHAPTER 25

About three hours later they had almost reached Inverness, and it was time for Amelia and Anders to head back south. On the edge of the city, they found a roadblock. A sleepy policeman beckoned them to continue.

'Lucky we weren't asked to show the car documents,' said Amelia sighing with relief.

'That would have been a problem. Usually, the police stop lorries, and often it's just enough to look sleepy and annoyed, and they let you pass.'

'You know about these things too?'

'I have passed some checkpoints in the past. Do you still have Romanov's letters?' asked Anders.

'Yes, in my jacket pocket, why?'

'Because it would be extremely challenging to go back and get them. By this time Dimitra's house will be full of police.'

'I don't want that money,' said Amelia, 'perhaps we should destroy them.'

'And how would you explain that to the guys who are after us, if we get caught?' Anders continued to drive into the night, without looking at his companion. 'Maybe you should go to the police. Deliver the letters, report the matter publicly. Once the newspapers write about this story, they wouldn't dare to harm you, they wouldn't have any more reason to do so.'

Amelia seemed to reflect. 'Perhaps it would be the right thing to do. But at the moment everything scares me. Just the thought gives me the creeps.'

'Let's take a few days, then. I don't think anyone is following us. We find an isolated village to spend the night in, and tomorrow we keep going south. At least until you have a better idea.'

'Sounds like a good plan,' said Amelia, who was making every effort not to think. Sleeping would definitely help.

Anders drove on for about forty minutes; they arrived in a village called Aviemore and began looking around in search of a hotel. They wouldn't waste time choosing, the first that they came across would be the one they'd pick. They parked the car in front of an old two-story building, a bed & breakfast, and entered.

It was one of those typical places with rough wooden planks, smoothed from years of use and spilt beer. On the walls, there were low-quality paintings, evidently representing the surrounding landscape. A lady came forward to greet them, and they asked for a room. She had to repeat the price twice, due to the almost incomprehensible accent. One hundred and forty pounds for one night.

They sat in the main hall for a beer, although both were sleepy. Only then did the full extent of what had happened hit Amelia, the tension was fading, and she became fully aware of the horror of what had happened.

'You're shaking,' said Anders.

'My God! Poor Dimitra.'

'We had a lucky escape. Someone must want that money at all costs. They were not Russians, though. One looked Middle Eastern.'

'From the Middle East?' Amelia tried to remember what she'd read when going through the bank documents, but she couldn't remember anything that could justify the attack. The customers were mostly Russians, not Arabic.

'Mercenaries for sure. Maybe the same ones who killed Romanov,' noted Anders.

'Let me get this straight. We have the money belonging to the Russian mafia, and probably their thugs are in hot pursuit, and as if that wasn't enough there are also Arabs who are chasing us.'

'It is not a given they are Arabs. As mercenaries, they work for anyone with money to spend,' replied Anders.

'Then they may have been hired by the Russians, no?'

'In the movies, the Russian mafia manage these things on their own. Perhaps we are in an even bigger mess.'

Amelia couldn't stop grinning at the comment, but it was definitely something to worry about. 'Come on, let's go to sleep. We are not going to figure out what's going on tonight. I'm dead tired.' Anders finished his beer and stood up, inviting Amelia to do likewise.

'Good idea.'

They headed slowly toward the stairs leading to the upper floors. The room was nicely decorated, and a double bed awaited them, but both were too tired to think about making love.

CHAPTER 26

When Logan, Splinter, and Domino arrived in London, they took a taxi to a hotel near St Paul's Cathedral. Tim Whitley had insisted on meeting them at his office in Canary Wharf, but Logan had declined the offer. They agreed on a pub not far from the Basilica of Saint Paul, the Red Herring, between Wood Street and Gresham, because Whitley was supposed to visit a prominent client in that area. One of his last tasks before leaving everything behind and heading for the United States. Just walking through the streets of London again had invigorated Logan; it had been years since his last visit and seeing the swarm of people around moved him inside.

'Shall we have a beer while we wait?' asked Splinter.

'A Coke for me would be just fine,' said Logan. He had almost screwed up with the cognac a few nights before, he wouldn't want the risk of relapsing at that time. 'And for you, Domino?'

'I'll have a beer, too.'

They hadn't talked a lot during the trip, except Logan briefly describing the rules of arbitrage, and receiving glassy stares in return from his two stakeholders.

A man of about fifty, red-haired, thin, and with a nose too large for his face, came into the pub, he looked around and headed towards their table. Logan rose from his chair, embraced him as he would a rediscovered brother and made the introductions. Not long after that, Whitley had ordered a beer for himself too.

'Ryan says that you are interested in making investments in my brokerage firm.'

'Let's say that we will invest on behalf of third parties,' said Splinter. 'Is your company already operating?'

'Oh sure, it has been for about a year now. I invested all my bonuses from past years, and I finally decided to take the big step. Considering only this year's return, and believe me, we've had a lot of expenses, I earned more than twice what I did at Barclays. And in my industry, bonuses are substantial,' said Whitley. The enthusiasm was visible in his eyes.

'Please explain to me how this arbitrage works,' asked Domino. 'I don't think I've understood it too well.'

Whitley couldn't wait any longer. 'Well, it's pretty simple in theory, but hard in practice.' Then he looked towards Logan, to seek confirmation on how to proceed. Logan beckoned him to continue, a simple nod of assent, signifying you can trust them.

'Don't leave out anything.'

'An arbitrage occurs when a stock is sold on several markets at the same time. There are times when the same title has different values on two markets. I'll give you an example. An investor wants to buy one hundred stocks of Hewlett Packard at 25 dollars, the price the stock trades at that moment on the New York Stock Exchange. On the BATS, another stock exchange, you can find them for sale at 24.95. In this case, the arbitrage is to buy 100 shares on BATS at 24.95 and simultaneously sell them on the NYSE at 25 dollars. Basically, you search for differences in price, you buy and sell without being exposed and, in the case above, earn 5 cents per share without any risk.'

'I think I understand,' said Domino giving him her doe eyes. 'If I buy and sell the same title, at the same time on two different markets, I don't run the risk that the stock price changes. But why people aren't doing that all the time?'

Whitley had a resonating laugh. 'Because arbitrages will cancel out, eventually. These differences don't go unnoticed, investors will start to buy on the more favourable market, and the price would go up. Cancelling the difference.'

'Then I did not understand,' said Domino disconsolate. Meanwhile, the waitress had brought the drinks to the table, and for an instant, the dialogue was interrupted. Whitley sought the right words to explain the issue again.

'During a day in the stock market, there are billions of transactions. These differences happen all the time, but the hard part is in finding them and putting them into practice, which is what we do with our company.'

Logan realised that his old colleague was talking too technically and intervened. 'Maybe the example above has confused you. Imagine a large investor who wants to sell 10 million shares of HP in the market at twenty-five dollars; that would be two hundred fifty million dollars. If Whitley can get hold of the same number of shares at 24.95 dollars and can sell them all to that investor at twenty-five, it would be a gain, without risk, of approximately five hundred thousand dollars. And that on a single transaction.'

Domino and Splinter's mouths opened simultaneously, but no sound came out.

'And if you fail to rake in all those shares?' insisted Domino.

'Simple. We buy everything available on the market before that investor. We buy the shares at 25 dollars, the investor won't find anything on the market at that price I'll then sell the same shares at 25 dollars and five cents. In fact, I'm stealing away all the available stocks from under his nose, and I sell to them at a higher price.'

'Now Tim will tell you how he does it, then I can translate it into common language.' Laughed Logan.

Whitley began to tell of how he got into business with some colleagues in the industry. The first thing they had to do was to hire a group of programmers who specialise in that kind of financial transactions. The idea of exploiting arbitrage came at the same time as the NYSE had become fully electronic, by completely removing the human factor from stock transactions, entirely relying on computers. As a matter of fact, all the stock exchange transactions were made by computers that communicated with other computers. Of course, the dealers were part of it still, but they only entered the parameters for buying or selling onto their computers. The association between seller and buyer was dealt with automatically by a myriad of servers in New Jersey. A recently passed law also forced investors to buy stocks on markets where the price was more favourable.

'But if you always have to buy where the price is more favourable, then these arbitrages go down the drain,' said Splinter.

'Theoretically yes, practically no,' said Whitley. 'What my company does is market on a daily basis hundreds of reasonably low-valued securities, on a specific stock exchange. Those shares serve as bait. Large investors should always buy at a more favourable price, and the shares we are selling are always the first to be purchased. When we detect an order from a big bank or a hedge fund, then we rake in all the available shares on other markets and sell to them at a higher price.'

Marcus drank another sip of beer, to disguise his embarrassment. He couldn't understand much of what this chap was saying, and the fate of his plan was in the hands of this individual who seemed to speak another language. It was Logan who came to his rescue.

'How can you tell when a large investor comes into a market willing to invest millions?' and then nodded to make it clear to his comrade that it was time to tell the full story.

'We have maps of the internet paths that connect to the various stock exchanges. We hired a technician who worked at a telecommunication company, and when he left, he had, shall we say, stolen those maps. We know how long it would take for each individual operator to reach each stock exchange. At that point, we are in business. There is no certainty, but the odds are always in our favour.'

'So, can you spot when a big investor enters a high number of shares on the market?' said Domino.

'Exactly.'

'But how? I don't understand,' insisted the woman, 'if I run a hedge fund and I want to buy, say, a million shares of IBM on the market, that request goes to all markets simultaneously.'

'Not really, and it is for this reason only that we make money.'

'I'm getting a headache,' said Domino. 'Tim, what do you say we get together again tonight for dinner? There are still a lot of details I don't understand, but I seem to be getting too much information all at once.'

'I'll pass,' said Logan, 'I have a couple things to do while I'm here in London.'

'I have another customer to visit,' lied Splinter, leaving the field open for a dinner for two between Whitley and Domino.

'That seems an excellent idea to me,' said Whitley savouring the last sip of his beer. For dinner with Domino, no man could say no.

CHAPTER 27

Amelia awoke suddenly. It was morning and a faint light filtered through the shutters, revealing the wooden interior of the room. Her purse, left on the desk the night before, caught part of the sunbeams which projected an almost unnoticeable shadow towards Amelia's hand. She tried to move, but Anders' arm held her tightly. She made a slow movement to slip out from under the covers, causing a short moan from her companion.

She tried again, and this time she managed to break free. Amelia prepared instant coffee and began to observe the scenery from the window. It was a cold and crisp day, perfect for taking photographs, she thought. She could see the village boundaries and, beyond, the green hills. Some isolated cottages stood on the horizon.

It was a peaceful place; it wasn't exactly a tourist spot, no museums, and the village had nothing special, but Amelia could understand how that place could be appreciated, even in a situation such as hers.

The coffee was not great, but at least it was hot.

She was immersed in her own thoughts when a voice from behind called her. 'Have you been awake for long?'

'Only about ten minutes. I was lost in the panorama of this charming village.'

Anders smiled. 'When you're on the run, options are limited.'

'No, I didn't mean that. Quite the contrary, I like this village, it gives me a sense of serenity, I don't know how to explain it, but I could live here. A small community, evenings at the bar with friends instead of my busy life.'

'If it were in the south of France, I would prefer it,' said Anders.

'And stop wandering around the world? I have my doubts about that.'

'I'm not kidding, that would be nice. But I admit that I might well get bored after a while. How about some breakfast?'

'Great idea.'

Anders slowly rose from the bed and headed for the bathroom, and soon after, Amelia could hear the rush of the shower. The woman walked into the bathroom moments later. She could see Anders' shape from behind the frosted glass of the shower screen. She opened the door and joined him.

After breakfast, the two sat at a table at the hotel bar. The liveliness of the previous evening had disappeared entirely, and they were alone, apart from a waiter moving around from time to time. 'What do we do now?' asked Amelia.

'I have no idea, but maybe we should watch the news to see what's said about Romanov's daughter, things like that.' Anders opened the computer and started looking at the news, until he exclaimed out loud, 'What the hell?!'

'What's going on?' asked Amelia across the coffee table.

'Come and see for yourself …'

Amelia moved her chair until she managed to peek at the computer screen. There was a chat window open saying, 'Well awakened Amelia and Anders.'

'Could it be one of our trackers?'

'I doubt it,' said Anders, 'they would kick the main door in with a gun in their hand.'

- Anders: who are you?

- Guest: I am your new best friend.

- Anders: This does not help, how did you manage to log on to this computer? What do you want?

- Guest: Let's start with the introductions. I am Konrad.

- Anders: Hello, Konrad.

- Guest: Good morning. Regarding your question, I am a hacker, and accessing computers is one of my specialities. We need to discuss business.

Anders and Amelia looked at each other.

- Guest: The business proposition is a simple exchange of data. According to the instructions

Romanov gave me, you should have part of the access to some foreign bank accounts. I have the missing information.

- Anders: How do we exchange?

- Guest: Simple, we do it here in the chat window.

Amelia and Anders looked at each other again. 'How does he know that *we* also have the codes from Romanov's daughter?'

- Guest: Because I hacked into Dimitra's computer too. I could see and hear you when you were in her house. I'm glad you survived the shooting, it would have been a problem otherwise.

'But how does …'

- Guest: To be honest, I'm looking at you too, from the cam built into the computer, and I can hear you speaking also. They should just change these privacy laws.

Amelia sighed and motioned to her companion to go ahead; meanwhile, she took the letters from Romanov from her purse, ready for the exchange.

- Guest: I go on trust, I give you the first code. Landau Bank, xxxxxx-674566456-xx GARTER975 – MRS xxxxxxxxx

- Anders: How do we know that you are giving us the correct ones?

- Guest: Just go on the bank website and look at the account. Follow the instructions to log in.

Anders was ready to open a new window in his browser and then suddenly stopped. If his computer was compromised, this Konrad could redirect him easily onto a fake website. He took the phone and googled the Landau Bank website. He entered the login and looked at the bank statement. Two million dollars. He showed the screen to Amelia who nodded.

- Anders: I think we're in business.

They exchanged the rest of the account details, and they were surprised when the hacker said he would only go for one of the accounts, the Colman Affiliates of Panama. That was what the deal had been with Romanov, and he didn't intend to profit from the death of his daughter. Amelia and Anders had nine million dollars in their hands.

- Anders: Okay, everything looks fine. It was a pleasure, Konrad.

- Guest: My pleasure. If you need my help in the future, I'm here.

- Anders: How do we contact you?

- Guest: I'm always there for my clients. Use your imagination.

Then the hacker came alive with the last post.

- Guest: A piece of advice. Get rid of Amelia's phone as it does not seem to be the only wire on you. Pack your bags and get out of the way because you are about to receive a visit you might not like. RIGHT NOW.

Once again, the two looked at each other, without moving. Then Anders closed the computer and put it in his bag. The tension in the air was almost palpable, and Amelia panicked, looking around the room, but no one could give her an answer. Anders took her by the hand and just at that moment a big black SUV parked in front of the hotel.

'Fortunately, we travel light,' said Amelia, who at least had not left her bag in the room. They had all their belongings with them. Anders strode quickly towards the kitchen and out of a back door. 'Wait here, I'll get the car.'

'They will see you.'

'Don't worry about me. It will take them five minutes to speak to the manager and invent an excuse, and then they will have to go up to our room. At that point, the game is set, they will start looking for us in the village. If I do not return in three minutes, start walking in that direction. And don't look back.'

Amelia was going to argue, but Anders gave her his wristwatch. 'Three minutes, then start walking.'

He pulled the hood over his head and left her; he disappeared around the corner in a flash.

Amelia stared at the watch, waiting at the back of the building; every now and then she turned toward the door with terror that someone would come out and surprise her. *To hell with the three minutes,* she thought, and she started running in the direction indicated by Anders.

She heard several gunshots echoing in what would otherwise be a quiet morning and began running faster. Her breath was fading, and she could feel the lactic acid building in her legs. Three hundred meters. Four hundred. Then the noise of a car approaching at high speed. She looked back and saw that it was the same car that they had used the night before; no black SUV in pursuit.

Anders stopped the car, and Amelia lost no time in jumping in.

'What happened?'

'I'll explain later,' was the only answer. They drove out of the village and headed for the countryside.

CHAPTER 28

'Who's in charge here?' asked the Inspector Corrigan entering the police station in Brighton. A policeman at the entrance, engrossed in the computer, raised his head to regard his new visitor.

'And who are you?' he asked puffing. He still had a foot-high pile of reports to update and no time to lose, given the recent spate of petty crime.

'Corrigan, Interpol,' said the man taking out a badge and slapping it against the glass partition. The officer seemed to scrutinise the badge for an infinite time and then, reluctantly, took the phone.

'Chief Superintendent Ross, please. Yes, I know … A guy from the Interpol … OK, thanks.' After laying down the phone, the man looked up with renewed respect for the gentleman who faced him and mumbled, 'Follow me.'

Inspector Corrigan dragged one leg as if an old wound had begun to hurt against the humidity of the day. He sauntered behind the cop, with a slightly undulating pace. They climbed the stairs until they reached the first floor of the old brown building, and the policeman led him across corridors and through doors to Chief Superintendent Ross' office. He knocked once and, receiving no answer, he did so a second time.

Ross shouted, 'Come in!' and the constable opened the door warily, knowing too well the superior officer didn't welcome anything akin to work. Ross was on the phone and beckoned to the newcomer to sit on the chair in front of the desk. Once the conversation ended, he turned toward his guest.

'How can I help you?'

Corrigan, who didn't like to be kept waiting, pulled out a file from his briefcase and threw it on the desk. 'Corrigan, Interpol. What steps you are taking to stop these guys?'

Taken aback, Ross lost no time flipping through the file. There were names, photographs, whole pages about a gang of crooks in London. He lingered for a moment on Marcus Splinter's picture, a grizzled sixty-year-old man who could have been a 1950s actor. He had committed every sort of scam according to the information in the dossiers but had never been caught in the act. Other pictures were of seemingly ordinary people, except for a quite charming woman, Domino Gravis, and a young man, Anders Nilsson, who could pass for a model in one of those fashion magazines.

'We're actively looking for them,' lied Ross, 'but it's no easy feat. I mean, we're understaffed and …'

'You're not doing a damn thing! This is the truth. You settle for catching a few pickpockets or catching some car thief, but you let the big fish slip through the net.'

Ross, his pride wounded, threw in the towel. 'How can we help you?'

'They have a beachfront suite in a hotel, we believe they are trying for something big and their target is Bruno Mortcombe's daughter, Amelia. As you know, she recently took possession of her father's bank.'

'Sure, I think I read something in the newspapers,' he said trying to remember as much as possible. 'Mortcombe Bank, the one behind Regency Square?'

'Which, as you know, is a base for the Russian mafia for money laundering,' continued Corrigan. Then, seeing the wonder on Ross's face, he asked, 'But you don't even know that? They launder millions under your nose, and you're ignoring all this?'

'For all I knew, the mob leaned on tax havens such as the Cayman …'

'And now they've decided to slap you in the face right before your eyes,' said Corrigan. 'I need a team to work with. The primary focus is on Marcus Splinter and his clique of crooks. Here's a warrant from Interpol that allows me to work with the local forces,' he said passing a paper across the desk which he had removed from his inside jacket pocket. 'Secondary objective will be to stop the Russian mafia operating in this country.'

'How come the mafia is not the primary goal?'

'Because to catch them will take months, if not years, while Marcus Splinter is ready for a scam in a short period. If we can convince her to cooperate, then we will also have access to the data from the bank. Trust me, Amelia Mortcombe is the key.' And then as if the thought had slipped into his head at that moment, he added,' Obviously you can keep the credits for this operation if we are successful.'

'Of course ... of course ... thanks. Maybe we should find a meeting room as a base of operations,' said Ross looking around. His office was a modest one and although the idea of scoring big, seeing his face in the newspapers and on TV news attracted him, the idea of spoiling his daily routine he was dreading. No, a meeting room would be ideal; he would leave Corrigan to the bulk of the work and every so often he would go and monitor the developments. *Keeping a fresh and detached mind*, was his justification.

He accompanied Corrigan into a meeting room with a large oval table at it's centre; a blackboard on the wall near the window would serve to keep notes on the case. Then he called two constables and assigned them to Corrigan. If they were able to progress, he would be able to allocate more people.

'Well,' said Ross, 'from this moment onward you will be working with Inspector Corrigan on this case; I want a daily report on how things are progressing and, of course, you know that my door is open. Whatever you need, let me know. Please keep Inspector Blake up to date, also.' And having said that, he was happier than ever to return to the comfortable space of his own office. An investigation of that magnitude was not up his alley, Ross was bureaucratic by nature. Politics was his forte, getting the budget for the following year approved, doing end-of-year staff performance reviews, managing the crime statistics. But throwing himself into an investigation, no way, not if he could avoid it.

****

Corrigan updated the two officers on the case. He drew a team profile of Marcus Splinter and hung pictures and documents to the wall, along the side of the blackboard. A secretary had meanwhile brought some fresh coffee into the meeting room. It would take hours to bring the two officers up to speed.

'The most important thing is to convince Amelia Mortcombe to cooperate. Go to her office and summon her for tomorrow morning. In the meantime, I will pay a visit to Marcus Splinter.'

One of two officers rose his hand tentatively, as if still in a classroom, and asked, 'Do you think it is going to be wise to announce yourself? You'll put them on alert.'

Corrigan snorted. 'Of course, that's a possibility, but if they know we are breathing down their necks, we raise the tension, we force them to evaluate quickly instead of taking time to plan. And decisions taken by impulse are a recipe for disaster. No, we have to keep them under pressure.' He poured a cup of steaming coffee, drank a sip, and placed his mug on a folder. In retracting his hand, a finger slammed against the cup handle toppling the contents across photographs and documents. 'Jesus Christ!' swore Corrigan. The two officers rushed to help with several paper towels, trying to stop the big patch of coffee that was spreading on the table. Several documents were irrevocably stained.

'I have copies on my computer,' said Corrigan as if to apologise. 'OK, thanks for your help, I'm going to print new ones. You can go to Amelia Mortcombe in the meantime.'

The two officers stood up and left the office.

CHAPTER 29

Tim Whitley did not waste time. For half the afternoon he had called friends, implored favours, promised the impossible, but in the end, he had succeeded. A friend of a friend, for a fee, was ready to give up his reservation at one of the most renowned restaurants in Mayfair. In certain places, you had to call at least one month in advance, especially when it came to a two Michelin star, but he managed to succeed. Bringing Domino to an ordinary restaurant would have been a personal failure. The woman was charming, but if what Logan had said was true, she was also an ideal partner to enter into his new venture with fresh funds.

He sent a text message to Domino with the address of the restaurant and briefly imagined a life full of beautiful women, luxury yachts, Michelin star restaurants around the world, and a factory to make money in New Jersey, that would work for him twenty-four hours a day.

****

Whitley arrived early at the restaurant; he gave a fifty-pound note to the waitress to ignore the sudden change of names on the reservation. He also made arrangements to accompany Domino to his table when she arrived.

He ordered a bottle of Laurent Perrier Rosé. It was not the most expensive wine on the list, but the Perrier was for him the symbol of success. It was what Aunt Mary drank. The uncles had made money doing business in oil fields, having started with a simple candle factory. Over the years the company had flourished, and new contracts followed suit, the first oil deal had been to build a plant in the Mediterranean, and then others followed. At Christmas, Aunt Mary always carried a couple of crates of Laurent Perrier when she came to visit her family and the driver took care to transport them from the Bentley and bring them into the house. When Whitley had to celebrate something, he always did it with a bottle of Laurent Perrier Rosé, he didn't care if there were other more expensive wines.

Domino arrived about ten minutes later, and the waitress led her up to Whitley's table, who stood up upon the arrival of the guest.

'I like this place,' said Domino looking around. The restaurant, Amaze, was stylishly decorated, with dark wood and cream-coloured tables. It had the right atmosphere for Londoners who appreciated good food and were not afraid to spend more than necessary to prove it.

'It seemed appropriate. If we do business together in the future, I would like to discuss it over lunch in a place like this.'

They both chose the tasting menu, ten small dishes allowing the guests to appreciate the chef's style and why he deserved his Michelin stars.

'Tim, there are things that I do not understand what you're doing with this new company in the United States.'

'Understandable, it's not that simple. What are your concerns? I will try to explain to the best of my modest abilities.'

'How did you start this venture, to begin with?' asked Domino.

'About the business in the USA? Simple, there are more and more stock exchanges now. The more stock exchanges, the more probabilities to find arbitrages.'

'That would be, buy on a market at a lower price and sell at a higher value on another,' said Domino, more to explain it to herself than to her dinner companion.

'Exactly.'

'But then these arbitrages cancel themselves out,' she continued.

'That is also correct.'

'What you said today intrigued me when you said you try to work on orders from large investors. That is where I got lost. The market is the market, how do you know when one of those big investors place an order? I mean, many orders arrive every hour on the market, and nobody could possibly know who they belong to.'

'In principle you're right, no one should know. But investors must follow certain parameters. At first, they are investing in the bank's *dark pools*, then they have to buy first on the market where the price is more favourable and finally on the other markets.'

'What is a dark pool?'

'Banks can buy and sell shares on the stock market, but they have to pay commission. So, they created these little domestic, in house stock markets. Let's say a client A of the bank wants to sell 100 shares of Apple and client B in the same bank wants to buy it. There is no need to enter the order on the stock market. The bank matches these orders inside their dark pool, and they don't have to pay commission.'

'Seems beneficial, but I don't see what use it has for someone else,' said Domino.

'The banks want to make money, and, in time, they opened these dark pools to the outside world, to those like us who do electronic transactions. This allows us to see in advance who enter orders. Then there are other things happening behind the scenes. Everyone thinks about electronic transactions as if they were immediate. People see on the screen, for example, Facebook's stock at 107.1 dollars and they think that that's the value of the share at that moment.'

'And isn't it?'

'No, far from it. There are always changes, minimal fluctuations. Computers manage the stock exchange nowadays: the human eye can't see beyond one-tenth of a second, a blink of an eye, but in the computer world we work with milliseconds, even lower values. In that world, it doesn't matter what the human eye can see, computers are exchanging information at a speed which is difficult to understand. A millisecond makes all the difference in this world. Also, the data must travel from the bank to the stock exchange.'

'But aren't those transactions instantaneous?'

'Far from it. Our data centre is right next to the building which houses the New Jersey Exchange. Orders coming from banks from New York always take a fraction of a second longer. Over time we've mapped all banks. We know how long it takes them to go to the NYSE, to the BATS, or any other markets. On each of the markets, each operator comes with a different delay, even though it's milliseconds. It is all we need to beat them to the punch. Sell them what they want to buy and collect shares at lower prices even before their order has come into play.'

'So, aren't you exposed by buying all those shares in advance of an order?'

'That's one of the tricks. Finishing the day with zero shares, what we buy and what we sell must balance at the end of the day. Maybe we transact a million shares in one day but by balancing what we buy and sell, what remains is only the gain. Keep in mind that we don't buy physical actions, there isn't an exchange of shares on paper. It's all electronic. So, if you buy a million shares of Hewlett Packard and then resell them on the same day, nothing is owed. You pay if you lose or gain if you win.'

Domino was not yet convinced. 'But there is always the risk of chasing a wrong order, maybe you think there shall be a million shares ordered, and there isn't.'

'Well this is true, there is always an element of risk, but we have moved the odds so much in our favour that the risk is minimal.'

'But why are the banks are not doing the same thing?' insisted Domino.

'Because they are greedy. Banks like to earn money, not spend it. Their programs to handle these things are slow and obsolete, created over time. Computer programs that changed so much over the years that they became inefficient; they should throw them away and write new ones. This involves investments they don't want to make. If it works, and believe me when I tell you that banks still make a tonne of money, why change it? We have young people, Indian mathematicians who create amazing algorithms, young Russian programmers who care little about the money, but they take these challenges as if they were chess games, hackers who know everything about how to optimise systems but who wouldn't be considered as employees by a bank. We reinvest most of the money, and once a year we give some nice bonuses to our own people.

But then comes the time where we have to go full speed ahead. If we have enough liquidity, the real money will come, hundreds of millions. We'll do it with or without you, even if with your capital things could be much easier and faster.'

The waiter arrived with the first course. The bottle of Laurent Perrier was already empty, so Whitley ordered another.

Domino, for once, saw the chance of making money, the amount of money that could sort her out for a lifetime. She could forget the everyday scams, running from the police, avoiding entire neighbourhoods for fear of being recognised by one of the scammed.

No, this Tim Whitley had bright ideas and a plan, it was just a matter of convincing Price about the deal of the century. Tim was also good looking despite his age, and Domino decided that perhaps they should remain friends after all. Just in case. He was a bit tipsy at that point, but Domino knew all the tricks to get him to stop drinking and get him to invite her to his house. Making sure that Whitley thought it had been his idea in the first place. A bonus, given that they were about to become partners in that enterprise.

CHAPTER 30

'What the hell happened?' insisted Amelia.

'Two guys didn't much like when I tried to take the car back,' said Anders continuing to watch the road.

'Anders, you will get killed if we continue at this rate.'

'Well, we are already in trouble, nothing we can do about that.'

Amelia was aware the situation was becoming too dangerous. She took a road map from the back seat and began to study it.

'Which way are we going?'

'Towards Glasgow and then down as far as London. Maybe we should keep going to the channel tunnel and go to France,' said Anders.

They took turns driving for several hours, stopping only occasionally to fill up with petrol and eat a sandwich, until they arrived north of Birmingham.

'Can we go south towards Oxford?'

Anders briefly took his eyes off the road. 'You have friends there?'

'No, Oxford is where I graduated and where we part. I'll take a train to Brighton, I'm tired of running and hiding like a rabbit. And I don't want you to accompany me, you have already risked too much.'

'Do you want to get yourself killed?'

'I don't think so. If they know that I ran away, they wouldn't expect me to come back to Brighton.'

'Oh, now you're a strategist, aren't you?' asked Anders. 'Don't be a fool. If they catch you, and sooner or later they will, what do you think will happen? They'll kill you.'

Amelia remained silent and then said, 'Let's go to Oxford.' It was an order, not a request. Her voice was not as loud and determined as when she spoke to her clients, and all she wanted to do was cry, but showing any kind of weakness would have made her fail in her intent.

'OK, OK. Is it going to be a goodbye then?'

'Not necessarily, we can always find each other …' And then he had an epiphany. 'They must have another way of tracking us. Think about it. They were able to find us in that small village, and that was no coincidence. We took a random exit on the motorway, and they certainly didn't spend the night visiting each and every hotel in a hundred-mile radius. Check your bag and clothes; they must have planted another bug somewhere.'

'I hadn't thought of that,' said Amelia. And then, after a long pause, Anders slowed down the car and looked in the rear-view mirror.

'It doesn't look like they're chasing us now, but actually it's not a coincidence. When the hacker, that Konrad, told us to run, I was immediately on guard expecting the worst, and then, after the shooting, the adrenaline didn't give me time to relax. But it's not a coincidence. Konrad knew they were in hot pursuit. They must have some way to track us.'

'He said to throw away my phone, which we did, so there must be other bugs.'

They had arrived on the outskirts of Birmingham and Amelia began searching frantically in her bag. She opened her lipstick. Nothing. The diary didn't seem to have anything unusual, and all the other items seemed fine. She searched the bag again, looking for a transmitter, even though she had not the faintest idea what one would look like. Nothing. She searched her clothes, and even those seemed fine. Anders couldn't have any transmitter, thought Amelia; a pursuer couldn't have predicted a casual encounter with a person met in a bar. And then Anders was too smart, they wouldn't have planted a bug on him without him noticing.

As a last resort, she checked her shoes. She once saw a movie where they had planted a transmitter in Will Smith's shoes and, having no other options, she decided to check. The left shoe heel rubber did not seem to adhere correctly, and Amelia strove to lift the flap completely. She took out her office key and wedged it between the rubber and the heel, using it for leverage.

It took her a couple of tries, but she finally managed to remove the heel. Right in front of her eyes, in a carved recess of the heel, there was a small electronic device and a coiled wire.

'I don't think I bought this with the shoes,' she said showing the small object to her companion.

Anders briefly perused the object. 'Nice gadget. That is why they found us over and over again, it probably sends the GPS coordinates of where we are. It doesn't have a battery, so maybe it works by pressure: when you walk you upload and send a signal. That's why they couldn't find us last night. But as soon as you put the shoes on and walked in them, to go downstairs for breakfast, it reactivated.'

'Shall I throw it out the window?' asked Amelia.

'I have a better idea.' Just past Birmingham Anders parked the car next to a petrol station. He picked up the bug and went toward a van that was filling up. Nonchalantly, Anders dropped the transmitter inside. Then he returned to the car in a hurry.

They didn't notice Margot's car, parked behind theirs at a distance of about a hundred feet. The woman watched them like a hawk who had their eyes on the prey.

'That should slow them down for a while.'

'Don't stay on the motorway,' said Amelia, 'go through villages. If they suspect anything, the highway is a trap. They know we're ahead of them and they just have to accelerate to pick us up. If we change direction, each country road opens many possibilities; going east, west, or south. Or retrace our steps back north.'

'Good thinking.'

'I've considered this for a long time, Anders. As soon as I'm back in Brighton, I'll go to the police. I'm sick of it, I want to see this story over. But first I want to give you a gift, here.' Amelia took the notes where they had marked the access to the secret accounts and passed them to Anders.

'Are you kidding me?'

'No, not at all. I'm not giving this money back to my brother-in-law, or to the mafia. If the police get hold of it, it will remain in evidence for centuries. Make good use of it. I will only show Romanov's letters to them, and I will say that the hacker never contacted me.'

'Amelia, I don't think …'

'Stratford-upon-Avon. Stop here and take me to the station, please. It doesn't make any sense to go further.'

Anders was reluctant but did as asked.

'Come on, come with me and let's see if I can find a train to Brighton. Perhaps, one day, our paths shall cross once again.'

Anders realised that there was no need to make further objections. He put the papers Amelia had given him into his pocket and parked the car.

CHAPTER 31

It was a quiet afternoon at the Grand Hotel in Brighton. Or at least so it seemed watching the number of tourists come and go from the modern building, some with city maps in hand, others with shopping bags full of purchases, which they'd barely have room for in their luggage once their holiday was over.

Price was sitting at the bar and sipping a single malt, satisfied to have gained valuable time with Sokolov. He was not out of the woods, not yet, but by doing some illegal movement on Russian mafia accounts, it had helped him stall the situation. *Robbing from the rich and giving to the rich …?* he thought. There was not a single mafia in Russia but many different organisations and thanks to the work done by old Mortcombe, most of them had at least one account in that bank. Some more, some less. Brighton was an ideal place, outside of the usual money-laundering path, a police force with little attention to specific issues and easily corruptible; remove money from a group of accounts and move it to another. He would have been in trouble if all the representatives of the various mafias rushed in to check at the same time, but that was a highly unlikely scenario. The important thing was to save his skin now that Sokolov was in town.

He had just finished a meeting with Sokolov in one of the suites in the hotel, and what he needed was a glass of something substantial, to take off the edge. How to put the accounts in order was something he would have to deal with at a later stage.

'Excuse me, is this your wallet?'

Price turned and saw an elegant gentleman in his sixties, with a pinstriped tailored suit, probably made on Bond Street in London, and an affable smile.

Price checked his jacket pocket. 'No, it's not mine.'

'It was on the ground right under your chair, and so I thought ...' Marcus Splinter placed the wallet on the bar, sat next to Price, and asked, 'What's your poison?'

'Laphroaig, smooth.'

'I am a bourbon person. Waiter, please a Laphroaig and a Jack Daniels on the rocks.'

While waiting for the drinks to arrive, Splinter began to look inside the wallet.

'Blimey, a nice amount,' he said pulling out a wad full of fifty-pound notes, laying them on the counter, right under Price's nose. 'Ah! By golly! An ID. I was already looking forward to sharing the loot with you.'

'We can always do that,' said Price, whose eyes were glued to the stack of money. He was a greedy man, and for him, any amount fed his hunger for money, though clearly, from his reaction, the more, the better. It did not matter much to whom it belonged.

'Ah yes, if it were an anonymous find, I wouldn't bother taking it to the police, especially here in Brighton, but with a document, we cannot do that.'

'Maybe he has already left for another destination,' suggested Price.

'Maybe. Why don't we finish our drinks and then go check with the concierge? It will be our good deed for the day.'

Price was vexed. He took the glass and drank it in one gulp. He didn't wait for Splinter to finish his drink and rose from his chair, forcing his partner to do the same.

He looked around, and four of the receptionists were busy with guests. He went to the only free person, who seemed busy with their computer. 'I wonder if a certain Anthony Edwards is a guest of this hotel,' said Splinter.

The young boy found the room number immediately, 'Do you want me to call him?'

'No, don't worry,' said Splinter laying a ten-pound note on the reception desk. 'He shall be glad to see us.'

The two made their way to the elevator. 'My name is Marcus, by the way,' he said holding out his hand to the other man.

'Robert Price, nice to meet you. What are you doing here in Brighton?'

'Investments. I'm mainly in real estate. I'm working on a renovation project in the outlying areas. Those 1950s buildings are awful, in fact, we're buying them and replacing them with much more modern dwellings. Groups of villas for those who want to sell their house in London and move to the coast. Buying in central Brighton has become increasingly expensive, and it won't be long before people start looking at the surrounding areas, and at that time we will be ready with a series of new housing. And what do you do, Robert?'

'I deal with investments for a private bank.'

'Ah, I see. Fast cash. I've always admired those who invest in the stock market, in shares, and all those modern things. Unfortunately, I'm a bit old school, I'm still stuck with bricks and mortar, I don't understand much of the financial sector.'

'It's not that difficult ... but behold, we've arrived, room 405,' said Price. He knocked vigorously at the door, and a tall and handsome man came to open it.

'How can I help you?'

'Actually, we're the ones that may be useful to you; we found your wallet down in the bar,' said Price, taking over the discovery and the reins of the conversation. The man seemed surprised; he checked his pants to verify the fact of the disappearance, not finding anything.

The man turned his head towards his jacket, leaning on a chair, but instead of going to check he turned to the two strangers at the door and said, 'Please, come on in. I'm Hank.'

'My pleasure,' trilled Splinter.

Hank had booked the suite the same day after they had followed Price to the hotel. There was a large living room with sofas, a vast round table in the centre that could host a dinner with friends, upon which instead were a myriad of dossiers and documents and further on, towards the window, a large desk and an open laptop. It was towards the desk that Hank directed the two guests.

Price took back the initiative. 'As I said we found your wallet.' Making a nod in the direction of Splinter, who promptly pulled the object out from a jacket pocket, putting it on the desk.

Hank surveyed the wallet for a moment, evaluating the contents, and then pulled out a handful of fifty-pound notes. 'There aren't many honest people these days. Hang on a second, to show my gratitude...'

'Don't even think about it,' said Splinter, stopping Price who acted instinctively, already rising from his chair to grab the bills. 'It was our duty, you would surely have done the same.'

'Well, certainly,' said Hank, 'but are you sure? You've returned a tidy sum ...'

'Of course, don't worry, it's been a pleasure.'

Seeing the displeased face of Price, Hank smiled inwardly and made an alternative suggestion, 'If you do not accept a monetary reward, allow me at least the chance of investing this money, which would otherwise have been lost, and share the gains with you.'

The two guests looked at each other, and before Splinter could utter a word, Price said, 'Why not?'

'Then we have a deal, I will invest these few thousand pounds on your behalf today. If you're in town and you have the courtesy to come and see me tomorrow night, I'll give you the rightful earnings.'

Splinter choked back a half laugh. 'Oh, these young men, always betting. Be careful because with gambling, sometimes people win, but they often lose.'

'No, don't worry, no gambling, of course. I care too much about money to risk losing it stupidly.'

'But then how would you *invest*, if I may inquire?' insisted Splinter.

Hank grinned broadly and said, 'Don't worry, if I don't get a significant return, I can always invite you for a drink,' then he turned his eyes towards the bar, right behind the two speakers, where there were several bottles of liquor, mostly expensive.

'If you have a good bourbon, it's a done deal,' said Splinter.

'But certainly,' said Price, though he was not very excited about the opportunity.

The two left the suite and immediately Price hastened to share his thoughts.

'I think we missed an opportunity. Cash now, in exchange for a promise. It is certainly not a good deal.'

'You see, my dear friend, I feel differently. First of all, we got a glass of the good stuff just for doing an act of kindness. But what interests me most, if you want, is to understand people. That young man, Hank, seems to know his stuff. With an ounce of arrogance maybe, but he never gave me the impression of someone who exaggerated his achievements. I'd bet that within two days he will keep his promise.'

'If you say so,' said Price.

'I'm convinced. So, see you back here in a couple of days?'

'Why not? If the investment turned out to be rubbish, you would have to buy me a bottle of whisky.'

'Done deal,' said Splinter smiling, 'done deal.'

<u>CHAPTER 32</u>

Stratford-upon-Avon station was a small red brick building, no bigger than a house. An anonymous station as many others in England. However, unlike many other stations, this was crowded with tourists. Amelia walked at a fast pace toward the ticket booth and looked at the trains map to evaluate how to get to Brighton. She bought a ticket from the vending machine and then turned to Anders, who was patiently waiting.

'You are doing something foolish, you know?' he said, 'when you arrive in Brighton, you will be helpless. Those are professionals, what are you going to do, hide?'

'As I said, I'm tired of running. Don't worry, I'm not going to get myself killed. As soon as I'm off the train, I'm heading straight to the police station.'

'Yeah, sure. And you believe they will do something about it?'

'I'm a respectable person, they should listen, and if they don't, I will turn my attention directly to a judge. I made some friends these past few years,' said Amelia.

'May I come with you? At least until we reach the police station,' insisted Anders.

'You've done enough. Keep that money away from me. The farther you are, the less motivation those thugs will have to hurt me.'

Anders did not seem convinced, but he finally nodded. He couldn't convince her, but one way or another he would follow her to Brighton, and he would try to protect her.

Five minutes were left until the train departed and it was time to say goodbye. They approached the first carriage, and Amelia turned toward Anders, stopping him in his tracks. She kissed him hungrily on the mouth, and the man kissed her back, holding her tight. That kiss seemed to last forever, and for a moment Amelia almost decided to change her plans. Leave everything and flee to some remote village, away from everyone and everything. The money would have been enough to build a new life, with new identities for both, but she didn't feel quite ready. Too many loose ends. They looked into each other's eyes, and Amelia leaned her face against Anders' muscular chest.

'Go, before I change my mind,' said Amelia.

Anders nodded. He had waited in vain for the woman to make the first step, hoping she would suggest they run away together, but now the moment had passed. Anders didn't want to be the one asking, Amelia had a life in Brighton, albeit in danger, a law firm, and maybe even an entire bank to manage. How could he ask her to renounce everything, for what? A life in hiding?

Without saying more Amelia boarded the train and soon found a place by the window so she could see Anders one last time, from behind, walking away.

Have I done the right thing? She asked herself without being able to give an answer. She sat down and picked up a magazine someone had forgotten on the table between the seats. It was at that moment that Margot, unseen by Anders, made her move and climbed onto the last carriage of the train, undisturbed.

The trip would last several hours, and there would be enough time to prepare a plan. Margot lightly stroked the Glock she held close to her side, relishing the image it conjured in her mind. Yes, she would have accomplished her mission even if she had to shoot Amelia on that train in front of witnesses. Margot had never failed a target.

Amelia was unaware of the danger and that Margot was observing her, sitting in the same carriage a few rows away. The killer was wearing a headscarf and a pair of sunglasses and pretended to be sleeping. Every now and then she looked out the window, where she could see Amelia's reflection. She could only see her shoulder and locks of hair, but that was enough.

Amelia and a couple of other people that afternoon dismounted at Leamington Spa where she was supposed to wait for about twenty minutes before the train to Reading. It was at that point that Amelia walked to the public toilets to refresh herself, the tension of the day and the adrenaline still flowed through her veins. She had to be calm and relaxed when she reached her destination. There were too many things to do. She washed her face as best as she could and entered a cubicle just as Margot made her appearance in the toilet. The assassin looked around, assimilating the contours of the environment. It was an isolated toilet, away from the main entrance and if she acted quickly, maybe she could get the job done. She drew her Glock and screwed on the silencer. Then she put a round in the chamber. As far as trying to remain silent, the mechanism of the gun was never free from noise. She moved slowly in front of the cubicles, trying to understand if they were occupied. The first three were empty while the last two she could see the occupiers' feet. She cursed herself silently for not paying attention to what kind of shoes Amelia was wearing.

The question was whether to kill both: she could shoot through the door, but there was still the risk of missing the target, then she would have to kick the door in and check. *Too complicated*, she thought, *the body of the victims may fall forward, preventing me from opening the door*. She didn't care about killing an innocent person, only about completing her mission.

She decided to take action, she violently kicked the first door and fired upon an overweight lady, who looked stunned for a moment before she crumbled to the ground. Margot's bullet hit her in the chest. There was a loud bang despite the silencer, but the killer fired a second shot to the back of the head of the unfortunate, just to be sure not to have witnesses.

She was turning around, heading toward the second cubicle when a fist to the face propelled her backwards; she stumbled into the victim's body and lost her balance. Margot pointed the gun towards the threat, but Amelia was quicker, and with both hands she grabbed the woman's wrist, pushing up. The barrel of the weapon danced, swinging between the faces of the two opponents, each trying to find an edge. Margot was in a precarious position, with her back to the wall and the toilet seat beneath her; Amelia had her back to the door and did everything possible to avoid being killed. She had thought to flee, but she knew she wouldn't get the chance.

'Who sent you?' she asked the killer while fighting.

Margot did not answer.

'Who sent you?' she asked again.

'Your dear brother-in-law. Not that it matters much, you'll be dead soon.'

Amelia not used to fighting, felt her muscles harden and hurt from the effort. The only advantage was that the killer was in a somewhat awkward position and it would have been hard for her to overcome Amelia. They fought again and then a shot echoed around the cubicle.

The train station was almost deserted and the muffled echo of the shot didn't reach the few bystanders on the opposite platform, nor the car park. Only one woman emerged from the toilets a couple of minutes later; she was wearing a large overcoat and a pair of sunglasses, which she didn't remove when she glanced at the train timetable.

Checking she hadn't been followed, she hurried on to the next train.

Job done.

CHAPTER 33

Chaz Lubbock and Lenny Carlton were busy setting up a new office in Brighton. The offices did not have a view of the Channel, but that was not important. Since they'd arrived in Brighton, they had worked almost continuously.

'Shit, if I wanted to work, I wouldn't have started these scams,' said Lenny as he was about to put false paperwork and containers on a shelf.

'At least we don't get paid a pittance unlike those poor souls who have to do this work eight hours a day for a lifetime, for real,' retorted Chaz.

'This is also true. Do you understand why Marcus changed his mind?'

'No, he had Anders working on that beauty of a lawyer, but then he changed his mind. There is another target apparently, who is also affiliated with the bank. Jesus Christ, how could she possibly refuse to own an entire bank? You'd have to be blonde and stupid to do such a thing,' said Chaz.

'How comes your parents didn't leave you a couple of banks as an inheritance? I've got five,' laughed Lenny.

Lenny and Chaz were the gang's fixers. Lenny's responsibility was to organise all aspects of a scam, from finding offices and providing furniture, to finding luxury cars, sometimes also took care of creating websites that would support a story. He had just finished one for Hank. Resurgence Financial Equities was the fictitious enterprise they would use to perpetrate the con against Robert Price. It had taken him almost three days, but now it was online: he had copied the website content from others, there was a switchboard that sent all calls to Domino's phone, and a picture of Hank as company CEO. The other members of the board were anonymous faces taken at random from LinkedIn, no one in particular, but Price would search that website, so no harm done. He also spent the whole week posting, under different names, in various blogs and finance message boards praising the merits of the Resurgence; each of these fictitious individuals had a story to tell, of unexpected achievements and investments all of which went to fruition. He had also forged false reports by the leading *Securities* firms in the world, fake articles from *Forbes* posted on the website and interviews with leading financiers.

The important thing was to have several sources, which would create noise and attention around their fictitious organisation, so that even a simple Google search would show several references.

Lenny had worked for a computer company and had a family and a mortgage that would have crippled anyone else. He had done his part for several years, pulling the cart, generating money for shareholders who he did not even know the name of. He had always been a model employee, judged by everyone as a hard worker and a good person.

Then there was the incident. The tumour was diagnosed soon enough, but it was the chemotherapy that had almost killed him. He was not surprised when he got the letter of dismissal.

When the insurance company refused to pay for his treatment, he changed his life. He would never again work for someone else.

The offices where Chaz and Lenny were, were empty and waiting for a buyer, and Lenny had convinced the owner to furnish them. Lenny pretended to be an office furniture seller and those places would serve as a showroom for his newly built company. As far as the company that provided the furniture, he instead presented himself as the owner of the building.

'Where the fuck did you get all this furniture?' asked Chaz.

'Tricks of the trade. Come on, hurry up assembling that desk, you're training for when you will have your own house and you'll have to buy Ikea furniture.'

'Like hell,' said Chaz. 'If this scam goes as expected, I shall retire and won't lift a finger anymore.'

'Have you decided where to go?'

'Caribbean. I don't know which island yet, but the Bahamas is a prime candidate. After a lifetime in England my bones are full of humidity;

I've already decided how to spend the first two years. To bake in the sun, drinking Bacardi, and getting massage sessions by three beautiful girls.'

'It seems a bit trivial. Hand me that screwdriver,' said Lenny who was finishing one of the last desks.

'Ah yes, the Caribbean is now out of fashion. Go to hell, Lenny! So, what are you going to do with your share of the loot?'

'I will go to Scotland, the Highlands. I've already seen a couple of places that are right for me. There is this farm north of Edinburgh which has been for sale for several months, in the middle of nowhere. An ideal place for me, in complete solitude. Fifty miles away from the nearest bullshitter.'

'Will you bring Lucy and the child?' asked Chaz.

'We haven't spoken in a lifetime. We finalised the divorce and they say she has found someone else. No, I think I will go there alone, maybe I'll take a dog.'

Lenny thought about the never-ending fight with his ex-wife. He didn't want to get a job after the cancer, and she nagged him every single day. He started painting, an old passion of his which he had never fully explored. It was one day by the riverside of the Thames while he painted a landscape, when he met Gavin Neil Tiddington. They spoke about painting techniques at length and became friends. Then he told him how to make a fake and Lenny continued to listen. Only years later, by which time Tiddington had taught him all the tricks he knew, had he started doing his own art scams. Rumours had spread and Marcus Splinter approached him for a 'small job'. Then a second and a third. If painting was his passion, working with computers was his talent.

'Look, how much do you have left to do?'

Chaz sat down on the ground and breathed a sigh of relief. 'I'm done. How did you manage to get fake employees?'

'Well, for that I had to spend some money, nowadays almost nobody works for free,' said Lenny, 'they are all actors or aspiring actors. I finished the auditions just yesterday: we are doing a reality show and the actors will pretend to be in a working environment, of course under the watchful eye of hidden cameras …'

'Non-existent cameras, you mean,' corrected Chaz.

'Exactly. We are impersonating their bosses and will give them paperwork and tasks. A sort of *Apprentice.*'

'How did you choose them,' asked Chaz intrigued, 'I mean, did you interview them and everything else?'

Lenny blurted out a loud chuckle. 'Ah yes, their CVs all ended up in the trash and in fact the only criterion for being hired was to show up. Although they don't know that. I gave them instruction not to talk to the guests.'

Chaz finished assembling the last desk and looked with admiration at the work he and Lenny had achieved. They should to be proud of it, it looked like a real office, where money was made in spades.

The only question now was how to convince Price to fork over the money, but that would be a job for Hank.

CHAPTER 34

'We have the funds,' said Anders on the phone.

'Well done, lad, we need you here in Brighton to outfox Price. Was it difficult?' asked Splinter.

Anders hesitated. He never had scruples about scamming people, but with Amelia it was different. He had gotten to know her, maybe he had even fallen in love, and for a moment he thought about running away with her and all that money. It would have been enough. He had almost been on the verge of asking, but Amelia seemed so determined to return to Brighton and talk to the police, that in the end, he didn't dare ask. It would have been difficult to abandon his companions in the middle of that scam, but the temptation was too strong. For once he had had the opportunity to leave behind a life of cheating and go away. Amelia would be worth it.

'No, everything went smoothly. Aside from the fact that Price wants Amelia dead at all costs. I left a trail of bodies between Inverness and London to rival Jack the Ripper.'

'How much money did we rake in then? From what you told me there were hidden accounts,' said Splinter. He did not notice the tension in the young accomplice's voice.

'Yes, when we understood Amelia wouldn't take the reins of the bank, I was about to break up with her, since you're now working the brother-in-law angle, but then these slush funds came out of the blue. A fortune, we have nine million dollars. It allows us to go along with the scam without risking a cent of our own.'

Anders had been a vital element of the group at that time. If Domino was perfect to attract men and make them turn when she worked as a distraction, Anders was at the same level, if not higher. He knew how to play the role wonderfully, he was a born actor. Artist, young banker, penniless guy, naïve heir, he was able to play any part.

Anders joined the gang by accident. Or rather, he entered by force. The group was well established but one day this young man, with eyes as blue as the Aegean Sea and ash blond hair, approached them. Splinter and the gang had been, as usual, at the pub discussing the next scam when that kid showed up in front of them asking, no, pleading to be allowed to work with the famous and infamous Marcus Splinter.

Marcus began by pretending not to know what he was talking about, but Anders came back the next day and the day after. He had become a shadow for the group. A habit.

It took little to turn him into one of the stable members of the gang.

'Nine million? I'm tempted to abandon this con altogether.' Laughed Splinter.

'Actually, I thought about that too. I retire and start a new career as a writer and drinking margaritas on the beach; I already have a title ready, *Farewell to scams*.' Laughed Anders.

'Ah, Hemingway's style? It wouldn't be a bad idea,' said the older companion. 'Seriously, we need you here, we have a part for you to play.'

'I'm almost there, I'm almost in town right now, I will be at the hotel in about ten minutes.'

Splinter paused and then said, 'No, I'm sending you directly to the office space Lenny and Chaz have put together. I will explain your role later, Domino has also prepared a change of clothes for you.'

Hank was now down in the hotel lobby along with Splinter and Domino when a voice from behind caught them by surprise.

'Marcus Splinter, what a surprise to see you in Brighton.'

The gang turned in unison and faced a stocky man, with sparse grey hair and a direct and penetrating gaze. He was standing in front of the band of crooks as if he were ready for a fight. Next to him stood a police officer, a thin man with thick glasses who would pass easily for an accountant if it wasn't for the uniform he wore.

'Do we know each other?' asked Splinter looking the man directly in the eyes and without showing any surprise although in his mind the worst scenarios were starting to make inroads. The presence of a police officer had definitely taken him off guard.

'You don't know me, but I know you and your associates. Inspector Corrigan, Interpol,' said the man waving a badge under Splinter's nose. Then, pointing to the person who accompanied him. 'And that's Chief Superintendent Ross of Brighton Police.'

Splinter remained calm, looked at his watch and said, 'How can I help you, gentlemen?'

'If I'm not mistaken, that is your crony Hank Edwards, right?' Without waiting for an answer he went on, 'We know you're entangled in a scam of some sort, I have a dossier this thick on you guys in my office. But don't count on getting away with it this time, we are checking you out, and at the first mistake you will be arrested.'

'We really are here on vacation,' said Splinter.

'Ah! Nice one. Nothing to do with Amelia Mortcombe and her bank?'

Hank stiffened for a moment, but that was enough for Corrigan to note it. 'Ah, so she is your target this time. You can go home today because I'm gonna tell her about you myself.'

'Do what you have to do, inspector?' said Splinter, 'we have nothing to hide. As I said, we're here on vacation.' And with that said he headed for their car, followed by the rest of the gang.

'Who the fuck is this Corrigan?' asked Hank glancing behind, as if someone was still spying on him.

'I've never heard of him,' said Domino, 'although he isn't one of the usual Interpol guys who come knocking at our door from time to time.'

'And then, how did he know about Amelia Mortcombe?' asked Hank.

After a long pause, Splinter said, 'Calm down, guys. They have nothing on us, and we have not done anything illegal. Not yet. And we have invested too much into this to back down now. It is true that we were working on Amelia Mortcombe, but that's old news. We have to be careful, because they will keep us under surveillance, but they haven't mentioned Robert Price, our real goal. We'll just have to keep our wits about us, be careful, and keep in mind that they're watching us. A nuisance, but not yet a disaster.'

Splinter started the car and headed toward the centre. Occasionally he looked in the rear-view mirror trying to discover if they were indeed being followed. He changed direction a few times and when he was satisfied with not being followed, he relaxed.

****

'Why did you let them know we were on to them like that?' asked Ross. 'They'll obviously be on the lookout for us.'

Corrigan lit a cigarette and blew a puff of bluish smoke and then smiled. 'Of course, they're going to be on the lookout, but they'll also be under pressure. And when there is trouble, that's when you make mistakes, and we'll be there waiting for them at the gate.'

CHAPTER 35

Lenny and Chaz had done a fabulous job with the offices. The furniture and marble at the entrance oozed wealth; whoever came in would stop to look around before heading to the central desk where two receptionists were pretending to work. The instructions were clear, it was a reality show, anyone who was not on the visitor's list would be dismissed with courtesy and grace. Although it was an anonymous building from the outside, once inside the spacious reception area you could see the Resurgence logo everywhere together with different posters, with the typical faces of happy customers who had chosen that company for their investments.

Splinter was surprised, it looked just like a real company and Lenny had surpassed himself. 'But where did you get all these guys?' he asked.

'Smile, you're going to be on a new reality show called *The Office*. I know, the name is a bit dull, but all these people you see are extras and were looking for a job. I got them mixed up, and they are pretending to work, the important thing is not to look at the cameras and interact as if they were in a real office,' said Lenny filled with pride.

'Do we have cameras?' asked Domino.

'No way,' said Lenny laughing out loud, 'but they don't know that. For the actors, since this is a pilot, there is a promise to put the best ones through as part of the cast, when the series begins. For the unemployed an opportunity to win a job. For today they have a day off, so to speak. They pretend to work and things like that. In the days that follow we will prepare the script for the pilot, things to be said and so on.'

'I'm impressed,' said Splinter looking around, 'but how many people did we recruit?'

'About thirty. Most of the offices are empty, and we strategically place most of the actors on the path leading to the meeting room. Here, follow me,' said Lenny making inroads. He was dressed in an impeccable pinstriped suit that made him look like a 1930s Chicago gangster. Splinter and Hank instead looked like elegant businessmen.

At that moment Anders arrived, dressed like a Dolce & Gabbana model. 'Hi, guys. Lenny, have you got a good suit for me?'

'Of course, upstairs there are showers and your new uniform. Come on, follow me.'

The group walked up the marble staircase, passing through offices where young individuals were dressed smartly and pretending to work industriously, and reached the large meeting room.

'So,' said Hank, 'just to recap the plan. Marcus will take Robert Price to lunch and will come to our office to collect the fruit of their investments. Chaz, did you bring the cash?'

'Of course. Your office is the one opposite this meeting room. In the top drawer, there are two envelopes, one for Marcus and one for Price. The first full of waste paper, it has a pen mark in the corner, the second obviously is swollen with cash.'

'Perfect. Then we need a *persuasion*. Shall we do it before or after the meeting?'

The persuasion could happen in several ways, it was a way to give credit to what was promised during the scam. The first investment, usually a meager figure, was the first step. To make the mark believe that there was a quick way, albeit illegal, to make money. The second *persuasion* was a fairly high amount that was invested by the victim. Many scammers were content to stop at this point, disappearing with the investment, but the band, in this case, wouldn't settle for a few hundred thousand pounds. They were ready for the rip-off of the century.

The third *inducement* usually happened with a person not known by the victim, in this case, Anders. He had to prove that what Hank was promising was real.

'I would say to do it earlier,' said Splinter, 'if Anders enters the scene at the end, Price may not take the bait. Maybe he would decide to leave just when our Swedish friend arrives and before he has time to explain how much money he had earned thanks to the Resurgence Equities Enterprise.'

'To me, it sounds better,' said Domino, 'we lead Price into the office just in time to see you giving a nice briefcase full of cash to Anders, ensuring Price will see the contents. Then Anders leaves the scene.'

'Approved,' said Hank, 'OK, everybody knows which way to act. Marcus, it's up to you now. Go get our future benefactor and let's get the ball rolling.'

****

Splinter fetched Robert Price in a luxurious Mercedes S-class 600. There had been a lengthy discussion with Chaz the day before, who had arrived with the 500 model. 'Nothing sounds more as if *I hadn't made it in life* as a model 500!' said Splinter visibly enraged. 'It's like shouting to the world I would like an S-600, but I can't afford it!'

Despite the grievances by Chaz, explanations of how hard it would be to find that particular model, in the end, he had succeeded. *Chaz was young,* thought Splinter, *one day he will learn that appearance, in certain things, is everything.*

Price left the bank a few minutes later, and Chaz opened the right rear door of the Mercedes to let him in.

'My dear, Marcus, my wife thanks you for the beautiful flowers you sent,' said Price shaking Splinter's hand.

'Oh, nothing, just a gesture.' They had spoken earlier on the phone when they had arranged their lunch. Maybe they could discuss business, Splinter had hinted.

'I booked us into a downtown restaurant, and then we could go see if that Anthony Edwards has kept his promise,' said Price.

'Ah right, I'd almost forgotten,' lied Splinter. 'Why don't we go there first? That will give us the occasion to have a bit of gossip in case those promised fabulous earnings are a disappointment.'

'Why not? Your driver knows the way?' asked Price.

Splinter took out his diary and gave instructions to Chaz, which he inserted into the GPS. They arrived outside the offices of the Resurgence Equities Enterprise a few minutes later. Price was not fooled by the old building that housed the headquarters; in the centre of Brighton, it was hard to find offices and often old buildings were being converted. Splinter announced himself to the receptionist, who made them sit on a leather couch in the elegant marble lobby. Shortly afterwards Domino came to greet them.

'Hello, gentlemen, Mr Edwards will be pleased to meet you, please follow me.'

Employees were moving briskly, young men who spoke on the phone, secretaries who roamed the stairs and offices, moving folders and boxes of documents; the headquarters of Resurgence Equities Enterprise were in full swing. Price lingered longer than usual to admire Domino's hips swaying in front of his eyes.

They arrived at Hank Edwards's office, and from the window wall, they could see him talking with an impeccably dressed young man. A briefcase was open on the desk, and it was filled with cash. Domino went into the office announcing the two new guests, and Anthony made a broad smile, greeted the two with his hand, and motioned to enter.

Anders was closing the case and saying goodbye to Hank, '…and thanks again, this was the best investment I've made in years. See you next week? I have another proposal that might interest you.'

'Sure, sure. Domino, please make an appointment for Mr Nilsson for next Tuesday.'

'You already have an appointment on Tuesday with the Ministry,' said the woman looking at a tablet she had in her hand, 'but you are free Thursday afternoon at four o'clock.'

'Thursday will be fine,' said Anders. Then he saluted the two newcomers and left.

'If I'm not mistaken, you owe us a bottle of whisky,' said Price recalling their conversation.

'Hello, gentlemen, please sit down, and you are wrong. The bottle was if I had not had a *significant* return on the investment. Here,' said Hank opening the desk drawer and pulling out two hefty envelopes. 'As promised!'

Splinter slipped his envelope into his jacket pocket while Price started to count the money. 'There are about five thousand pounds in this envelope, there is nothing in the world that can guarantee such a result in the financial field,' said Price staring straight into his benefactor's eyes.

'Well, apparently there is something.' Smiled Hank. 'And if you want, I also invite you to celebrate with me. It was a wonderful week.' With that said, Hank moved toward the elegant cabinet that contained the spirits.

'Difficult to say no to a glass of good whisky,' said Splinter. 'In what kind of business is your company?'

'We invest in the stock market like everybody else,' downplayed Hank.

'You mean insider trading? If you earn this kind of return, that's the only way.' Price had not mentioned that insider trading was illegal, a fact immediately seized upon by Hank and Splinter.

'No, nothing like that, what we do is totally legal. I mean sometimes we bend the rules to our advantage, but I wouldn't say it's illegal. Maybe one of those famous grey areas that we often talk about,' said Hank with a mischievous smile. He poured the whisky into three glasses and handed two glasses to his guests.

'Could you be more specific?' pressed Splinter.

'Sure, we rely on an algorithm that identifies the arbitrages on the different stock exchanges. We buy low, and we sell at a slightly increased price, without any risk for our investors.'

Price laughed out loud. 'Arbitrages cancel each other, you'll make nothing more than a few thousand pounds at the time.'

Hank continued to smile but said nothing. He had to leave that idea developing in Price's mind, let him come to doubt that someone had actually found the goose that laid the golden egg, the system of making money without having to worry about losing. Then Hank added, 'That was true in the old market when there were only humans making transactions. Today it's all electronic, orders are exchanged in milliseconds, a title which is now listed at, let's say, twenty dollars undergoes minor variations during the day, maybe just a few pennies. But during all those hours that it's on the market, it fluctuates. Think about how many milliseconds there are in a day, multiplied by all the shares on the market.'

Price gasped. He had a solid financial background, but he was old-school, he had never thought about the technological side of a transaction. For that there were programmers, the only thing that mattered was to buy and sell at the right price. He remembered about some transactions he'd tried in the past and not succeeded in. Shares that were available on the market at one moment and had disappeared as soon as he introduced an order. It was hard to imagine that thousands of transactions, perhaps tens of thousands, took place simultaneously on the stock market every second without anyone actually understanding what it meant. It was something too difficult to fully comprehend. The blink of an eye was a tenth of a second, something that most people could barely register. Who could imagine how the stock market world behaved in a split-second? But Price still wasn't convinced. 'And how do you find them before everybody else?'

Hank had studied the part, thanks to Logan, and now he could speak like an expert. 'Our data processing centre is right next to the stock exchange building. This means that we receive the data a split-second before everybody else. Also, our software is very slender. New programs, cutting edge. We hired the best technicians in the world, and we pay them a fortune, traditional banks instead cannot afford to rewrite all of their software. They are already making plenty of money from commissions. This means that they are far behind from a technological point of view: their information systems are old and slow, and we beat them to the punch. Every single time.'

'Damn,' said Splinter, 'I never heard of anything like that, despite having been in business for a lifetime. But if I think about my damn phone, which has more features than I could possibly learn, I begin to understand your logic. You are telling me that others aren't there yet. We are exploring uncharted territory, here.'

'So, if I'm building my own data centre near a stock exchange, I can do the same?' asked Price, looking for a weakness.

'Ha, ha, ha, not really.' Hank had him in his grasp, he had interested him to such an extent that Price kept asking questions. It was clear he was trying to understand. 'We have a few aces up our sleeve. First our programmers. Chinese, Indians, and Russians, people that write exceptional software programs. And then we spent more than a year mapping the major investors. We can calculate how long it takes them to reach the various stock exchanges.'

Splinter saw a worried look in Price's face, for sure he was thinking about it. But to avoid misunderstandings, he kept asking questions himself.

'I don't understand why you're mapping large investors. And how would you map them?'

That enquiry was the correct one. Price watched him with admiration as if Splinter had read his mind.

'Large investors are key. They are those who buy and sell millions of shares at a given time. Think of the large investment funds, pension funds, etc. We want to know when they move, this is the fundamental point. If a major investor wants to buy two million shares of IBM, for example, it will be extremely difficult for them to be able to fulfil such an order on a single market, so the order is broken down across several stock exchanges. And that's when we have the opportunity to beat them on time, gather the same shares before they are able to at a lower price and sell at the right price. Or buy what is available and when their order arrives we resell the shares at a slightly increased price. We gain in the process, without taking chances.'

'But how do you know which market the order will enter first?' asked Price.

'According to recent US laws, a stock trader must always look for the best price for a share. It is a recently passed law, and its goal was to protect investors. Since we are right behind a stock exchange, we place a small number of shares on the market at a lower price, waiting for a major investor to buy them. If you want to give it a name, this is the lure. Since we sell stock at low prices, they are forced to buy on the stock market where we operate. We just sell a few hundred titles at a time and wait for the fish to bite,' explained Hank.

Price couldn't believe how the system was so simple, but still, he was not convinced. His head was bursting, it was one of those moments where he could see a solution to a big problem and something was missing to complete the picture, to fully understand how the system works. 'But how do you find the big fish? Maybe a pensioner in Nebraska has decided that very day to try his luck on the stock market.'

'As I said, we have mapped large investors. We know where they are located and how long it takes to place an order. Some are in Manhattan, others in Chicago and so on. There are infinitesimal differences, mere milliseconds, but the transactions arrive at different times, the farther the investor is, the longer it will take them to reach a market. The same operation entered in Manhattan will take longer to get to the data processing centre of the stock exchange in New Jersey than the same transaction made from our offices, which are right next door. As I say, a thousandth of a second, but that's enough.'

Price sipped his whisky and began to think about what he had learned, trying to reach a conclusion. They were all silent for a few seconds, they needed to digest this information, and fully understand the implications.

Splinter was the first to speak, there are no risk-free operations. 'What's the catch?'

'There aren't setbacks, but there are risks, quite frankly. First, every day we have to buy and sell shares to attract our prey. And this has a cost; we have those orders running at every hour of the day hoping someone takes the bait; we need a decent amount of cash to begin with. The first year we couldn't do many transactions, so we closed just in profit. This year we have more funds and can deal with more transactions. Therefore we have a wider net if you like. The risk is always there, but the chances are so much in our favour that we always win in the long run. As the house does, at casinos, when playing roulette.'

'If I wanted to invest, what are your fees?' Price asked finally.

'Twenty per cent profit. I know, it sounds usury but consider that such operations have a cost;

I assure you that our costs are very high, but conditions are so favourable that the operation is almost without risk.

'What do the authorities have to say about it?' asked Splinter.

'All legal. In fact, we are among those who, as they say, provide *liquidity* to the market, so there is no reason to investigate. If you ask me, the financial authorities don't even have a clue what we're doing.'

'I do not invest cash,' said Price, remembering the man who had just left the office with a suitcase full of money.

'No cash. We have our bank accounts, and we transfer the funds into the United States. Some of our clients ask us to pay the profits in cash to avoid telling their wives,' said Hank.

'Or the tax man,' said Splinter.

The three laughed loudly, almost at the same instant. Now their tones were relaxed, and Price would definitely invest.

'What do you say, Marcus. Shall we have a go?' asked Price of his companion.

'I would say that we can try, just to see what happens.'

Hank looked at his watch and saw that Domino was waiting at the door with a new client, played by Lenny.

Price and Splinter realised that their time was over and it was time to leave, but they also registered that there were other interested parties to do business with Hank Edwards. If they wanted a piece of the pie, they would have to act quickly.

Hank accompanied them to the door and, before sending them on their way, he said warmly, 'If you'd like to leave your details with my assistant, she will give you all the information you need to make the first investment.'

The two nodded. The trap was set.

CHAPTER 36

'Chief Superintendent Ross, Brighton Police,' he said after lifting the receiver. As the conversation progressed, Ross's face went from disbelief to surprise to settle back down on resigned. He got up in a hurry to get to the office that had been assigned to Corrigan.

'Incredible news,' he said breathlessly upon entering the Interpol agent's room.

'What's going on?'

'Amelia Mortcombe was killed in Leamington last night,' said Ross, no half measures.

Corrigan was shocked. 'That's not possible,' he faltered. 'How did this happen?'

'From the account made by the local police, she was found dead in the train station public toilet. There was another victim, and they think it was an execution. The company doing the cleaning spotted a closed bathroom, and after repeated attempts to try to open the door, they called a supervisor. When they prised the door open, they found these two women killed by gunshots. Maria Benhauer of Stuttgart and our Amelia Mortcombe. There will be an autopsy of course, but the cause of death is evident, several gunshots that shattered her face. They found the victims' documents and they are discounting a robbery gone bad since there was cash on both of the victims.'

'Who could have wanted her dead?' said Corrigan.

'At the moment those are all open questions. Who killed Amelia? What was she doing in Leamington? All issues that need to be addressed. The local police said they will keep the investigation going and keep us posted, but I think we have a duty to do our homework and investigate ourselves,' said Ross. Then, after a moment's pause, he added, 'Perhaps your theory about those scammers was incorrect.'

Ross never had liked Corrigan. He had entered his life like a bull in a china shop and, shoving that Interpol badge in everyone's face, he had started controlling everybody and demanding results. Ross didn't like when his daily routine was disrupted, and Corrigan was undoubtedly a troublemaker. Maybe he'd be gone soon.

'Could you let me have a copy of the investigation documents from the local authorities?' he finally asked. 'If Marcus Splinter and company are here, there must be a reason. I'm sure they're up to something.'

'Maybe they aren't aware of her death. When they learn that fact, they will go away,' said Ross. *And with them, you too*, he thought.

'We will need to inform her family.'

Ross sighed. Maybe it wasn't over yet. 'One of my officers is trying to track them down right now. She has a sister, from what I learned. We will find her.'

'Do you mind if I accompany your officers when they go to break the news? There could be important elements that we haven't discovered yet.'

'Go ahead,' ruled Ross. He was confident that Corrigan's permanence in his department wouldn't last long. A little more patience and everything would be back to normal.

Ross had never been wrong. Not until that moment.

CHAPTER 37

'We have the funds,' said Anders without looking away from the computer. 'That jerk Price dropped a hundred and fifty thousand pounds. What a deadbeat!'

'This means that our friend Marcus will have the better hand, what do you think?' asked Hank.

'That wouldn't be a bad idea. Price seems a competitive type if we pretend that I've invested three hundred thousand pounds it will piss him off. He's young and ambitious and seeing that an old man like me got the best return will send him on a rampage. Obviously, he won't show it openly, but rest assured he won't be happy,' said Splinter.

'What return are we going to give him back?' asked Anders.

'I would say at least three hundred thousand pounds. That might tempt him to make a much higher investment later.'

'From what I read in Romanov's letters,' said Anders, 'he is exposed by ten million. If he wants to cover his loss, he could well invest five million.'

'That means there would be thirteen million in our pocket, without the risk of exposing our own money,' said Hank. 'What makes me smile is that this whole thing is legal, or almost. Obviously, we are not a real financial institution, but these types that Logan found really are a piece of work. I thought I'd seen many scams, but these guys are head and shoulders above us and some.'

'You've decided to invest regardless?' asked Anders stupefied. The last time they had talked about it, the gang had decided to use Amelia's money to subsidise the scam. Logan had been useful to find the mechanism to hook Robert Price. That *High-Frequency Traders* company was registered in the United States, was mentioned on websites, there were employee profiles on LinkedIn, would have been useful if Anders had not managed to get his hands on Amelia's money. When they received the news of his success, Splinter and Hank decided to continue the old way and use the funds already available. Hank had thought investing Price's money for real would have been a gamble they could afford.

'We blackmailed Logan, we went to London to meet this Whitley, why not try? We have the money. We're going to be cautious and only invest Price's funds to see what happens. By the way, where is Logan?'

'He's just arrived,' said Domino, 'he now comes here every day, for lunch, eyes me up while he stuffs his face and then returns to where he came from. A pathetic old man.'

The woman went to call Logan, who joined the others in the main room. When Hank explained what he had in mind, the old lawyer nodded, he asked them to transfer the money to the account as previously agreed and called Whitley on the phone. The two were old friends, and they spent most of the time reliving memories and sharing bad jokes, increasing the irritability of everyone present. They were not used to working with strangers and Logan, although he looked old and tired, remained a wild card to them.

'They will do us special favour: today they will invest all the money, and they'll work for us all day. They will send us the transaction log by email. Not that it's necessary, but if it serves to demonstrate to Price that the transactions are legitimate, so be it. I'm going to have to stay up all night to make a copy for Marcus. It doesn't have to be precise, but not a duplicate of the original either,' said Logan without particular enthusiasm.

'Do you think it's necessary? Why not just the front page and the rest blank?' asked Splinter surprised by the unexpected offer.

'That depends. If Price is curious, he would want to give a sneak peek at your sheets, maybe just hoping to steal some secret.'

'When you say they will work for us, what do you mean?' Domino interjects.

'They will start investing the hundred and fifty thousand, and then they will continue all day to buy and sell. If at eleven in the morning they reach, say, three hundred thousand pounds, they will continue to sell and buy with all the money and profits, to maximise earnings,' explained Logan, without entering in further details. The others did not ask anything further.

'We just have to wait. When do you think we will hear from them?'

'When the market closes. They could, in theory, continue on the banks' dark pools throughout the night but at 5 p.m. New York time they will send the money to us, less their percentage, of course.'

'That will be about eleven o'clock at night GMT,' said Domino doing a quick mental calculation.

'We will wait.'

****

Corrigan and Inspector Blake arrived at Robert Price's luxury apartment rather late in the evening.

Price made them sit as soon as he saw the badges, fearing for the worst. He had ordered the killing of Romanov, he was dealing with the mafia, and had ordered the murder of his sister-in-law. He relaxed only when they demanded the presence of his wife. If they wanted to arrest him, they wouldn't have made so many compliments.

Carla arrived a few minutes later after she'd sent their children to bed.

'The police', her husband stated in hushed tones.

'Let's hear what they have to say. Can I get you something to drink?'

'No thanks, we're on duty,' said Blake, with a tinge of embarrassment. A glass of something strong would certainly help him deliver the bad news, he was young and still was not used to such situations. 'It is about your sister,' said the inspector, 'she's been killed.'

Robert Price and Carla looked at each other, one not at all understanding precisely what the detectives were saying, the other, on the other hand, knowing all too well what had transpired.

'Don't … It's not possible. How did it happen? I spoke to her not long ago … certainly, we weren't very close but …' She covered her face with her hands. Corrigan failed to see if the woman was crying or not.

Even Price gasped, but for other reasons. With the death of Amelia, Carla would automatically take possession of the bank while Mortcombe was still in a coma in the hospital. Not understanding anything about finance, she would turn to him to lead the bank.

'She was found murdered, along with another woman, at the train station in Leamington. She had been shot in the face a staggering number of times, we barely recognise what little of her face remains intact, and only IDd her from the contents of her handbag,' stated the officer.

And bang goes making it look like an accident, thought Price, but the fact that Amelia was killed in another county would have minimised the suspicion on him. Of course, he had a motive, but his wife seemed to be sufficiently stricken to divert the investigator's attention from him. Margot had done an excellent job and had earned her pay.

'Are there any suspects?' asked Price, 'I don't understand what she was doing in Leamington, the bank has no business in that region, and I don't think her law firm has clients in that area.'

'The investigation is ongoing, but it will be conducted by the local police,' said Blake, 'of course we will keep you informed of developments. We have a warrant to search her office; we would like, if possible, if you could come along. There could be clues that might get us on the right track.'

'Of course, no problem,' said Price, 'I will take care of that myself by getting in touch with Mr Logan, who is … was Amelia's business partner.' Then he cursed himself silently, some incriminating papers were still in Amelia's office, and he should make them disappear before the police went there. If he had entrusted that job to Margot, she would have botched it. Not knowing what to look for, she would have turned the entire office upside down shifting the focus of the investigators to Brighton. No, he should recover the documents himself: Amelia's death gave him that right. Doing it before the inspectors arrived and outfox Ryan Logan was another matter.

He would deal with the matter that very night.

CHAPTER 38

'How much did you say?' Hank asked, not believing his ears.

'Two hundred and twenty thousand,' confirmed Anders unable to take his eyes away from the computer screen.

'Doesn't seem much to me,' said Domino, 'I mean, would it be enough to convince Price? I expected, like, a million at least.'

Logan laughed out loud, causing them to all turn in his direction. 'Dear girl, with that return, one hundred and fifty thousand pounds becomes two million in just one month. Twenty-five million a year. Doesn't seem to me like a gain to be underestimated, for an investment done honestly. Of course, if you want a million, you can always try the lottery, but if you manage to convince Price to put tens of millions, you might keep your share of the profits without committing any crime.'

It was Splinter's turn. 'Guys, let's not be greedy. We know that greed is the spring that pushes all our buttons. You can't cheat an honest man. We have nine million, we invest them for a few months, and we see them doubled or tripled with this history of high-frequency trading. For once, we have the opportunity to make money without risk. I say we should wrap this up and withdraw. Many thanks, Mr Price, we give him what he is due, and we dismantle the operation. What do you say?'

The gang members didn't seem very willing to listen to him at that point, everybody was doing the maths in their own head. Invest, receive the fifty per cent gain, reinvest. It would take quite some time to reach a significant amount. Conversely, if they had hooked Price for good, those millions would multiply very quickly. It was the difference between a beautiful house and a villa, between a regular luxury car and a Rolls Royce, between a decent life and one made of glitz.

Lenny was the first to speak, 'I say we continue to rip off Price. We invest the nine million plus whatever the banker is forking, and when we reach three hundred million, we disappear.'

Splinter was getting nervous. 'We know that the first priority for Price is to recover that ten million. Once he reaches that figure, he will be much more cautious in investing. Currently, he has the motivation, the Russian mafia is breathing down his neck, but if he can recover that money, the biggest problem is past. He will make inquiries, he will ask around, he will look at our credentials in more depth. We can't keep it going for too long.'

'Then we hurry him up,' said Hank, 'with the next investments we keep him below the ten million threshold. Eventually, he will relent and invest a large amount.'

Also, Domino, who was usually calm and rational when it was a matter of money, was dreaming about the big hit, the one that would have made history. 'I am with Hank, we keep Price on a leash until we hit him big and then we can leave.'

Seeing the situation slipping out of control, Splinter contacted the last two constituents, hoping still to receive a majority. 'Chaz, Anders, what do you think?'

'Both situations are good for me,' said Chaz, who was the youngest and least experienced. 'I'm with the majority.'

'And you, Anders?'

'Hell, I vote to scrub Price and make him pay. I nearly got myself killed by following the money and Amelia. I'm almost convinced that he was the one who sent those killers after us. If we don't cheat him as a team, I shall do it on my own, he deserves it!'

Seeing that the decision had been made, Splinter did not resist further. 'OK, it seemed right to put all options on the table. We continue with the scam, as agreed.'

Everybody relaxed, all except Logan, who remained on the fence, worried.

CHAPTER 39

Price couldn't sleep that night. Despite having given the order to kill Amelia, he hadn't considered the boxes of banking documents would be in her office. What if they impounded every single scrap of paper as part of the murder investigation? An amateur mistake, one which he would have to remedy. The problem was how to do it. If he forced the door, the investigators would notice, Logan would do a check and tell the police what was missing. And the suspicion might fall back upon, the bank.

But then how do you force a door? I'm not a burglar, he thought.

He could send a courier to collect the documents, but Logan might have objected, and if the police were there, it would have aroused suspicion.

There was no way out.

He looked at his phone screen again, and then he dialled the number, despite the late hour.

'Sokolov,' said a voice on the other end of the phone on the second ring.

'This is Price, I have a problem.'

'You're not alone. We worked with that assistant you assigned to us, and it appears that

Bruno Mortcombe stole ten million from our accounts.'

Price breathed heavily. There was no point in denying what Sokolov already knew. 'It's not like that.'

'Then explain how it is,' said Sokolov. His voice was calm, but that meant nothing.

Price told him about Albert Romanov, how Price hired a hit man to kill his sister-in-law, of the failed attempts and how Margot eventually managed to kill her. It was at that moment he realised Margot had not contacted him yet. What happened to that money? Maybe the killer had decided to keep it and disappear? He cursed silently.

'Can you go to the bank tonight and pick up a couple of boxes of paperwork with no value?'

'I think so, the bank is closed, but the guard won't say anything if I show up. What are you planning to do?'

'I plan to save your ass, this time. I'll send you one of my guys. Follow his instructions to the letter, and when he arrives, do not keep him waiting.'

Then there was silence.

Price dressed quickly, trying not to wake his wife and silently walked out of the apartment. The fresh night air enveloped him, and he wanted to smoke a cigarette, seeing the condensation leave his mouth. He had stopped years earlier because he realised the health issues caused by smoking. He smiled, thinking about the damage he risked by working for the Russian mob; the possibility of going to jail for the rest of his life. The harm of cigarettes appeared insignificant.

A black Audi stopped right in front of him about ten minutes later; he entered the car without waiting to be asked, and the man drove to the bank. He had already seen him driving Sokolov on other occasions, the mobster had a hard face and tattoos on his neck that made Price cringe. He could see a skull and a dagger, symbols indicating that the man was a murderer. They stopped in front of the building, and the man got out of the car along with Price. 'Now we enter,' he said bluntly, 'you get the paperwork, put them in a container and then we go. Do not provide explanations to anyone about what you're doing.'

The nightshift guard came to open the door shortly after. He recognised Price and sized up his escort, but he wasn't paid enough to ask questions. Price was also known for his short temper, so the guard avoided asking him to sign the entry register.

The two made their way to the elevator and went to the upper floors until they reached the archives. After about an hour of work, Price had filled two boxes with documents. Old statements, reports of low importance, but that would assist the investigators from wasting precious time. The gangster took charge of bringing the two boxes out of the building before placing them in the car trunk, then he asked for the new address.

The Russian did not waste time talking more than he should, but Price understood, despite the strong accent, and gave directions on how to reach Amelia's office.

Once they'd arrived, the man opened the locks, and in the blink of an eye, they were inside the office. 'Search for the paperwork,' said the Russian, after lighting a cigarette and sitting in an armchair. Price didn't criticise that gesture; he would have liked to smoke a cigarette himself.

The bank documents were in Logan's office, and Price took charge personally of replacing them with those he had just removed from the bank. Maybe they would get away with it. The investigators would take them away, deem them uninteresting, and send them back. Job done.

When Price collected all that he needed, he headed toward the criminal who once again took charge of bringing the documents back to the car.

He left Price on his doorstep, with the two containers placed on the ground and he vanished into the night.

CHAPTER 40

The next day Price escorted the investigators to Amelia's law firm. Five officers followed him, including Inspector Blake and Corrigan.

Logan opened the door and let them in.

'Apparently, we meet every time one of your employers is killed,' said Corrigan in no uncertain terms.

Logan looked him straight in the eye, trying to match the face to a name.

'Inspector Corrigan, Interpol. I arrested you during the investigations into Saunders' murder,' he stated.

'A colossal fiasco. I was innocent, although it took about twenty years to prove it,' said Logan. Price watched the bickering between the two in disbelief, but he didn't say a word.

'Where were you yesterday?' asked Corrigan.

'In the office. A row of meetings with clients, one after the other, you can check my diary.'

'We will do so,' Corrigan explained in detail the fate of Amelia Mortcombe and Logan's face went from disbelief to shock. He did not cry, but it was evident that he was upset.

'We need to figure out what Amelia was working on. Did she have any enemies?'

Logan looked at Price for a moment, and then his gaze turned to his office, but then, biting his lips, he kept quiet.

'Mr Logan, do you know if Amelia Mortcombe had any enemies?' insisted Corrigan.

'No, I don't think so. We take care of the usual things, divorces, real estate, I don't think anyone would go to the trouble of killing Amelia for things like that. However, my office is at your disposal, go ahead and search the premises, you have my full cooperation.'

'Can we bring the documents to the police department?' asked Blake.

Logan thought about it, trying to remember if anything incriminating was contained in their paperwork and then nodded in assent. 'Take what you need.'

Then he slumped in a chair and began to stare at the empty space in front of him.

While the officers were busy searching the premises, Price approached the old man and asked, 'If I remember correctly, the firm is registered in Amelia's name, right?'

Logan replied without looking up from the floor, 'Yes, both the company and the premises are in her name. There was the talk of splitting it fifty-fifty, but for one reason or another we never bothered to formalise the matter.'

'Now all this belongs to my wife,' said Price, hissing the words as if he were a snake, 'when the police have gone, take your things and get out. Leave your keys with me, your services are no longer required.'

'We still have cases to work on...' Logan said.

'I told you, this is none of your business anymore!' cried Price, a couple of officers looked in their direction, 'bugger off, old man. And screw the pending cases! It is no longer your problem, do you understand?'

Logan did not answer but, resigned, nodded.

****

When Price returned to his office, he was surprised he had received an email from Resurgence Equities Enterprise. They informed him about his investment, they'd attached a transactions log and said they had already moved the money into his account. At the end of the letter, they thanked him for doing business with the Resurgence Equities Enterprise.

He opened the document on his computer and gasped reading the revenue column. Resulting from the one hundred and fifty thousand pounds invested he had received back two hundred and twenty thousand pounds. *That's impossible*, he said to himself, *someone is taking me for a ride.*

He opened the attachment and was gobsmacked by what the transaction log was telling him. There were pages and pages, one after the other, purchases and sales made at almost the same instant, earnings. Next to each line there was the date of the transaction, hour, minutes, and seconds. It didn't specify the milliseconds, as explained by Anthony, but he clearly saw that hundreds of deals were made during the same second. *How was it possible?*

He searched for a phone number in the corporate diary and called the IT Department. He knew they kept a log of all stock titles in the archive to do statistical analysis. He had personally approved the order to purchase additional servers and disks to store the data. The idea was to hold a stock historical archive to use for analytical purposes. He had also seen some presentations by computer giants that promised immediate analysis of large amounts of data to make decisions. *Big Data,* they called it. Often needed by supermarkets to analyse consumers' profiles and understand what products were more popular and what were the most successful ones? Although sceptical, he had approved the budget, but still had yet to see the results.

'Richard, I need a data analysis on the American stock exchanges. Yesterday's data,' said Price.

'What did you have in mind exactly, Mr Price?' said the computer engineer. The bespectacled young man who ran the database knew that data requests made to his office were often too general; the result was hours of work to provide answers that no one had ever asked. Figuring out exactly what people really wanted was winning half the battle.

'I have an Excel spreadsheet that I'm sending you now. It contains US markets transactions from yesterday. They are sorted by the stock exchange. I want you to analyse the data and confirm their validity.'

'You are unclear, Mr Price. If you already have the data, which kind of confirmation do you need? Wait a moment, please … I've just received the file … OK, I've opened it,' said the technician.

'Look at page three, those IBM titles. There are dozens of purchases at the same time at different prices. I cannot explain it.'

The technician was silent for a few minutes, and then he said, 'Maybe I understand. You are wondering why, at the same time, on the same stock exchange anyone could buy a stock at different prices,' said the technician, trying to unravel his ideas in turn.

'Exactly!'

'From the log you sent me I see that it shows only the seconds, not the milliseconds. Maybe I've got it, give me a half hour, and I'll call you back,' said Richard.

'If I am busy, try again until the phone is free. This is a priority!'

There were always priorities, thought the poor technician. Every day there was something he had to do with the highest priority. He set to work immediately.

Price picked up the phone and called Marcus Splinter.

'Marcus, my friend.'

The old swindler was sitting in an armchair and was sipping a cup of coffee. Around him, there were his accomplices, who remained in religious silence. 'Robert, nice to hear you, how are things going?'

'Very well. Did you get anything from the Resurgence Equities Enterprise?'

'Actually, I haven't checked it yet, wait a minute ...' Splinter pretended to press keys on a keyboard and then exclaimed, 'Wow, that's great. Three hundred and fifty thousand pounds for an investment I thought would give me ten per cent at most. What happened to yours?'

'Two hundred and twenty,' said Price through gritted teeth. He wasn't pleased that his new acquaintance had gained more than him.

'You did the right thing. In certain affairs it's better to be cautious,' said Splinter. The irony pervading his words was noticed by Price.

'Have you looked into these Resurgence guys?' Price then asked, as if it were something reasonable, a casual business discussion, while he was fully aware. Instead, he had found the goose that laid the golden egg.

'I asked around a bit. The company looks legit, although almost everything is based on secrecy. No customer names, nothing much specific on their website. A friend in the States said they are making money hand over fist; they dealt with almost three per cent of all transactions on various stock markets in the past couple of months. Amazing, for a newcomer. No one has been able to get more information, but they've certainly noticed them. Are you thinking of having another go with these guys?'

Price thought it over for a moment. 'I'm not sure. Maybe they were lucky; as you said, it's better to be cautious in certain things.'

'You are right, my boy,' said Splinter, 'to be cautious. I'm going to see them this afternoon.'

Price hung up the receiver without saying goodbye.

The phone rang again, it was Richard from the IT Department.

'What have you got?'

'All the operations are legitimate, I received a sample of transactions, I went through them to see what happened in those seconds and that's something amazing. I mean, they take advantage of small price changes on the titles of the different stock exchanges. It seems they can sell on the market at the highest price while almost instantly they glean whatever share they can on other stock markets. Or anticipate, I do not know how bulk orders. They seem to have a magic wand: buy large amounts of securities a few moments before a big bank, or a fund manager make an order. And as soon as a big order lands on the market, they are ready to sell. It might be inside trading, except that they make thousands of trades a day. It wouldn't be possible. If these guys have found the formula to take advantage of the arbitrage, they are getting seriously rich.'

'Thank you, Richard,' said Price hanging up the phone. So, it was true, how come nobody had done that before them? Then he remembered an article he had read some time ago, where the journalist had said that the big banks were losing market share, to the benefit of a small group of newcomers.

There was no time to waste; he needed to have another meeting with those Resurgence guys. Letting Splinter have the upper hand was not an option; the next time he would be the one to be humiliated.

CHAPTER 41

That same day, Price booked an appointment with Hank Edwards to discuss a new investment.

'There we are,' said Hank as soon as he ended the conversation with Price, 'the fish took the bait.'

'You've given me the jitters,' said Lenny turning to Splinter, 'with all your cajoling on being cautious.'

'Ah, it wasn't so difficult,' explained the older man. 'Price is ambitious and competitive. He loves money more than his own children, and it was evident he was getting upset when I told him how much I'd invested. I would have loved to have been a fly on the wall to see the look on his face. And when I told him to be careful, that was the famous straw that broke the camel's back. Telling a man that kind of thing is the equivalent of challenging him. It seems to me, all went for the best.'

The band moved their operation to the Resurgence offices; Price could show up at any time.

'What happened to Logan? We need to inform our new overseas associates about an incoming investment.'

'He had things to do in his office,' said Domino, 'he should arrive any minute now.'

'Was it necessary to bring him here?' asked Hank. 'If Price decides to make a surprise visit, he will suspect something.'

They were interrupted by shouting from the lobby. The receptionist was raising her voice to someone and threatened to call the police. Just hearing the word *police* made all gang members jump up from their chairs in that elegant meeting room and run to see what was going on.

Logan was right in the middle of the main lobby and screaming like a maniac. 'Bastards! They took her from me!'

'Sir, you're drunk, if you don't leave immediately, there will be trouble,' said the blonde who had now left her post and was trying, in vain, to push Logan out the door.

'Wait a minute,' cried Domino from the top of the stairs, 'I've got it.' So saying she hurried to reach Logan. She could smell the alcohol from three meters away.

'Ryan, what's up?'

'They took her from me,' he said crying, 'my baby girl!'

'Come on, come on, come upstairs and tell me more,' insisted the woman. Logan had always been a quiet and a soft-spoken man, addicted to work. No one had ever seen him in that condition, at least none of the gang had.

'I'll take this,' said Domino removing a half-empty bottle of whisky from Logan's hand. The stench of alcohol filled her nostrils. Then she held

Logan under his arm in an attempt to lead him toward the elevator. Splinter tried to approach and help, but Domino froze him with a glare. They went into a room, and the woman helped Logan lie down on a bench, the man was reduced to a rag and continued to mumble meaningless phrases.

The remaining gang members sat in the same office, waiting.

'What happened, Ryan?'

'She is dead, don't you understand? They killed her like a dog!'

'Whose been killed? I don't understand?'

'Amelia. They killed her, my poor daughter.'

They looked at each other. Anders was petrified. Logan's wrath unleashed against him. One moment Logan was lying on the couch and seemed to be in pain, but as soon as he saw the Swede, he lunged at him with all his might. 'It was your fault, you filthy bastard! You left her alone and look what happened!'

Logan grabbed Anders by the throat, but Lenny and Chaz stopped him in time, forcing him to stretch out on the couch. Then the man started sobbing like a child, invoking the name of the dead woman.

A tear fell down Anders' face.

He knew that Amelia had been taking a significant risk, but she also seemed determined. He had left her on a train at Stratford-Upon-Avon and had waited until it set off. How had this happened?

He thought back to Amelia's offer, to take the money and run away; he thought back to the times they spent together when they had made love; his heart wrenched in his chest. He should have stayed with her. In that very moment, he realised how much he loved her, albeit only having known her for a short time, how he felt at ease with her, as had never happened to him before with anybody else in his life.

He wanted to go back in time and say, 'Amelia, let's run away, from everything, just the two of us,' but it was far too late for that.

He would pay for that mistake with remorse, for a lifetime, if necessary.

'That bastard should pay,' said Anders.

'Domino, keep Logan hidden in one of the offices until he recovers. And especially prevent him from doing anything stupid. Try to put him back together, tonight we will have to talk to his friends from overseas for new investment,' said Splinter after he glimpsed at the computer. 'Price has just forked over ten million pounds.'

****

Inspector Corrigan was sitting in the car in front of the building of what appeared to be the Brighton branch of the Resurgence Equities Enterprise. They had stalked Splinter, and he and Chief Superintendent Ross were making assumptions about what the gang were doing.

'From what I see, it's a financial company,' said Ross perusing the information on his mobile phone. 'I don't understand much of what they do. Looks like stock trading.'

'They have been inside for a couple of hours now, what the hell are they doing?'

They saw a drunken man staggering towards the building. He paused for a moment at fifty feet from them, just after the crossroad and then headed for the Resurgence Equities Enterprise offices.

'Hey, that's Ryan Logan,' said Corrigan.

'Are you sure about that? The one who is working in Amelia Mortcombe's law firm?' asked the surprised Chief Superintendent Ross.

'Who worked there. After Amelia's death, he was fired by Price, the brother-in-law.'

'No wonder he started drinking. At that age, another job will be hard to find.'

'The question is, what is he doing at Resurgence Equities Enterprise? Maybe is he working with Marcus Splinter and partners? We knew they wanted to rip her off, but we never found a connection. Now that appears to be Logan; in my opinion, he is the inside man.'

Ross was puzzled for a moment and then said, 'But now that Amelia Mortcombe is dead they don't have any motivation to continue with a scam? They definitely haven't killed her.'

'This is also true. But then why don't they dismantle everything and go? They must have some other target, although we still don't know who it might be. I find it disturbing that Logan is involved with those thugs.'

The traffic flowed slowly into the street. A bus stopped right in front of the building covering the visual of the two officers of the law.

'What do we do? Are we going to see what they're doing in there?' asked Ross.

'No, wait. We continue to follow them until we find out who their victim is. Then we act accordingly. Making a move now wouldn't make any sense.'

****

Igor Sokolov arrived at Mortcombe Bank at that same instant, asking to see Robert Price immediately. He was wearing an elegant grey, tailor-made suit and a red tie which gave him the appearance of a prominent businessman having just arrived in town. The receptionist, while awaiting Price's arrival, kept looking in his direction. Sokolov was an attractive man, but with a hard and cruel countenance, the likes of which promised ecstatic nights and terrifying days. And he knew he had that effect on women, on any woman.

He noticed it and smiled at the receptionist, who in turn looked away, guilty of being caught staring too intently.

Price arrived a few minutes later and made him sit in his office.

'Can I get you anything to drink?' he asked hoping it was a courtesy visit, although in his heart he knew that Sokolov never made such things.

'No thanks. We have a problem,' said the Russian, who in the meantime had removed his wristwatch, starting to wind it with infinite slowness. 'We are missing ten million from our accounts, money which we have not spent, and we don't know where they ended up. The assistant who helped says that the money was moved by Bruno Mortcombe. We didn't authorise him to do so, and of course, we want our money back. We need it because, as I told you, we are in the process of buying a company.'

Price had done everything to mask the shortfall caused by Romanov, but if Sokolov had noticed, it was useless to deny it. He would go on a rampage. He poured a shot of whisky, he briefly tasted the peaty aroma and then sat at his desk.

He sighed and began to tell all his problems, from the killing of Romanov until the disappearance of Margot.

Sokolov listened in silence, continuing to wind his wristwatch. Price's tension was mounting, which would he rather have, someone angry in front of him, even indignant about the choices he had to make. But the Russian remained silent, which what caused his legs to shake.

'Is that all?'

'No, there is more. I tried to retrieve the money, I swear. I found this American company that invests …'

Sokolov raised a hand to stop him talking. He was the one driving the conversation, and he ensured there was no doubt whatsoever about it. Sokolov would ask, and Price would respond. In one way or another.

'What makes you think this investment will be successful?'

'It is safe, they have a system that allows you to buy and sell stocks without exposing yourself.'

'And how much more of our money have you invested with them?'

'Another ten million,' said Price embarrassed. He had never experienced rigorous questioning. Usually, he was the one giving orders.

'So we are exposed by twenty million,' said Sokolov, more to confirm to himself the shortfall than looking for confirmation from Price. 'I want to meet these people, and I want my twenty million. Set up a meeting for tomorrow, I smell a scam.'

'For tomorrow. OK, I've got it,' said Price.

CHAPTER 42

When Hank hung up the phone, he cursed, attracting the attention of those present in the room.

'Price wants to see us tomorrow, no explanation about why he just says it's urgent.'

Silence fell upon the room, and they looked at each other, trying to make sense of the unusual request.

'We told him it will take a few days for that investment, didn't we?' said Lenny.

'Of course,' said Domino, 'Hank explained that for significant sums it takes more time, I was there at the time.'

'So, what the hell does he want? I'd say that he has smelled a rat and wants to withdraw the money. We have nine million from Anders, plus ten which Price gave to us, I think we should close this business and bugger off. It's a lot of money,' said Lenny.

'Until yesterday you said you wanted to con him, and today you change your mind?' said Splinter. 'Let us not panic. He invested the money and wants to make sure he receives a good return. We play this as agreed: we make him earn some money, but not enough to cover the hole that Romanov has created. At that point, he will be forced to reinvest. In my opinion, next time he will give us twenty million. Still, a few days of patience and we go our own way happy and enriched.'

Nobody commented further. In previous scams, they had managed to earn a few hundred thousand pounds at a time. Seeing millions in the account was something they were not used to, and the temptation to flee was strong. The only ones who seemed to stay calm were Hank and Splinter.

'So, what is the plan for tomorrow?' said Lenny.

'Marcus, tomorrow you stay away. Price must not see you around or he will suspect something. How is Logan?' asked Hank.

'After the rabid phase he went into depression mode,' said Domino, 'he is drunker than a spinster on Valentine's day, but today we were able to put him in touch with Tim Whitley and the Americans, although most of the time I was the one talking. Apparently, in the past Logan liked his drink, so nobody asked questions.'

'OK, let him sleep on the sofa tonight. Tomorrow after breakfast we put him back on track, we need him one last time. Make sure he doesn't show up when Price arrives. If the two meet, we are out of business.'

'It will be done. Did I ever mention to you that my middle name is *nurse*?' said Domino.

'Every day we discover something new about you. You could have told us before, I needed nursing attention after the incident in Eton,' laughed

Lenny. During a scam against a London gangster, Lenny had been recognised by a former crony who was passing by at that moment. Having sensed the fraud, the victim had viciously beaten Lenny up, and things would have turned for the worse if bystanders had not intervened. He ended up in a hospital with a couple of cracked ribs and spent a month in bed. From time to time, he complained about that, with the change of season.

'Chaz, you're going to be the accountant, as usual. Transferring funds from Price to the Americans. You will be in the office opposite mine, just in case I need to call you. Anders, you disappear, if he sees you're still around, he might suspect something was amiss.'

****

The next day, just after lunchtime, Robert Price entered the headquarters of the Resurgence Equities Enterprise, accompanied by Sokolov and two of his henchmen. One was the guy who had broken into Amelia's office, the other looked even more menacing, and they carried a gym bag. The receptionist informed Domino of the guests waiting at the reception.

When the woman arrived in the main lobby, her blood froze in her veins. Nobody had mentioned that there would be other people besides Price, and those other guys promised trouble.

Price didn't introduce his companions to the woman, after all, she was just a secretary. It was only when they were in the presence of Hank Edwards that Price spoke.

'This is Igor Sokolov, one of the most important clients of Mortcombe Bank.'

Hank started looking for a way out, he knew that those facing him were nothing more than representatives of the Russian mafia. They were dressed smartly, but that man introduced as Igor was definitely the most fearsome. Hank had dealt with the Russian mafia before in Manchester. They once targeted the wrong person, and he had almost lost his life in the process. He still got chills thinking about the months he spent looking over his shoulder with the fear of being kidnapped and tortured every time he stepped away from home.

'Nice to meet you, to what do I owe the pleasure?'

'Mr Sokolov ...' Price attempted to say, but he was interrupted by an abrupt gesture from the Russian, forcing him to keep quiet.

'Price manages our accounts, but in this case, he acted without our authorisation,' said the Russian.

'Please, sit down,' said Hank, pointing toward the chairs in front of his desk. Price and Sokolov sat down while the two bodyguards stood by the door. 'Can I offer you something to drink, a coffee perhaps?'

'No thanks,' said the Russian. Silence had fallen on the room, and the guests made no sign of wanting to add anything else.

After a moment of embarrassment, Hank said, 'I understand, there are no problems. Every evening we invest the money, and at the end of the day, we put it back into the personal accounts of our clients. Your money is still on our accounts after last night's investments.' Hank looked at his watch, 'For another thirty minutes. We can make a transfer immediately to your bank account. Do you want to know what the balance is?'

'Yes, please.'

Hank turned to his computer, he typed at the keyboard for a few moments and then said, 'It's around fifteen million, to which account do you want us to transfer it?'

Sokolov took a pen from his breast pocket and began to write in a notebook; then he passed the message to Hank.

A few seconds after, Sokolov received a message on his phone. The money had arrived into his personal account, then he turned to Price and said, 'You can go now.'

Price remained dumbfounded for a moment as if he had not understood and it was at that point that Sokolov was forced to repeat the order, 'Go home, Robert, if we need you, we know where you are.'

The banker muttered a *thank you*, rose from his chair, and walked toward the door, turning a few times in the vain hope of being recalled. Which was something that did not happen. He passed by the two thugs and was escorted out of the building by Domino.

****

'For Christ's Sake! That was Robert Price!' swore Corrigan, in his car stationed opposite the Resurgence Equities Enterprise. Inspector Blake had joined them and was sitting in the back seat of the vehicle.

'Amelia Mortcombe's brother-in-law,' said Blake more to confirm it to himself than anything else. They had met when he had given him the news about Amelia Mortcombe's death; there was little doubt.

'What the hell is going on here? We were trying to frame Hank Edwards and associates, we thought the goal was Amelia, and now the brother-in-law pops up.'

'Those three guys who went in with him,' said Blake, 'they are Russian mafia.'

'What makes you say that?'

'The tattoos on their necks and hands. I've seen enough of them when I worked in London, and then from how they move, they appear ready for a robbery. What are we going to do?'

'We wait, we have nothing else to do.' Then, thinking aloud, Corrigan added, 'Edwards,

Mortcombe, the Russian mafia. How the hell are they connected? I can't figure it out.'

A few minutes later they saw Robert Price leave the building and take a taxi.

'Come on, let's follow him,' said Corrigan. 'We take your car, Blake. Chief Superintendent Ross, we may need help. Can you get reinforcements to guard this damn building? This time we'll catch them all red-handed.'

'Don't worry, I've got it,' said Ross, who already had his hand on his radio.

The two followed the taxi to Price's home, despite that they had bet that it would go to the bank. They saw him exiting the vehicle and enter the luxurious condo they had previously visited when they brought the news of Amelia Mortcombe's death.

'What do we do?' said inspector Blake.

'We question him, that's what we are going to do.' They parked the car about fifty yards ahead, and they headed for the building. Corrigan showed his badge to the doorman while Blake, in uniform, was awaiting a step behind the inspector. The man at the front desk made a phone call and then pointed to the elevator down the hall. Price was on the fourth floor.

The two introduced themselves and entered the apartment. 'What's this all about?' asked Price, 'is there any more news about Amelia's death?'

'No, we're here for another matter. Do you know these people?' said Corrigan showing Hank Edwards and his gang's picture.

'Of course, they work for the Resurgence Equities Enterprise down in the centre of town. I've just returned from their offices.' And focussing his attention on another picture he said, 'And this man is Marcus Splinter, a businessman I met recently. Would you like to explain what this is all about?'

'Please sit down,' said Corrigan.

The man remained standing, and Corrigan explained his role with Interpol, on how he had been chasing Splinter and his companions for years and how he had tracked him down to Brighton.

Price slumped in the chair behind him. If he had indeed introduced Sokolov to a gang of con men, his life was over. There wouldn't be a bank left to manage, and he would have to persuade his wife to leave everything and flee. He knew he was in deep trouble; just trying to explain to his wife what was going on would lead to endless discussions and questioning. And he didn't have time for that.

'Are they the ones who killed Amelia?' he asked finally.

'Oh no, far from it. Amelia was a target for sure. A rich heiress who would receive a fortune, but those people aren't murderers. No, the reasons for Amelia's murder must be sought elsewhere,' said Corrigan. 'What interests me is your involvement with the Russian mafia.'

Price stiffened in the chair. *How much did they know about Sokolov and the bank accounts?* If the police approached Sokolov, even to just question him, Price would be a dead man. 'How do you know …'

'Don't take us for idiots, Price. What we want from you are facts. Help us to get our hands on Splinter and his companions, help us to incriminate the Russian mafia, and maybe there will be a way out for you and your family.'

'And if I refuse?'

'If you refuse, someone will make an anonymous phone call to leak the story to the newspapers concerning who we are investigating. We're going to break into the Resurgence building, and we will book Splinter, his gang, and the Russians. And even if we can't catch them this time, the law is patient, there will be an opportunity tomorrow, next week, or next year. Think about your interests, I find it needless to remind you that you are in a serious amount of trouble. One way or another.'

Price sighed. He knew it was over and perhaps the only thing to do was to negotiate his own salvation with the police before they investigated his sister-in-law's death further. Resigned, he made a sign of assent with his head and stood up. 'I would like to call my lawyer.'

'Sure, why not? You can do it from the police station,' said Corrigan.

Inspector Blake handcuffed him, and together they headed for the car.

CHAPTER 43

It was three o'clock in the afternoon and Hank had explained to Sokolov the basics about Resurgence and how they worked the arbitrage. It was at that point that the Russian drew his Tokarev TT-33 and set it on the table in front of Hank. Despite its age, that gun had accompanied him for years and had never betrayed him. Being a remnant of the Second World War it was also the gun with which he had started to shoot as a boy. It was a simple gun, it wouldn't jam for any reason in the world, but it was also an extremely dangerous weapon, not being equipped with a safety pin.

'I will explain what will happen,' said Sokolov looking Hank straight in the eye. The sour face of the Russian gave no margin for negotiation. 'You will send home all employees except those needed to make an investment tonight. I will transfer funds into your account, and we'll stay here all night until the market closes. At that point, you will transfer the gains to the same account that I provided you the details of earlier.'

Hank tried to think quickly about a solution, something that could take them off the hook but, uncharacteristically to him, he failed to think of a way out. The most important thing was to save all those aspiring actors who they had employed for the scam. He called Domino.

'Send everyone home, including Lenny and Chaz and then get Anders and Ryan in my office.'

The woman glimpsed at the gun laid on the table and nodded in assent. When she exited the office, she was followed by one of the Russian's killers, to ensure she would be unable to call the police. They returned a few minutes later, along with Logan and Anders.

The young Swede watched the two Russians by the door carefully, trying to assess their skills and then settled his gaze on Hank, who shook his head. They wouldn't be able to overpower them, at least not without the risk of getting shot.

Sokolov made a sign, and one of the two thugs took out a laptop from the bag. The Russian typed some command and said, 'We are ready!'

'Now you have three hundred million belonging to the Russian mafia in your accounts,' announced Sokolov, 'do whatever you have to do, and nobody will get hurt.'

'Three hundred million?' interjected Logan. 'It is far too much, we cannot invest such a huge amount, we risk disaster!' The old lawyer perspired profusely from the tension that had arisen.

'Didn't you say you do arbitrage?' said Sokolov in a sarcastic tone. 'In that case, there is no risk. Aside from what you are running now, I mean.'

'It is not so simple,' said Logan, 'we risk sending the stock exchange into a panic. No one will understand what's going on; we are in danger of bankrupting banks, sending some investment funds belly up. There will be investigations.'

'We're used to being investigated. So, we're in business or not? The stock exchange opens in fifteen minutes,' said Sokolov holding the gun. The man was laid back, a calm that was putting their worst of fears into everybody else in the room.

'I need to make a phone call,' said Logan.

The old man called Whitley on the phone and explained the situation.

'It is not possible,' said Whitley. 'The SEC will open an investigation, we will be in every bloody newspaper around the world. It's suicide, Ryan!'

'Wait, I remember you said you had Russian programmers there? Are you in New York?'

'Yes, we have a couple of Russian guys, why?'

'Bring one to the phone! Fast.'

After a few minutes of silence, a voice with a strong accent showed up on the phone, 'I'm Yuri Belikov.'

Logan put his hand on the receiver and then turned to Sokolov, and said, 'Talk to him.'

The Russian took the phone and began to speak in his own language. It seemed like a friendly conversation, there was almost a melody in his words if anyone in the room didn't know perfectly well that instead, they were threats. The Russian mafia was everywhere, even in New York and New

Jersey and Sokolov was telling his fellow countryman what would happen to him and his family, all his friends and relatives, all co-workers, neighbours, and their dogs if they did not obey.

Sokolov returned the phone to Logan.

'For Christ's sake!' said Whitley, 'what kind of shit did you drag us into? Is it true what Yuri just told me?'

'You can bet your skin. Indeed, you did it already. Why don't we do a video call, so everyone can hear and see what's going on?' Questioned Logan.

'Good idea,' Whitley asked for Hank's email address and sent a link. In a matter of minutes, they were connected via computer. Hank posted the image of the video conference onto the giant screen hanging on the wall.

Whitley was visibly panicking. 'You know how things work, we have to wait until someone decides to make big investments today. If today is a quiet day, there is nothing we can do.'

'And then make them change their mind,' said Logan. 'You received the money, put a few million shares on the market and then cancel the order before it's executed. And then do it again until someone starts asking questions.'

Yuri was explaining something to Whitley, but the people in Brighton couldn't understand what he was saying. Then Whitley began to speak aloud. 'There could be a way. In a specific stock market, some settings are available only to high-frequency traders. If we do our things right, maybe there is a way. Give us half an hour, Yuri must write a program for this purpose.'

Silence fell on the room. Now it was just a waiting game. Sokolov got up to stretch his legs, and meanwhile, he put the Tokarev back in his holster. He approached one of his assistants and took his inlaid axe from the bag. Then he sat down on a couch and slowly began to sharpen it with a whetstone. It was a slow operation that Sokolov did whenever he was forced into waiting. The grinding of the slow-moving blade on the whetstone made people's skin crawl. All eyes of those present were fixated on that axe as if they were victims of a spell.

'OK, here we go,' said Whitley returning to screen. 'Keep your fingers crossed, if we get away with it this time, I'm retreating to some remote island. And if we don't … well, let's not think about that. Yuri, is everything ready?'

The Russian nodded and launched the program. Whitley had placed the computer so that the camera could show the screen where the buying and selling of shares happened. It didn't really matter because those transactions were made at a speed that the human eye couldn't record, but it provided an idea of what was going on.

Hank saw a variety of charts that rose and fell, not understanding the meaning of what he was seeing. To others, it seemed they were watching a sci-fi movie where amazing technologies were at work.

'For now, everything is going as expected,' said Whitley, 'we are entering and deleting orders, and the market is moving. See, someone is trying to follow us.'

Whitley was doing a live broadcast of any transaction that Yuri was doing. Actually, most of the work was being done by computers in their data centre, but on a screen, they could clearly see the accounts and in particular Sokolov's, and his three hundred million. The numbers were changing at every moment. In an instant, the counter changed from three hundred million to one hundred, then two hundred million for a moment, then went back to zero. Silence reigned in the meeting room in Brighton and the only one who didn't seem interested in what was happening was Sokolov, who now had started polishing the axe.

Gradually they saw the account grow again. Three hundred and ten million, three hundred and twenty. That went on for another hour until Whitley's voice woke them up from that spell.

'Jesus Christ! We had a flash crash.' Whitley took a handkerchief and wiped his forehead, beaded with sweat. 'Get us out of this mess, Yuri!'

Hank continued to watch the monitors, stunned. He saw Google shares that were falling from seven hundred dollars to pennies. IBM shares were sold at $100,000 apiece, and an instant later returned to normal. Then, for a while, the Nasdaq Index went to zero, and there it remained for about ten seconds before returning to the nominal values.

Then it was the turn of the BATS and later the NYSE. The market was in chaos, no one knew what was going on, except maybe for Yuri, and when the Chicago Stock Exchange began to trade, even that was not free from repercussions.

The counter which showed Sokolov's earnings had risen to nearly four hundred million and didn't even hint at stopping.

'Guys, we're in big trouble this time. If they catch us, it's jail time for all of us! I'd say it's time to stop,' said Whitley.

'Not yet,' boomed the voice of Sokolov from across the room. Everyone turned and saw him standing and looking right at Whitley on the screen. Then he went further toward the camera while holding the inlaid axe in his hands. He showed the axe to the camera and said, 'I decide when it is time to stop.'

Whitley wiped his forehead again and tapped his hand on Yuri's shoulder, urging him to continue. The young Russian programmer did not need encouragement. He knew what would happen to him if he did not obey.

CHAPTER 44

Robert Price had called his lawyer from the police station, he asked him to go to his house and pick up some boxes full of documents from the trunk of his car.

When the lawyer arrived at the police station, he went into a separate room with his client and had a long discussion. In the end, Price was ready to confess, said the lawyer, in exchange for immunity and protection for his family.

The full confession took place in Chief Superintendent Ross's office, who had personally taken over to call a prosecutor and to inform a judge in case they needed a warrant.

In the quiet office, Price told of Mortcombe's involvement with the mafia, his ambition and when he became, de facto, the mafia's banker. He did not neglect any details, except for the murders of Romanov and Amelia Mortcombe. That would remain a secret, unheeded.

Now and then he watched his lawyer as if seeking confirmation. The lawyer nodded to encourage Price to continue. Price was not ashamed of what he had done, his only regret was that he had been caught.

While he told the facts, a tape machine took care of recording every word of what would later become his formal confession. He spoke slowly, chanting the words, pausing from time to time to construct the right sentence to describe the years serving the most powerful criminal organisation in history.

When he had finished, Price felt drained. He had nothing left. The dream of leading Mortcombe Bank vanished. The vision of becoming rich out of proportion and even to live a happy life with his wife and children had disappeared. It would no longer be possible. And if his wife didn't ask for a divorce, they'd have to live a regular life, an ordinary one, probably in a country overseas. One of the clauses to remain under police protection was to stay inconspicuous, remain anonymous as much as possible. That was what terrorised Price most, much more than just dying at the hands of the mafia.

He read the typed confession, slowly, nodding from time to time. Then passed it to his lawyer for a second reading, before he signed it. For an instant, his gaze was directed towards the window, behind Ross's shoulder. He could glimpse the sea, silhouetted in front of a cloudless sky. He knew he wasn't going to see it again.

'I can't believe it,' said Chief Superintendent Ross, 'this will be a tremendous blow to the mafia. We will be in every newspaper in the country.'

Price's lawyer checked for one last time the letter from the prosecutor which had sanctioned both Price's freedom and the protection for him and his family, then passed it to his client.

'These are the documents we promised you,' he said then, showing the two boxes that had been left by the door. 'What you'll find there is enough to indict Sokolov and suspend all the accounts. When you have a warrant to enter the bank, you will find more information. Obviously, my client is happy to fully cooperate with you.'

'I guess it's time to go get them,' said Corrigan addressing Blake. Now the net was tightening, a patrol had followed Marcus Splinter, Chaz, and Lenny to the hotel and was waiting for orders. The Russians and Hank Edwards were still in the Resurgence Equities Enterprise building. Corrigan and Blake would go directly there, followed by other officers.

'I have an idea,' said Corrigan to Ross and the prosecutor, 'just to avoid our newly acquired friend, Mr Price, changes his mind about the story he told us today.'

The two listened in silence and then smiled malignantly toward Corrigan.

****

'We are in the news!' announced Whitley, 'CNN has just reported the news of the *flash crash*, if we keep going, we will be the richest convicts on the planet!'

Sokolov looked at the giant screen and saw how much money was in his account. The counter listed six hundred and ten million and was still growing. 'We can stop now,' he announced with his deep voice.

'Praise the Lord!' said Whitley. 'Well, guys, it was a real pleasure. See you in Patagonia, for that's perhaps the only place in the world where they won't search for us. Holy cow, we'll have to live as refugees. I'm going to transfer the money to you immediately, minus my commission. I'm going to pack my suitcase, and if you have some brains, you will do likewise.'

Hank's computer let out a slight *beep* in confirmation that the money had been transferred. Four hundred ninety-six million. He had to look at the number repeatedly, to make sure he understood what had just happened.

It was at that point that a sound of breaking glass interrupted the conversation. 'Go and see what is happening,' said Sokolov to one of his bodyguards, 'I wouldn't want that employees had forgotten to leave the building.' Then he leaned his axe, which he had held in his hand the whole time on the table and drew back the Tokarev TT-33.

Pointing the gun at Hank, he said, 'Now transfer the money to my account. Every single penny.'

Before he could comply, the office door was smashed open and Corrigan, Blake, and two other police officers raided in, immobilising the remaining guard. 'Put down that weapon, Sokolov. You have everything to lose if you make the wrong move.'

The Russian obeyed quietly, resting the gun on the table. Robert Price, accompanied by a police officer, entered the room. Sokolov looked straight into the traitor's eyes as he left handcuffed.

'We will meet again. It's a promise.'

It was at that moment, not noticed by the officers, that Logan picked up the Tokarev TT-33, pointing it in Price's direction.

'Bastard! You killed Amelia! You won't get away with what you have done!' Keeping the gun pointed toward Price, Logan ordered Hank to move the money into another account. He dictated the account numbers that Hank repeated aloud for confirmation. In an instant Logan's phone made a beep, confirming the transaction had completed successfully. He took the phone in his left hand and looked briefly at the notification, but that instant was fatal for him.

'Let go of the gun, Logan, it's not worth it,' said Corrigan pulling out his revolver and pointing it towards the old lawyer. Logan who was shaking while holding the gun with both hands and now there was nothing but hate on his face. He fired in Price's direction.

Corrigan fired in turn, hitting him twice in the chest. Logan slumped to the ground while his shirt became red with blood. His breathing was heavy, he could barely keep his eyes open. His shot had missed Price by a whisker.

'Someone call an ambulance!' cried Corrigan as he tried to take Logan's pulse, 'and for Christ's sake, make sure there are no other weapons around.'

While the officers handcuffed Hank, Anders, and Domino, Corrigan looked again toward Logan's body. He picked up the Tokarev which had fallen a short distance away and placed it in his jacket pocket. Then he felt for Logan's pulse again. He turned toward Ross and shook his head. 'A weak pulse, he's losing a lot of blood.'

The ambulance arrived a few minutes later, and two paramedics raced up the stairs until they reached Hank's office. Logan had passed out, and the two paramedics loaded him on the stretcher, after learning that he was still alive.

'Where are you taking him?' said Corrigan.

'The Royal Sussex, it's the nearest hospital,' said the younger of the two.

'What's your name, boy?'

'Konrad.'

'Well, Konrad. When you arrive at the hospital, ensure the doctor calls me immediately.'

'Absolutely, sir, yes,' said Konrad. The two paramedics hurried to load the wounded man into the ambulance and set off, the sirens screaming in the night. Only after a couple of miles did the driver slow down and turn off the sirens.

'We made it, guys,' she said talking to the three in the back.

'Jesus Christ, I shit myself when that Russian entered the room. I thought he was going to kill us all,' said Logan, opening a can of Coke. That day he was celebrating the thirtieth anniversary of sobriety.

'Cheers,' he said, tipping the can towards the front where Amelia was grinning at him through the rear-view mirror.

<u>CHAPTER 45</u>

Bruno Mortcombe awoke suddenly hearing someone calling his name.

He looked around. He was still in a hospital bed. A room with two beds this time, his and that of an old man intent on watching television. The pain in his neck and chest made him almost pass out while he tried to look around. In those rare times when he had regained consciousness, during the past two days, he had always been alone. Not now. And nobody had pronounced his name. Not in that room. The television was showing an attractive brunette, lean, and scatty; she was right in front of the Mortcombe Bank building. In the background, he could see the blurred flashing lights of police cars, high-visibility yellow jackets moved around indistinctly, like ghosts, on the TV.

Mortcombe closed his eyes and continued to listen to that voice. Investigators had not released a statement yet, but it was evident that Mortcombe Bank had ties with the Russian mafia, according to some indiscretions. There was plenty of evidence. Everything had been put on lockdown, and the local police were searching for more clues on the bank's computers. Several bank accounts had been frozen.

According to the journalist, it was not yet clear whether there was a link with the recent death of Amelia Mortcombe and another man named Ryan Logan, killed during a police raid at the company headquarters of Resurgence Equities Enterprise.

The woman went on, telling how Resurgence was a fictitious company, unrecorded and the mysterious disappearance of Logan's body; she promised more news as soon as it became available. Then she sent the link back to the studio.

Logan, thought Mortcombe, the natural father of Amelia.

With great effort, he reached the phone and composed a number he knew by memory. 'I must disappear immediately,' he said to the person on the other end of the phone, 'it's a matter of life or death.' He listened intently to the words that were spoken to him. 'I still have some money saved up, but not much. Make it quick,' he said.

The journalist on television was interviewing a police officer about the mysterious disappearance of Ryan Logan's body.

Logan was worse than cockroaches, thought Mortcombe, that do not die even after a nuclear catastrophe.

CHAPTER 46

La Bouilloire was an elegant, but not too much so, bistro in a side street facing directly on Boulevard de la Croisette in Cannes. Marcel, the owner, was a sixty-five-year-old man from Paris, who had bought the place as an investment many years before. That was his main job, buying ruined shops and apartments, putting them back on track and selling them for profit.

With La Bouilloire things had been different. Soon after restructuring it, he furnished the kitchen, just to entice potential buyers. Then he applied for a license and he finally hired a cook, two aides, and three waiters. It had been nearly two decades since that day.

It was a quiet morning and the only guests were a woman, an old man, and a young man with blond and straight hair, like punks used to have. The woman would be the new owner of the bistro. The time had come to retire and take that cruise around the world that Rosalie, his wife, had always desired.

'Have you decided where to go?' asked Amelia.

Before Konrad could speak, a solid man, with an undulating walk, approached the three guests. 'Inspector Corrigan, Interpol, may I sit down?' said the man, showing his badge.

'Good morning, inspector, you are welcome,' said Amelia, smiling. 'Can we offer you something to drink?'

'A glass of white wine will be fine. I don't have the pleasure of knowing this young man,' said Corrigan, aimed at the young blond.

'You should well remember him, Jordan. He is the guy who loaded me into the ambulance after you shot me,' said Logan, 'and his name is, or rather was, Konrad. Part-time paramedic, although his preferred job is to hack computers; he is now retired from public life.'

'Nice to meet you. You seriously have to work on your communication skills, guys. I had to find out what was going on for myself and improvise.'

Corrigan turned the glass between his fingers for a few seconds before continuing, 'Here's the latest news. Price was put under protection and disappeared from circulation. Bruno Mortcombe fled the hospital once he woke up from his coma; there is a warrant for his arrest. Sokolov got away with it. He lawyered up and passed as a potential victim. The documents Price gave us were enough to freeze all the accounts; they'll go bankrupt, but there wasn't enough evidence to condemn the Russian.'

'I only regret not having been able to see Mortcombe's face when he heard the news,' said Logan.

'He won't get off easily, even if he fled. The police blocked his accounts. He has no money, no support from the mafia. He has a life of hiding and misery in front of him.

'What happened to Whitley?' asked Amelia.

'The company is still in business. After a week, the newspapers were tired of trying to explain to the average American that the stock exchange is basically a scam in itself. The SEC slapped him on the wrist but did not find anything illegal. I mean, these high-frequency traders are growing like mushrooms. I was reading in yesterday's newspapers that they are going to link the London Stock Exchange with a high speed trans-Pacific internet cable. New markets for him and those like him,' said Logan.

'And new opportunities for arbitrage,' said Corrigan.

'Remind me not to invest my money in the stock market,' said Amelia.

'By the way,' said Logan, 'that old boyfriend of yours, Quentin. I convinced him to invest in Resurgence, I hope you don't mind.'

Amelia laughed loudly. 'What a bastard!'

'Who, me or him?'

'Him. But you too. How much did he toss their way?'

'A hundred thousand pounds. He is still hoping for a future together with you.'

Amelia shook her head amused.

'What are you going to do with your share of the money?' asked Corrigan.

'I'll buy a battery of servers as big as a house,' said Konrad.

'I'm doing nothing,' said Logan. 'It's dirty money, when I was released from prison, I learned that I needed very little to live in peace. I just want to stay here, in contact with my daughter. We put our life savings into this restaurant. What more do you want? Honest work, by the sea, in one of the most beautiful places in Europe.'

'By the way, here are your new documents, hot off the press,' said Corrigan.

'And what will you do?' Logan asked Corrigan.

'United States. I'll buy one of those luxurious camper vans and drive across America. I'll send a postcard to my ex-wife from a different place every day. She can try chasing my pension if she really wants.'

'What about you, Amelia.'

'As Ryan said, we begin a new career. It is certainly more exciting than spending my days dealing with divorces and buying and selling real estate. We have lots of things to catch up on, Ryan and I; we have been separated for far too many years. And I'll start writing novels, that's what I've always wanted, but haven't yet had the courage. I also have a personal matter that still requires addressing, but much of the money will go to charity.'

The rest of the group did not ask, although each of them had a suspicion of what Amelia would do afterwards.

CHAPTER 47

The last thing Price remembered was that he was returning home after work. He had entered the witness protection programme, and Interpol transferred him, along with his family, to Naples in Florida. They found him a job as a clerk in a travel agency, a new identity, and an apartment with a decent view of the Gulf of Mexico. His eyes were still clouded, but he knew he was not at home. He was lying on a table and any attempt to move failed. His sight slowly returned, and he understood he had been tied to a table, completely naked. It was a room engulfed in semi-darkness, a filament light bulb faintly illuminated the room. He looked around and panicked.

On the table beside him, equally bound was Bruno Mortcombe, also naked. White and motionless, but what terrified Price were the many wounds on Mortcombe's chest and arms. His face was swollen from beatings. He saw his chest rise, a sign that his father-in-law was not yet dead. Not yet, but almost. Mortcombe had disappeared months before, soon after Price had been arrested. Nobody knew where he went, despite several international arrest warrants. It seemed he had failed to escape the Russians.

Sokolov's inlaid axe was resting on a small trolley nearby, still stained with blood. At the base of the table upon which Mortcombe lay, a little dog, definitely a mongrel, was licking the blood that had fallen to the ground and had not yet clotted.

The door opened and three thugs entered.

The first one to speak was a giant with a red beard and biceps the size of basketballs, covered with tattoos.

'We want our money back. If you cooperate, your deaths shall be quick, otherwise you and this traitor will suffer like dogs. We will cut you piece by piece until you have given us the information we seek. Sokolov went to pee, he will return in a few minutes.'

Price did not know where he was and had no idea what had happened to the money. He wanted to shout that he didn't know anything about the money, that he had been the victim of a scam, but a knot in his throat wouldn't allow it. He no longer had any money and doubted whether Mortcombe had three hundred million. Even by selling houses and draining bank accounts, they wouldn't even come close.

He began to weep.

CHAPTER 48

It was a cold and rainy morning, and Anders Nilsson worked as a bartender at Julian's in Windsor. He had started working there a few weeks before, and the place was busier than usual. Domino had just finished breakfast and was posing as a regular customer. She was sitting at a coffee table next to a certain Roger Denton, local entrepreneur and greedy person.

They had got out of prison a month before, earlier than expected due to good behaviour, and they were following a reintegration programme. Not that it was working. After the conmen were arrested in Brighton, Interpol and the local police had focused their attention on the Russian mafia. Having found no conclusive evidence on the gang, they had been arrested for attempted fraud and had been sentenced to three years in prison, then discounted to only one, to serve in the homeland galleys of Her Majesty the Queen.

The Brighton con had been a disaster and had in fact dried up their finances; the biggest surprise came during the investigation when they discovered that their accounts had been emptied also. And so they were back to square one, doing short cons, just to get back on their feet.

Anders approached Domino carrying the bill.

'I think I forgot my purse at home,' said the woman, desperately looking in her handbag. 'I don't live far away. If you could wait, I could come back in about ten minutes with cash.'

'Really, I couldn't,' said Anders.

Domino was red in the face with embarrassment. 'Look, I have a proposal? This brooch belonged to my grandmother, it's an object that I'm very fond of. I don't know how valuable it might be, but my grandmother always said that one day it would help me get out of trouble. I think it's valuable. Why don't you keep it while I go home? I swear I will return in about ten minutes.'

'I don't know, I should ask the owner …'

'Please,' implored Domino.

'OK, OK but please don't rip me off. I've only just been given the job here.'

'Don't worry.'

Domino stood in a rush from her table and headed for the exit. Anders was back behind the counter when he heard someone calling him. They were two smartly dressed gentlemen, tailored clothes for sure.

'Would you mind showing me that brooch for a moment?'

'Of course,' said Anders approaching the table.

Marcus Splinter looked at the brooch for a few moments and then thundered, trying to be heard by their target, Roger Denton. 'Like I said, Hank, it's a Faberge brooch. See the punching here on the side? And then this aquamarine is a pretty stone, and the diamonds appear to be of excellent quality. Your client left a pledge of ten thousand pounds,' said Splinter, returning the brooch to Anders.

Domino returned a few minutes later and paid cash for breakfast, upon the return of the valuable brooch. Roger Denton followed her out of the bar, trying to gain the bargain of the century; he would offer her a thousand pounds in cash for that gem and if she did not want to sell, he would offer much more, there was an ATM machine just in front of the bar.

'So, going to jail taught you nothing!' said Amelia. The woman was sitting nearby, but due to the hat she was wearing, the big sunglasses and her hair having been dyed black she was unrecognisable.

'Amelia!' said Anders, flabbergasted.

'Look, our Miss Mortcombe is alive and well,' said Splinter composedly. 'You left us in deep trouble after cleaning us out.'

'Shall we kill her here or outside?' hissed Hank, 'As far as the authorities are concerned she is already dead, that shouldn't be too much hassle.'

'Calm down, let's hear what she has to say first,' said Splinter.

'I'm here to make amends, especially to Anders' she said, rising from the table and then standing in front of them, 'Do you mind if I sit down?'

'We like to hear a good story,' said Hank.

'I can't believe you're alive!' said Anders picking up a chair and sitting right at her side.

'I wanted to apologise to you, Anders, first of all. I didn't know you were part of all this when I fell in love with you. Yes, I'm not afraid to say it out loud. For us, you were just a group of con artists we needed for our own scam.'

'Hang on a second,' said Domino, who had returned and now sat between Splinter and Hank. 'We chose you, not the other way around.'

'That is not entirely true,' said Amelia. 'Corrigan, the Interpol inspector, pointed us in your direction. We paid a journalist for a series of articles on me and the bank; it was just a matter of ensuring you picked up the right newspapers. Failing that, we had alternatives but we didn't need them in the end.'

'Corrigan was in your pocket all along?'

Amelia carried on explaining that Logan was her natural father, not Bruno Mortcombe; she told them about the years Logan had to spend in jail, innocent. She explained how Corrigan was the one who arrested Logan and how he felt guilty for having contributed in ruining his life. He wanted to make amends. She also explained how she eventually met her own father, thanks to Albert Romanov.

'The one from the letter,' interjected Anders.

'Exactly him. He was like an uncle to me, and although in the end he went rogue, he still has a place in my heart.'

'It doesn't make sense,' said Splinter. 'We decided to switch target from you to Robert Price.'

'Not entirely true. At that point, you'd already approached Logan, so we knew we were in the game. We placed a couple of actors when I had lunch with Price, to spread some well devised rumours. We knew most of you anyway, thanks to Corrigan.'

'She is good,' said Hank, 'maybe we should ask to join us?'

They all laughed, which helped releasing the tension that was building up.

'I didn't know at that point you were involved, Anders.'

'When did you learn that?'

'On the way to Scotland. Logan got suspicious and asked me to send him a photo of you, he eventually checked with Corrigan, which confirmed who you really were. The fact is, at that point I didn't care. I was too involved with you and I would have left everything if you'd said the word. I was prepared to disappear forever with you.'

'Funnily enough,' said Anders, 'I had the same feeling when we were at the train station. I was ready to run away with you and leave everything and everybody behind. If only you'd said the word … You know, I' am also in love with you. Since I came back …'

'Get a room!' said Domino. 'But only after Ms Mortcombe here explains how in hell they managed to con us.'

'Conning is what you do best, so we let you run your game and we tagged along. There had been a few hiccups. For example, we didn't expect the shootout in Scotland, nor that a hired gun would try to kill me. That was a lucky escape which played to our advantage.'

'I trust Mr Logan is still alive?' asked Splinter.

'Alive and kicking. Corrigan shot him with blanks. I drove him away in the ambulance.'

Hank shook his head. 'I cannot believe we fell for that. We've used that trick ourselves, once, the only difference that the police raiding the office was real. I bet your friend Corrigan had something to do with it.'

'And you would win that bet,' said Amelia. She went on explaining how Konrad hacked into their computers and transferred the money away at the right time.

'So, was it revenge or did you do it for money?' asked Domino.

'For us, revenge, and we wanted to put right a wrong. We didn't think it would turn out badly for you and I'm here to make amends. A good amount of what we took went to charity. I hope this will be enough to compensate you for the trouble we gave you.' And then, turning toward Anders, she said, 'And for saving my life.' Amelia put an envelope on the table and Splinter opened it. He looked at the cheque for a few seconds and then passed it on to Hank.

'What's the catch?' asked Splinter.

'No tricks. Like I said, you saved my life, and you did a good job, all things considered. I wanted to even the score.'

'And we leave it like that?' said Splinter.

'With you, yes. As for Anders, well, he could drop me off at the airport if he feels like it. I have a private jet that leaves in a few hours to the south of France. He can even come along if he wants.'

Anders was stunned, he didn't know if it was because Amelia was still alive, because he really loved her, or just because he had been caught by surprise, but speech failed him.

'What are you waiting for, you dumbass,' said Splinter, 'take off that apron and bugger off!'

'Yes, yes …' Anders managed to mumble, unable to take his eyes off Amelia.

'What about your share?' asked Hank, looking at the cheque.

'Spend it! I already have everything I want,' said Anders as he took Amelia's hand.

THE END